Whispered Regrets

By Linda Van Meter

Cover design by Linda Van Meter

Linda Van Meter
Printed in the United States of America

First Printing: July 2018

ISBN-13:
978-1721771561

This book is dedicated to my parents

for giving

me many summers at the lake.

A special thanks to Lori, Michele, Jean and Kait

for your sharp eyes

and brilliant suggestions.

And always to Jerry

for his endless love and support.

1

He slammed the door of his old, red pickup, his mouth was a thin line. Lily Darby watched him advancing across the parking lot, his work boots crunching the gravel. She felt her heart speed up, was he upset with her?

Dylan was nineteen, three years her senior, a fact she hoped to keep from her mother. He would have graduated two years ago but a suspension for tobacco had pushed his absences too far, and he dropped out rather than make up the time to receive his diploma. Sharing that information with Lily, he sneered, "Who cares? I make plenty of money with my uncle, pouring concrete." Another fact she would prefer to keep from her mother, but she understood. Dylan had such a difficult life. While her parents were constantly breathing down her neck, no one seemed to care about him at all.

Lily had met him here three weeks ago; the Dairy Bar had just opened for the season. Dylan was in the habit of stopping for a milkshake after work, and most times she was working. His looks appealed to her from the very first, his stained and torn jeans, tattered t-shirts with the sleeves cut off and a dirty ball cap pushed over his dark brown, shaggy hair seemed tough, but he had the sweetest face, almost like a little boy's. Even his neck tattoos did not take the innocence away.

When he was happy, he had an infectious grin. Dylan had aimed that grin at her every day the first week. By Friday, he had asked her name. She had blushed crimson when he told her that milkshakes were the second reason he was stopping by. He had Lily's number on his phone before he left.

A devoted texter and caller, he sent her fourteen messages that very first night. Lily was thrilled. Dating encounters to this point were minimal. Her parents had said no car dates before sixteen. Other than that, she'd met boys in groups at the movies, at the Pizza Playground, had gone to homecoming dances. Lily's experience with guys was limited to quick kisses at the front door and some stolen touches at parties.

Dylan was a man next to the boys at her school. By Tuesday of the second week he was waiting for her when the shop closed, parked next to her blue Honda. Sitting on the merry-go-round they had talked until Lily's phone beeped. Her mom was looking for her.

At the door of her car, Dylan had leaned in and kissed her. It was a kiss of intention, different than any she had ever had. Though he tasted a bit like stale smoke, she liked the forcefulness of his tongue exploring her mouth. She had barely made it out of the park before he was texting to her that he wanted to do that again.

On Saturday, she convinced her best friend Olivia, to go out with her after work. Dylan had promised to bring a friend too. Lily needed Olivia as a cover; she did not want to drag Dylan over to her parents. They decided to drive into the bigger city, New Haven.

The night had not been terrific. Dylan's friend, Andy was a short stocky guy with bad skin. He leered at Olivia and she nearly made Lily leave at that very moment. Lily convinced her that they would go to a movie and straight home. Olivia agreed but sat at her right, Dylan was on Lily's left. Andy was stuck next to Dylan. At first, he just held her hand, and she loved it. He was so warm and strong. At one point he tried to kiss her, she was embarrassed with her friend next to her. When Lily pulled away lightly she swore she heard him say "Tease" under his breath.

Afterwards they rode in Andy's car to get some food. In the back seat, Dylan immediately began putting his arms around her and kissing her. The car was dark, the music was loud, so she kissed back.

Now, Dylan was approaching the stand with an angry air about him. Lily smiled sweetly at him, "Hi."

He glared at her, "You look at all the guys like that?"

Honestly surprised, Lily responded," Of course not."

He scoffed, "Really? Looked like you were trying to give it to the guy who just left." With his head he motioned to a car pulling out of the lot.

Not remembering who it even was, Lily saw the man in question with his two toddlers. "Dylan, I just took the order out to his family."

"Yeah, whatever. I know how you are Lily. Smiling, shaking your ass as you walk away."

"I was not," Lily flushed angry.

"I know what I saw," he threw back at her. Dylan saw her expression. With the possibility of pushing too far, he tried another tactic. His voice became soft, nearly whiny, "I just don't want to be screwed over again."

It worked; she put her hand on his forearm and oozed sympathy. “Of course not, Dylan, I would never do that to you.”

He gave a satisfied grin, “Then make your man a milkshake and get your ass out here with it.” Dylan sauntered over to a table and sat.

Thrilled to hear him refer to himself as “her man”, Lily whipped up the milkshake and headed out to deliver it to him.

**

Julia Darby stood with the rest of the parents and clapped as the girls soundly defeated the other softball team. Her middle child, Kelsey, had pitched a no hitter and scored two runs. At fourteen she was already an excellent athlete. Head coach, Ken stood at the end of the line to give his daughter a big hug. Kelsey’s dark, thick hair was pulled through her ball cap. The hair and her sturdy build matched that of her father.

Ten-year-old Seth tugged on his mom’s arm. “Can we leave for the Dairy Bar right now and beat the team? I’m starving.”

Julia smiled indulgently down at him. The mom next to them laughed, “Go ahead, I’ll tell Ken you’re already there.”

"Okay, hungry boy let's go." At ten, he already reached his mother's chin. Julia was five feet six; her son would one day be much taller. They walked down the tree lined streets of the small Midwestern town. Houses of varied structures flanked both sides. This was a town built around a few industries; on the north corner was a large candy manufacturer and at the other corner was a brickwork.

Two blocks from the park was the Dairy Bar. Julia was just about to ask her son what he wanted to eat, when she spotted Lily in the picnic area. A young man was sitting on a table and her daughter was leaning into his open knees, back to his chest. Julia was stunned. As far as she knew, Lily wasn't dating anyone. Who was this boy? Lily was obviously familiar with him.

Seth took off at a sprint, leaving his mother and at the sight of him, Lily moved away from the boy. She grabbed a rag from her pocket, wiping off the tables. It was then that she turned and looked at her mother.

The teen male sauntered over to an old red pickup. He climbed in and sat. Julia decided that Lily must have sent him away. Her mind was racing, why would her daughter hide a boy from her?

Lily tried to act normal, "Hey Mom."

"Who is he?"

"Who?" Lily nervously twisted a strand of long, wavy chestnut hair. Except for chocolate brown eyes, opposed to Julia's green ones, Lily looked remarkably like her mother.

"The guy who you were hanging onto two minutes ago," Julia looked pointedly at the pickup truck. The boy pulled his ball cap lower over his eyes.

"Mother don't," Lily hissed.

"Don't what, I was just looking, who is he?"

"Can we talk about this when I get home?" Lily glanced nervously at the truck. She caught his eye and shook her head slightly. The boy started the truck and drove away.

"You don't go anywhere with someone who hasn't been at the house." Julia looked with disbelief at this stranger her teenage daughter had become.

"Mom let's talk about this later, okay?" She turned and headed back into the ice cream shop.

Ken and Kelsey arrived with the team and parents; Julia decided to drop the issue until Lily got home from work. While they were standing around the table of giggling ball players, Julia watched a woman climb out of a car with out-of-state plates. There was something familiar about her thick, dark hair and solid build. From the passenger side of the vehicle emerged a young boy, probably close to Seth's age.

They moved up to the counter to place their order. Lily handed her soft drinks and the woman turned toward the picnic area, scanning the place for an open spot. She glanced at Julia, looked for a table and then back at Julia. At that moment, recognition dawned in both their eyes. Julia moved toward her.

"Julia?"

"Angie? What are you doing in Seneca?" Seeing Angie brought her back to her teen years, spending her summers at a small northern lake. Angie was a few years older and grew up on the lake. They had not been friends but had known each other well through another person.

Angie's son sat down and helped himself to a soda. "We're moving here. I got a job at Crystal Candy and just signed a lease on a house."

The women discussed the location on Sycamore Street, Julia recalled the nice white ranch with red shutters. Just then Lily brought out the food. Julia touched her arm before she left. "This is my oldest daughter, Lily."

Angie looked up surprised, “How old is she?”

“Sixteen. Is this your son?”

“This is Cody, my one and only.”

The precocious little boy held out his hand, “Cody Castile. I’m nine.”

Julia’s eyes filled with knowing, “That’s right, you married Marcus Castile.”

A shadow crossed Angie’s face. Julia read the message loud and clear, he was not here looking at the house. “When do you move?”

“That was the surprise, we can have the place on May 1. It’s a perfect location near the elementary and my job, it was hard to pass up.” A frown crossed her face, “But I can’t imagine pulling him out of his school for the last quarter, maybe we won’t move in until late May.”

“That’s a tough decision. We have a wonderful school system, you should talk to ours and his current one and seek their advice. This is such a nice community to raise children.” Julia glanced across the lot. “The rest of my family is over there. The girl at the table with the brown pony tail is my middle daughter, Kelsey. My husband, Ken, is the coach in the matching jersey standing in the group of men. My youngest, Seth, is over there with the other boys. He’s the one in the Ohio State

T-shirt." She glanced at Cody, "He just turned ten last month."

Angie took in the faces. "You have three children, that's amazing."

"Tell me about it. Never a dull moment. How's the lake?"

Angie's smile did not reach her eyes, "Oh it's fine, same as always. Mom and Dad are still in the old place. Luke built a house across the lake."

Luke, the name caused a flutter in Julia's stomach. A name she had not thought of in a long time. She forced a casual smile, "Good for him."

After a bit more conversation, the women exchanged phone numbers. The Darby family was ready to head home. Angie promised to call if she needed any help moving, or if she had any other questions.

He was with her, stretched out on her purple and yellow beach towel. The waves lapped lightly on the shoreline, but she could not hear their sound because his pickup was parked next to them and he had the radio on.

"Luke, I can't leave you," her voice had a tone of desperation.

He was in his typical attire of cut off jean shorts, no shirt, no shoes. The chain with her class ring was the only thing on his chest. He leaned over her, so close that his long dark hair brushed her forehead. His brown eyes glittered, "I'll call you every day and see you every weekend."

She propped up on one elbow to be closer to him. "That's not good enough," she pouted, "besides your boss won't let you have every weekend off."

His tan, slim finger traced the line of her jaw, "We'll make it work. I love you baby." They kissed.

"How am I going to survive every day without you?" Her tears dripped on his bare, tanned chest.

He tilted his head back and gave her another slow kiss.

In five days she was moving to a college that was two and a half hours away from him. His plan was to join her in a year. Now he was finishing a two-year program at a local community college.

She stood up, folding her towel. He had his arms wrapped around her waist. She brushed at the hair in his eyes. "I want you to come to school with me."

From the hill she could hear her father sounding the horn on their station wagon. This was her signal to leave. He grabbed her, and they kissed once more. She sobbed as she turned her back and walked up the road.

Julia was sitting at the kitchen table daydreaming about her own first love when her daughter pulled into the drive two hours later. She had not shared about the boy in the pickup with Ken.

The butter yellow kitchen was the center of this old farm house. The family spent their time around the large round, Amish built table or on stools at the matching island. Lily opened the door to the attached garage and saw her mother waiting for her and rolled her eyes. "What?" she snapped defensively.

"I'm just waiting to hear about your new boyfriend," Julia had her hands wrapped around a mug of decaf.

"Do we have to do this now? I'm tired." Lily was trying to edge her way to the hallway.

"Yes, we do, sit down."

The eye roll repeated and the sixteen-year-old slumped in a kitchen chair across from her mother. Her phone buzzed, and she glanced at the screen to read the message.

"Put it away, we're talking."

A heavy sigh and the phone disappeared into a jean pocket.

"Who is he?"

"Dylan."

"More details, Dylan who, from where, how old?"

"Specter. He is from school, well he . . . graduated."

"Graduated? Is he 18?"

Julia watched her daughter look everywhere but her mom. "Uh, yeah."

"Lily!"

"He's nineteen."

"What? Nineteen, I don't think so."

"Mom, I'm almost seventeen."

"You're going to be a junior in the fall; you're not dating a guy who has already been out of school for a year. No way. How long has this been going on?"

"We just started hanging out a couple of weeks ago."

"Why haven't I met him?"

Her daughter stood up, "Look you don't know him and you already hate him!"

Julia took a deep breath, determined not to yell back. "He's nineteen that's too old for you!"

"No, it's not, I really like him."

"How did you meet him?"

"He always comes to get a milkshake after work. We started hanging out."

Julia was continuing the deep breaths, "When have you hung out?"

Lily looked at her fingernails. "Just sometimes."

Julia recalled her daughter being gone overnight on Saturday and her heart began to pound. "Last weekend when I thought you were with Olivia? Did you see him that night?"

"Yeah, but he brought a friend to meet Olivia and then we went back to her house for the night. I swear!"

"I can't believe you find someone you like, and you immediately start sneaking around!" Julia was hurt.

"I have to; you already said he was too old. I know you're never going to give him a chance."

"Why would you say that when I didn't even know about him? I know what it's like to be a teenager, to date. Why wouldn't you come to me? Lily, you are starting this whole thing off on the wrong foot. I haven't even met this guy and already he has two strikes against him, he's too old and he thinks it's okay if you sneak around behind your parents' backs."

Both women were quiet for a moment; Julia's mind racing for the best way to handle this new ground. "I have to do some thinking about this and talk with your dad. In the meantime, you're grounded for lying to us about your weekend plans."

"But, Mom! He's so sweet; he comes to see me every day that I work."

"This is serious, we entrusted you with a phone, a car and freedom and you're taking advantage of it. The car stays parked for now."

Lily looked ready to cry, she mustered up her last bit of bravado, "Whatever," and headed up to her bedroom. In a moment, Julia heard her door slam and her cell phone ring at the same time.

Julia grasped her coffee cup in both hands, staring blankly at the liquid inside, "Here we go," she said. It had been a long time since she had felt that she was younger than she wanted to be to face motherhood. Now at 36, she was dealing with her daughter's teen romance. She hoped she was ready.

**

Over a week had gone by; Julia was headed home from the grocery. As she crunched down the long winding gravel drive, her German shepherd, Sophie, leaped off the porch and ran alongside her car barking. Before she was out of the vehicle, Seth had it open, grabbing bags, "Mom can I spend the night at Tyler's?

She grinned, "Is that why you're being so helpful?"

"Can I? We're going to set up a tent and his dad might build a bonfire."

Julia appreciated the simplicity of a younger son.

Once in the kitchen, she could hear the baseball game on in the other room. "Don't bother to get up, Ken, we can get the groceries." Her voice was laced with sarcasm.

"It's the last inning," came the reply.

"Until the next game begins," she mumbled to herself. Ken was a sports addict. He had a favorite team for each sport season, their family activities were scheduled around them. It was an obsession she had not fully realized when they began dating. Not that it mattered, when they had married this was not the kind of thing that was even important.

Julia's phone buzzed in her pocket. The screen revealed a text from Angie Castile. She had talked to the schools, both felt he would do well starting in Seneca. Cody was fine with it, so she was moving in today. She also included that she and Marcus were in a trial separation. Julia guessed that this was to avoid an awkward explanation in person. She responded that she could stop by on her way to drop Seth off at a friend's.

They agreed to get together in two hours. Julia rummaged through the cupboards looking for something to bake as a housewarming treat.

2

Julia put the pan of brownies in the backseat of the car, as Seth climbed in the passenger seat. She explained where they were going and promised not to stay too long.

Angie's home was in the middle of the small town on a quiet residential street. As she reached up to knock, the front door opened. Julia opened her mouth to say hello to Angie, but the words were lost when she saw Luke standing in front of her.

"Hi, stranger," his voice was still familiar to her. She sat the basket on the porch and reached to hug him. He wrapped his arms around her in a warm embrace.

"Luke, it is so great to see you," Julia said over his shoulder.

"You too," he spoke into the side of her neck. His hair, still slightly longer than most men's, brushed against her cheek as they moved apart. Tall and slim as ever, Luke was wearing dark jeans, a white button shirt and was barefoot.

"I don't think you've aged a day, Julia."

She laughed self-consciously, glancing down at her jeans and black T-shirt. Her hair must be a mess from driving with the window down. Just then Angie came to the door, "Are you going to let her in, or does she have to stay on the porch?" Luke placed a hand on the small of her back, guiding her in. It was a familiar gesture and terribly intimate.

They were in the process of setting up Cody's game system. The two boys joined together to finish the task. Angie took the brownies into the kitchen, promising to bring out a piece for everyone.

Motioning Julia toward the couch, Luke sat at one end, she sat at the other. She looked at him, "Tell me what you've been up to."

He smiled, "I have my own design business."

"Your own firm? That's marvelous. You're still at the lake?"

"Yes."

"Lucky, I miss being around the water. I wish my parents had never sold the place."

Something passed over his face that she could not distinguish. “It’s still in great shape, a family with young children own it. I built a place on the north point,” he looked at her to gage her reaction. He was not disappointed.

Angie came in just at that moment. “Sorry I took so long, I couldn’t resist filling the silverware drawer while I was in there searching for forks.” She handed a piece of still warm brownie to Luke and Julia. Sitting in a rocker by the window, Angie took a bite of her own piece. “So, tell me what you’ve been up to.”

“I teach history and psychology at the community college in New Haven.”

Luke smiled, “Impressive.”

Angie nodded, “I saw your family at the ice cream place. I can’t remember your husband’s name.”

“Ken.”

“And three children,” was Angie’s reply. Luke was silent. “How old are the girls?”

“Both teenagers.”

Julia turned to Luke, “How about you? Kids?”

He shook his head, “No.”

“Are you married?”

Again, he shook his head, “I was for a few years.”

"You remember Gina Logan, her folks lived next door," Angie chimed in.

Luke made a point of changing the subject, "Is Seth in the same grade as Cody?"

Julia was still processing Luke and Gina's marriage. "Yes," she murmured distractedly.

Angie spoke up, "I'd like to hear all about the school system." Julia shared with her the generalities of the small county school. It was designed as K-12 on one campus, each grade level in a different wing. The average size of a graduation class was 150. Not much different than the school where Cody was coming from.

Seth reminded his mom of his plans, the adults stood up. Julia turned to Angie, "Call me when you have a free moment, I'll be happy to tell or show you everything about this *big* city."

Impulsively Angie hugged her, "It's a relief to have a familiar face in a strange place, thanks for coming over."

Julia looked behind her, Luke had left the room, "I was going to tell Luke goodbye."

Angie turned, surprised also, "I'll be certain to tell him for you."

**

Reaching for the car door handle, she felt him standing behind her, and turned. His hands were shoved in his pockets, "I'm glad I got to see you again."

"Me too, Luke."

"It's been a long time, Jules," she smiled as he called her the nickname she hadn't heard for nearly twenty years.

"Are you staying here for the weekend?"

"Probably, it's kind of tough for her to be moving in alone."

"Sorry about that. Next time you visit, you'll all have to come over." She reached out and gave him a quick hug; he pulled her close and held on. Finally, she pulled back, "Bye Luke."

"Goodbye, Julia."

**

Luke had been Julia's first love. The image of him fueled her memories and she re-lived their entire relationship on the trip back home. She recalled her first semester at Ashland College. He'd managed to come visit nearly every weekend, staying in her room when her roommate went home or staying in a cheap hotel if not. Their phone bills were outrageous. Wouldn't cell phones have been fantastic back then?

During the spring semester, he got a job on a construction site and was not free on weekends. The overtime was helping him put money away for the high cost of the out of state university he would be paying for next year. But, their time apart began to cause problems.

Typical of any eighteen-year-old girl, she was insecure and always pushing to see him. Typical of a nineteen-year-old boy, he got tired of the arguments and rebelled. He began hanging out with the party crowd. He was a regular at local bars. Eventually it happened, one night he had too many beers and took another girl home. He made a mistake.

Consumed with guilt but afraid to tell the truth, he tried to blame their problems on her, she was always accusing him, he told her she was pushing him. Finally, she borrowed a car and drove to Spring Lake one evening. Face to face he confessed his mistake. She was furious and broke off their relationship.

For three weeks he tried to get her back. She wouldn't speak to him on the phone and the two times that he drove to Ashland, she refused to see him. Eventually he gave up.

It all seemed so trivial to Julia now. She remembered how she was certain that the world would end that summer. When school was over she got a job on campus and stayed there. She did not go to the lake with her family again.

Now, here she was, nearly two decades later remembering every precious moment with Luke Thomas.

**

Luke was also recalling what went on between them and the end of their relationship. He had tried so desperately to get her back.

"Why are you calling, Luke?"

"Please Jules, we have to work this out."

"What is there to work out? You got drunk and slept with another girl," her voice was icy on the other end of the phone.

Luke stretched the cord of the white kitchen phone until he was as far down the hall as he could be. His sister Angie was in the kitchen and he didn't want her to hear.

"Luke, you cheated on me, I'm here and you're there. Obviously, the long distance isn't working for you. I guess we're better off apart."

She could hear the catch in his voice, "It was once, it was stupid, and I was drunk. Please don't do this. We're not better apart don't say that."

Angie was suddenly next to him, "Yes, you are," she whispered. Luke shoved her away.

"What was that?" Julia said on the other end.

"Nothing, it was Angie."

"She wants us apart, Luke. She never liked me."

"So, your parents don't like me, it doesn't matter. I love you."

"You stayed home, when I moved here. You were supposed to transfer here."

Luke made a loud sigh into the receiver, "I needed to finish the associate program. I want to be there."

Her words were cold, "Actions speak louder than words, and after last weekend you're acting like you want to be there."

"Jules," he groaned, "please don't say that. I regret what I did, please forgive me." He could hear his sister shouting, "Just hang up," from the kitchen. Luke tried to stretch the phone further away.

"Don't call me 'Jules' ever again. This is over."

"I love you."

She was silent for a moment, "I loved you too, but you didn't care. Good bye, Luke." The phone went dead on the other end. Luke could not believe she had hung up.

He remembered showing up at her dorm, driving the two and a half hours in a fog. Her roommates had held him off, not telling him where her class was and somehow getting word to her to not come back. Maybe she hadn't even known he came down. Whatever happened? She never wrote responses to the many letters he sent or spoke to him on the phone. He gave up after a month, it was over.

Now after all these years, he had just seen her. Julia was right here in this town where his sister was moving. Julia had come to Angie's new house. She had visited this very house with her son! He was the youngest of her three children. She was married.

Luke had been married, too. At 22, he had married the girl next door, Gina. The relationship had been companionable, but within the first year she was ready for kids. In the two years they stayed together, it had never happened. Medical tests were inconclusive. It drove a wedge between them, they agreed to split instead of trying to adopt. He had heard from her mother that she and the man she married a year later had twins. Maybe it was him.

This hadn't bothered Luke. He went out with women regularly. In fact, in the small community at Spring Lake, he was famous for dating. Hardly a single woman moved to town or was divorced or widowed that did not manage to get him to take her out. There had been relationships that lasted for a while, some over a year. But, Luke had yet to commit to staying together.

3

Julia returned home without Seth. He had been thrilled to be dropped off at Tyler's house. The tent was already pitched when they arrived. In the living room, Ken was stretched in a recliner watching golf. "Hi, hon," she spoke coming up behind him. He waved noncommittally.

They had been married now for seventeen years. Seventeen comfortable years. Ken was a good husband; he had a great job in sales at a nationally successful insurance company. He was great with the kids, coaching Kelsey and Seth's ball teams. When Julia met Ken in college, she would never have guessed they would spend their lives together.

After her split with Luke, Julia spent the weekends going to the college clubs and dancing with her friends. She would occasionally have a date, but nothing serious, too soon after Luke. It was embarrassing to recall the few one-night stands that she threw herself into as personal revenge for his infidelity. Julia woke up one morning and decided that was wrong, she had even gone off birth control pills to avoid casual sex.

During her sophomore year in college, the girls were attending some frat parties in the fall. It was always a great time of year for free beers because all the fraternities were trying to recruit new members and held parties on their lawns. Her roommate, Teri, who was trying to get her hooks in a Sigma Nu guy, Doug, had convinced Julia to escort her to the party but soon disappeared with him. Julia found herself alone on a picnic table with a warm beer in her hand when a Frisbee flew across the lawn and smacked her in the head. Ken had been the coed who had thrown it and he came over to see if she was alright.

After that they began dating. It was a casual thing. Parties, dancing, sex. It was fun to have a guy waiting after class for her. Going to games with Ken and his friends was always amusing. Julia was not madly in love with Ken, but it was a good time. Six months into the relationship, Julia walked out of Ken's bathroom, the plastic stick still in her hand. "It's blue, I'm pregnant."

Awkwardly Ken put his arms around her, "It's okay, sweetie." Her tears made marks on his Sigma sweatshirt. "We'll get married, I graduate in a month, and it will be fine."

Julia glanced at the back of her husband's head, leaning against the leather cushion of his recliner. Life had been fine. One unexpected baby had turned into three children, a house, a dog, and a nice life in a quiet country town. Julia had finished college when Seth went to school and loved her job. Now, she walked up behind Ken and kissed the top of his head. He reached for her wrist, "What's up?"

"Nothing." He did not inquire further. They were not the kind of couple who spent much time sharing feelings or emotions about their relationship. It was an unspoken agreement that they were content in the marriage. Julia had adjusted to this, so different than her first love. She had spent the last two decades believing that this was what matrimony was like.

Julia went into the small office off the living room and opened the laptop. She logged on to Facebook. When she first got an account, years ago, she had looked up Luke. He had a private account and she had seen little more than his profile picture. At the time, she did not have to nerve to make a friend request. Now her finger hovered over the friend request button on his page, instead she scrolled through her news feed, liking friends' updates. Wishing an old classmate happy birthday and perusing a coworker's vacation photos. Julia was about to log out when the ding sounded, a message. She had a notation on the friend requests, it was from Luke. Her heart jumped a beat, he was thinking just like her. She accepted the request.

It felt almost scandalous, opening his page when he was most likely doing the same to hers. What was her current profile photo? Julia clicked on that first, she nodded confidently, it was a picture that was taken at a basketball game. She was in the stands in a school baseball shirt, laughing at Kelsey who had taken it. Okay, that would do, now back to his page. His photo was in front of a beautiful building, he was standing by a sign that read, "Designs by Thomas". This must be one of his. She thought the structure was lovely, but her focus was on the man in front of it. He was in jeans with a fleece pullover that looked as if it had the company logo on it. Luke's hair was blowing away from his face, he had sunglasses perched on top of his head. Julia thought he looked entirely handsome.

Luke's posts were few, most photos of places he had been or sports comments. Feeling nosey, she looked at his relationship status, none. What was he seeing in hers? Outside the study she heard Ken get up and head to the kitchen, feeling guilty, she decided to log out and quit stalking Luke Thomas. The private message lit up, it was him! *Great to see you today!*

You, too!

The conversation continued for a few moments, until Ken walked over to the door. Julia said *Nice to talk to you* and clicked off. Why was she feeling guilty?

A week went by and they kept in touch regularly. She found herself constantly looking at her phone, hoping for a notification.

Angie called one night, wanting to know if they could get together. They decided to walk the boys down for ice cream; it was just a few blocks from Angie's house. The walk was the perfect opportunity to talk, and Seth was taking pleasure from pointing out everything in town to Cody. This allowed Angie some time to discuss why she was here without her husband.

"Marcus has refused to put us first in anything."

Julia nodded her understanding.

"I knew when I married him that his 'gang' in town was always going to be around. I just thought that hunting weekends and every night fishing would change. I thought once we were married and had Cody that the guys wouldn't feel they could show up and hang out every evening. I wanted Marcus to tell them we needed family time. It took me nearly a decade to realize he wanted them around."

"That's rough. You're not the first woman I 've heard dealing with that when a man stays in the town he grows up in. He can't give up his boys."

"You didn't have that with Ken?"

"No, we moved to this area when he was hired by his company. I think it was good for us to have to start out knowing only each other."

"That sounds nice, if Marcus had been willing to move with us, I honestly think we could have made it. But he chose to stay there, even over being around his only son," Angie's voice cracked on the last word. Julia rubbed Angie's back lightly.

"We should do something together. I'm free on weekends. Something you don't know about Ken is that sports are his life. If a ball game isn't on TV, he wants to be out on the golf course. I have to be pretty tough to get him to stay around."

The women initially made plans to get together for a drink on Saturday. However, on Thursday, Angie cancelled. Marcus had agreed to come down with a truck to bring the rest of her furniture. She seemed nervous on the phone, so Julia suggested they go out on Tuesday evening. Angie may want to vent after the weekend visit.

**

Saturday afternoon was uneventful. Lily was allowed to have her best friend, Olivia pick her up from work for a visit. Julia could only pray that none of their plans involved Dylan. Seth was next door, at his friend, Kyle's. As the afternoon rolled into evening, Kelsey came into the kitchen, "I'm bo-ored! Can't we do something?"

Julia chuckled at her middle child, "Life is so rough, what do you want to do?"

"Can Vanessa come over?" Kelsey asked, pulling her cell phone out of her pocket. Julia nodded her permission. The girls talked for a few moments and then Kelsey held the phone away, "Her parents are out, can we pick her up?"

It was nearly seven, Julia suggested, "Do you girls want to go get a pizza?" When Kelsey agreed, she headed into the other room to inform her husband then up the stairs to change. Pulling on a clean pair of jeans; she added a pale aqua tee. As she touched up her makeup and hair, she appreciated that last weekend's unseasonable sunny weather had given her some color. Ken joined her in the room to change, throwing on an Ohio State pullover.

**

Typical for the Pizza Playground, the only pizza place in Seneca, it was packed on a Saturday night. The establishment was a pizzeria combined with arcade games. Seated in a booth near the game room, they ordered their food and the young teenage girls took off to play some games. Julia went up to the drink station to fill her Diet Pepsi. She took a step back when her glass was full and bumped into the person behind her. It was Angie.

The women laughed. "Cody has been begging me to come here. After the hard work today, I thought he deserved it."

Julia nodded, "Marcus brought all of your things?"

Her new friend's face flashed anger, then she said resignedly, "He had something else to do, so Luke brought our stuff."

Ignoring the flutter in her chest and the shame that accompanied it, Julia muttered how nice that was. She and Luke usually did a bit of Facebook messaging every day or two. It was causal, but she was ashamed to admit how much she looked forward to it. Her own thoughts nearly caused her to miss Angie's next sentence, "He's around here somewhere." The two women scanned the room. "Oh, there he is at the booth with. . ."

"My husband," Julia finished her sentence. There sat Luke and Ken having a conversation. She felt suddenly light headed. The women approached them as pizzas were delivered, both of their orders.

"Hey Mom," Cody said as they approached the table. Luke turned his eyes on Julia.

"So, we meet again," he said with a friendly smile.

"Hi," was Julia's weak response. She glanced at Ken, who seemed pleased with the company, "Have you two met?"

"Yes, after Cody spilled half his drink on Ken."

"I'm sorry," Angie jumped in apologetically.

Ken laughed," Oh, it's okay. With three, I'm used to messes." Julia touched her husband's shoulder so that he would slide over. The girls had grabbed pizza slices and headed back to the arcade.

Ken was drinking beer out of a large stein, as were Luke and Angie. As the two families ate dinner, Julia's phone buzzed in her pocket. It was Lily, she wanted to go to a movie and had no cash. She'd stopped by the house and it was vacant. Could she come there and get some? In what seemed like a few moments, she was tapping her dad on the shoulder. Ken looked up, "Hey, you didn't come with us."

"Mom said you were here, can I have some money for the movies? I don't get paid until next week." Luke watched the girl standing between her parents' shoulders and narrowed his eyes.

Julia noticed his expression, though it was unreadable. "Luke, this is our eldest, Lily." His polite response was met with a teen's quick "Hi". Soon she had cash in hand and was gone.

Putting his wallet back in his pocket, Ken said to Angie, "Just wait, the older they get the more they cost."

4

Luke sat on the mattress in Angie's guest room amid boxes and tied his tennis shoes. It was nearly midnight and the house was quiet. Though he should be exhausted from the day's work he could not get to sleep. He needed to take a walk.

A walk had always been his way of working things out in his mind. He had spent hours hiking through the woods behind Spring Lake. A fight with his parents, trouble at work, even planning to end it with a woman led to a walk. Through the years he could clear his mind on foot.

Now Luke moved quietly out the front door and looked at his surroundings. He had to admit to himself that if his sister was going to leave the lake, this was a good place to live. Seneca appeared to be frozen in time, perhaps from the 1950s. Bikes leaned against garages, flower boxes full of blooms sat next to front porch swings. Luke looked down the deserted street. He only hoped he would find his way back, he really preferred to get out of the town to walk, someone walking at night can look suspicious. He remembered what direction the country highways were and headed in that way.

There was a slight summer breeze and it blew his hair into his face, he pushed it out of his eyes. Julia's image filled his mind. Why the hell after all this time had she appeared into his life? Luke let out a rush of air, this brought the past racing back. He remembered every moment with her.

They had met when she was fifteen and he was sixteen. She was with another summer girl, Cathy. They were attending a bonfire one of Luke's neighbors was having. The guys had some beers and were eyeing the summer girls as fresh meat. Not Luke, in fact he had a girl with him, Gina Logan from next door. They were dating that year. Maybe that was why he was nice and chatted with the new girls. He wasn't trying to make the moves on them.

Julia was so cute and skinny then. She had crazy long hair that sprung wildly down her back. The two girls were wearing the normal attire, bikini tops and jean shorts and at their feet were sweatshirts they would later pull on to avoid mosquitoes.

When Gina's dad called her to come in, Luke had walked her home and came back. Two of the older guys were trying to get close to the girls. Luke could smell the many beers they had drunk. He offered to take the girls on a late-night boat ride. Cathy was enjoying the attention of one of the them, so she refused, but Julia joined him. By the end of the night, he had made plans to take her water skiing the next day. Before the weekend was over, Gina was ancient history and he had fallen hard for Julia Gordon.

That first summer they were an innocent young couple. They swam, skied, went to movies and did not do much more than hold hands and kiss. Her parents were okay with the summer romance; his parents thought she was nice. When the summer ended, they were sad but wrote each other endless letters. The phone bills were exorbitant.

The next year when they were sixteen and seventeen respectively, she returned for the summer. He was shocked to see the woman she had become. When he nervously kissed her that first night, he nearly fell back at her eager response. Before the summer was over, they had lost their virginity to one another. This was the year they declared their undying love for one another and only his summer job kept them apart.

For the next two years, he drove to her hometown to take her to school dances. Julia and Luke also secretly met on occasional nights and weekends. His parents were lenient on how he spent his time. Julia's parents had hopes that this "summer fling" would end and therefore she used a lot of her friends as alibis to meet him somewhere between her Ohio town and his Michigan lake.

They talked about going to the same college, but when he graduated a year earlier, it was wisest for him to take the local grants and attend the Spring Lakes Technical College for virtually nothing. They had a great associate's program in architectural engineering. That was when they made the plan that he would join her at Ashland for his junior and her sophomore year. The out of state tuition would be expensive, he needed to get as much cheap education as he could before he joined her.

Luke felt his speed increase as he recalled the break up. It was so trivial, but that was typical. The two of them had been so emotional and passionate about everything that now it seemed to make sense why one mistake was blown so out of proportion. He knew that he should have kept his mouth shut; he never would have repeated his actions.

Now he shook his head, and spoke aloud to himself, "What are you thinking?" Why think of what he should have done, Julia was Mrs. Darby, wife and mother of three. This was over. He thought of the daughter with the car keys, how long had she been married?

**

It was shortly after midnight; the house was quiet. Julia was alone in the kitchen. She had sat up and waited for Lily to return. Olivia's car pulled into the driveway right at curfew. Her car was the only one that pulled in, but Julia was certain that a truck had driven slowly by afterwards. Dylan?

She sighed, now what? She wasn't going to argue tonight. Tomorrow they would discuss having Dylan over. Before she completely wrote him off, Julia needed to meet him. In the past, Lily had never given her any reason to question her sound judgement, though she had reservations, Julia hoped she was making more of this than necessary.

Lily said a brief hello and good night, and then headed to bed. Ken had been asleep for an hour, Julia was not tired, and her mind was filled with thoughts and memories. Perhaps a cup of chamomile tea would help her sleep.

When the water had heated in the microwave, Julia poured the steaming liquid into a mug, over a tea bag. She picked up the mug and walked to the living room. The bright moon outside caught her eye and on an impulse, she headed outside. Swinging on her old front porch swing seemed very appealing, the air was extremely warm for May.

The porch swing moved silently with Julia, her mind racing ahead of its slow rhythm. Sophie, lying at her feet, suddenly lifted her head, flattened her ears and let out a low growl, staring at the end of the driveway. Julia strained her eyes to see if a raccoon was out there or a deer. She froze when she saw movement on the road by the mailbox, it was definitely a person, a man. Sophie stood up, still growling and Julia grasped her collar. Had he seen her on the porch? She watched as the figure stood facing her property. Suddenly a cloud floated past the moon and the light revealed him. It was Luke. He looked directly at her. The dog made a move toward the drive, and Julia knew she would bark loudly, possibly waking the house. "It's okay girl, it's okay." Luke remained standing at the mailbox. Julia moved down the steps and to the drive talking quietly to the dog the entire time.

"Lucas Thomas are you still wearing out the roads around Spring Lake?"

He grinned, the whites of his perfect teeth lighting up the midnight sky. She felt her response in her stomach. "You know me." He glanced at her as she stood in the driveway wearing shorts and a sweatshirt, barefoot, clutching a mug. "Still a tea drinker?"

Julia hadn't realized that she carried her cup with her, "Actually I usually drink coffee. I just didn't want the caffeine."

"What are you doing out at this time of night?"

She looked at him and could not answer. The truth came right to her tongue and all other excuses failed her. He gave her a sad knowing smile. "Me too, want to talk?"

How could she have forgotten his keen sense of intuitiveness? Not once had she kept a secret from him. She nodded in agreement, looking around and spotting the patio table in the yard. With a motion from her, they both moved toward it.

"How'd you find my house?"

"In all honesty, I wasn't looking for it. I was just walking and stopped when I recognized your last name on the mailbox." They sat on opposite chairs, facing one another. Her mug was on the table between them. He caught her eye, "Are you happy, Julia?"

She nodded as she spoke, "Yes."

"Is he a good husband?"

"Yes. And a great father to our kids," at this she unconsciously glanced at the house as if Ken may suddenly materialize at the front door.

He nodded. She was about to ask him about himself when he spoke again, "So he was better suited for you than me?"

"I wasn't comparing."

"How long after you met was it before you married him?"

Julia was beginning to feel uncomfortable. "About a year." She felt her heart pound, they were headed into territory she did not want to be in.

Luke looked almost angry, putting his hand flat on the table, "A year? We got together when you were fifteen, we split when you were 18. And a year later, you married him?"

"I was pregnant," she blurted out and regretted her confession immediately.

"You were pregnant?" His response was a choked whisper.

It took her a moment to answer, "Yes, five months."

After a beat of silence, he asked, "Would you have married him if he hadn't gotten you pregnant?"

The question caused a painful jolt to her heart. She couldn't tell him the truth; she knew she wouldn't have married Ken had she not been pregnant. Julia hadn't loved Ken, but now she did. Not the reckless, all-consuming love of a young girl, but a love of appreciation and companionship. She had been foolish enough to allow him in her bed. He also paid the price for that, now she could not betray him. Julia saw Luke's eyes bearing down on her; he could see the truth in her. She turned away from him.

There was silence between them. With a deep breath to compose herself, Julia prepared to speak, but as she turned to face him, Luke looked at her and said quietly, "I wish. . .."

"Don't," she stood.

He reached across the table and grabbed her hand, “Please don’t leave now. Too much has never been said, we never got a chance.” Their hands were still clasped.

She sighed and sat back down. “Luke, I am sorry for the way things turned out. I know I was hard on you, we were so young. I was so unforgiving.” With a ragged breath, she reached for her mug and took a drink of the now ice-cold tea.

“It would have made things so much easier,” his voice was husky with emotion.

“What would have?” Julia looked at him, so beautiful across the table, the early morning light shadowing his sculpted jawline.

“If we had gotten pregnant, then we wouldn’t have thought about jobs or college or anything. We would have married and worked the rest out. You made the right choice with the wrong guy. Look how everything has worked out for you.”

Julia put her face in her hands for a moment absorbing his words. She rubbed her eyes and looked up. He just stared back for a moment. “I imagined finding you.” He stroked her hand with his thumb, she allowed him to. His long slender fingers sent heat shooting up her arm.

Now she gently placed his hand on the table and stood up. “It’s a million years too late.”

He dropped his head down for a minute, composing himself, and then he too stood, “I can see that.” They were silent. “I should head home,” he spoke finally.

“Do you want me to drive you?”

He shook his head, “No, I want to walk.”

“It’s a long way, can I get you something to drink?” she looked down at her drink, “Want this before you go?”

Luke reached for her mug and put the liquid to his lips and grimaced at the taste. “Still think you’re sweet enough that you don’t need sugar?” He attempted a weak smile. The phrase was one he always had teased her with. Now watching his mouth where hers had just been and hearing it was almost too much. Julia felt her skin shiver. Luke sat the mug on the table and turned to her, “I’m glad I finally got to talk to you.”

She kept control of her voice, “Me too.”

He laughed ruefully, “I’m not sure I feel any better because of it.”

This time Julia had no words with which to respond. Luke suddenly put his arms around her and pulled her close. Their lips were so near, it seemed natural to kiss.

When they made contact, Julia wondered how it could be both soft and rough, every sense in her responded. Her fingers burrowed into his hair. His hand accidentally skimmed under her sweatshirt, turning her skin to fire. After a long moment, she pushed back. “I can’t Luke.”

He reached up and stroked her face, then grabbed her in for another kiss, and this time it lasted longer. At last, Luke stepped back, looked into her eyes, smiled and walked away. As he moved down the road, Julia felt the tears streaming unchecked down her cheeks. She turned with Sophie at her heels and ran to the porch swing.

“How could it feel like I’m still in love with him? I ‘ve been a liar every day of my married life. I never got over him, now I don’t know if I ever will. I’m so sorry Ken.” Her words turned into sobs as she leaned against the chains of the swing and closed her eyes.

5

The newspaper carrier drove his old Chevy, without the muffler, up to the mailbox and dropped off the Sunday edition. The rattle of his car woke Julia, still on the porch swing. She jumped up disoriented, stumbling over Sophie at her feet. Glancing at her phone, beside her, Julia saw that it was 5:45, she sighed with relief. No one would be up yet.

Ken was still snoring in the bed, having not noticed her absence. Silently pulling her robe from the hook, she snuck into the bathroom. Julia swore she could still taste Luke on her lips and regretted that the cascading hot water was washing him off her mouth. Try as she might she could not clear the memories of last night. She had one more good cry and told herself that was enough.

**

Angie leaned on the window of her brother's silver Range Rover. "You sure you're ready to travel? You look pretty beat."

Luke gave her a forced smile, "I'm fine."

"Did I make you work too hard?" Just then Cody came through the garage.

"Uncle Luke, you forgot your shoes." The boy was carrying the shoes Luke had slipped off at the back door, still covered in the morning dew.

Angie glanced at the shoes being passed through the car window with a raised eyebrow. "Were you walking last night?"

"Yes, I couldn't sleep," Luke sighed.

"Did you walk anywhere in particular?" She was watching her brother for signs and didn't like what she was picking up on.

"Ang, I've got to get back to the lake."

"Luke, she's married with three kids." Angie rubbed his arm sympathetically.

"I'm very well aware of that. It's okay."

"Did you see her?" she pressed on.

"Please sis, I need to hit the road."

She impulsively put her arms around her brother's neck. "Should I hate her?"

He hugged back then looked at her, "No, not at all. She'll be a good friend to you."

"Okay," Angie moved to let him drive away.

Luke turned back to her, "But do me a favor, don't make any hasty decisions about your marriage. You're here, this is a chance to spend some time apart and see how it is. Don't rush into anything. Promise?"

"I promise, Lucas. Thanks for everything, I love you." She watched as her brother pulled out of the drive and disappeared around the corner.

Luke didn't need to be reminded of Julia's life. He'd found her cell number in Angie's phone when he returned last night. They had exchanged texts since dawn. What happened between them had affected her too, but she wasn't offering or suggesting that they get together again. Luke was not ready to give up.

**

Lily's phone buzzed on the nightstand. She picked it up, it was 9:00 and it was Dylan. She flipped the button, "Hey," she said groggily.

"Be ready in half an hour."

Lily sat up, "What are you talking about?"

"My buddies want to go four wheeling' and they're takin' their girls. I'll pick you up."

"But Dylan, it's Sunday, I have to go to church."

Dylan swore on his end of the line. "Skip."

Lily remembered her conversation with her mom last week. There was no way she could get out of it. She wouldn't be able to sneak away today. "I can't, Dylan. I really want to."

He swore some more, then his voice became whiny, "But everyone else will have their girlfriends."

She smiled, she was his girlfriend. "I wish I could."

"I don't know if it's worth it going out with such a baby."

"Dylan, I'm sorry. Don't say that."

"I'll call ya." He hung up, not waiting for a response.

Lily lay back in her bed, reflecting on Saturday night. There had been no movie, no time with Olivia. Getting money was just an extra assurance that her parents believed her. She had gone to Dylan's house. No one else had been home. He had turned on the television as they sat down on his sofa, but she never saw a moment of it. Dylan had kissed her until she couldn't breathe. His hands had explored under her top, lifting her bra to expose her breasts. Then his hands had trailed down to her jeans, dipping into the low waist. Lily had never been touched down there, she flinched at first. He had teased her; at least she thought it was teasing. He sounded a little mean, but surely, he was joking when he called her a baby with no experience.

She had stopped him when he tried to unbutton her jeans. His coaxing did not work. Finally, he just climbed on top of her. She could feel his erection straining against his own jeans. Dylan pushed it against her, moving as if they were actually having sex. Lily remembered the sensation it had caused between her own legs. He continued to move against her, his tongue probing her mouth, his hand squeezing her breasts. Finally, he had achieved his own release and laid his face against hers. Giving him that moment gave Lily a sense of power, he must really like her.

Afterwards Dylan had rolled to his side. "What time do you need to head home?" he had asked sleepily.

Lily checked her phone, it was time to go. Dylan gave her a kiss, but never moved from the couch as she left his house. Lily had climbed back into Olivia's car and drove to her friend's. Now Lily reflected on those moments and still convinced herself that it had been something very special between them.

6

Hours later, Julia was pulling chicken breasts from the oven. Kelsey had been assigned to serve up the mashed potatoes and green beans. Seth was getting drinks around the table. Lily wandered into the dining room at the heels of her father. Her mother looked at her daughter for a moment as if thinking. "Lily, why don't you have Dylan come over tonight and meet us?"

Surprised Lily spoke up, "I'll check."

"Good," Ken nodded.

While texting, she looked at her parents, "So will you hang out with us the whole time?"

Julia shook her head, "No, we just want to meet him."

**

Lily looked in the foyer mirror again, smoothed her hair and adjusted her very short jean shorts. Gravel crunched in the drive and the dog barked. "Shut up, Sophie," she hissed. The dog dropped her ears and quieted down as Lily opened the door to Dylan. He was wearing a black racing T-shirt and baggy jeans, on his feet were sneakers. His cap was a Corona beer one. She silently groaned, would her mother throw a fit about that?

"Hi, sexy," he said.

"Hey." She turned and led him into the living room where her mother sat reading. Julia looked up, smiled and put her book on the table beside her.

"Mom, this is Dylan."

Her mom stood up, "Hi, Dylan, nice to meet you."

"Hi."

"Come in, have a seat." Her mother gestured toward the sofa. The young couple sat a foot apart. Dylan did not offer to begin any conversation.

Julia jumped in, "Lily says you graduated from Seneca High?" He nodded. "What do you do now?" She did not pick up on the look exchanged between the couple.

"Pour concrete for my uncle."

"Well, that must be hard work." He did not respond.

"Is that what you want to do in the future?"

Dylan shrugged slightly, seemed to think about it and spoke, "I'd like to have my own construction company. But if this works out, a lot of guys from school travel to the Carolinas to do concrete work. It's good money."

"How did you meet Lily?" Julia could see her daughter making a face that said this was enough questioning.

"I like milkshakes, so I always go to the Dairy Bar."

Julia nodded. The room fell silent; it was obvious that Lily was not going to enter the conversation. She stood up, "Well, Dylan, thank you for coming over here to meet me. You're welcome to visit here tonight with Lily. Nice meeting you."

At that moment Ken entered the room. "Oh, sorry, I didn't hear anyone come in. I was upstairs, just catching up on the end of the race, I missed it."

Dylan looked up eagerly, "NASCAR?"

Ken's eyes lit up, "Of course. Hell of a race today."

"I wasn't home, who won?"

Ken launched into a detailed explanation, treating Dylan as if he was his long-lost son.

Julia headed out of the room. What was her daughter thinking? She imagined her dating the popular athletes in her class, not a guy who rarely spoke an entire sentence. In the kitchen, she opened her phone to play music. The hearty racing conversation in the other room was nauseating, didn't Ken see that this guy was not for Lily? Perhaps baking some cookies would get her mind off what was going on. She could imagine her daughter and her ideal boyfriend hanging out in the kitchen with her, munching on cookies. Dylan did not fit this picture.

Kelsey came down the stairs and into the room. "Whatcha baking?"

"Chocolate chip cookies."

"Yum, need help?" Her middle child swiped a chip from the bowl.

Julia smiled; she loved the early teens when it was still cool to hang with mom. But, she knew this was limited, it wouldn't be long before Kelsey would be scowling at the prospect of forced parent/child time.

When the first batch was done, she took the spatula and placed half a dozen cookies on a small plate. Julia retrieved two tall glasses from the cupboard, filled them with milk and placed it all on a tray. "Kels, I'm going to take this out to Lily and Dylan. If the timer goes off, take the cookies out of the oven."

"I want to see him."

"Not now, you can spy later," Julia grinned at her daughter.

She walked silently through the hall and glimpsed the teens before they saw her. He had his arm around her shoulder and it looked as if they had just quit kissing. Julia raised the volume of her voice and said to the sleeping dog in the hall, "No Sophie, quit sniffing, these are not for you." Lily moved away from Dylan as her mother walked in. Julia worked up a smile and spoke, "Thought you two might be hungry."

Lily opened her mouth to protest, but Dylan looked more animated than Julia thought possible. She barely had time to place the tray on the coffee table before he scooped up a cookie and shoved it whole in his mouth.

**

Luke tipped up his tumbler, trying to pour the last drops of Captain and Coke down his throat. With the final swallow, he propped his legs up on the deck railing, tilting back his chair. The sun was setting, and he admired the expanse of orange and pinks across the sky over the lake.

He wanted Julia back. Not just in his bed, though his sleeping was becoming more interrupted with those possible images, Luke wanted her here in this house.

Always interested in architecture, he had loved filling graph pads with plans for dream buildings. When he and Julia were together, they had made the first design sketches for this house. The sandy point at the north end was uninhabited, this was where they were going to create their home. Several times in the building of it, he had considered himself a fool for sticking with it. When the last board was placed, and final coat of paint was complete it had become more than a dream with Julia. It was a showpiece that served a self-employed architect well.

Now a few weeks after seeing Julia, kissing her, it was once again a pathetic representation of what he had lost. A boat passed, a wobbly skier on the back. The driver, a former classmate, waved heartily. Luke returned the gesture.

Would she ever leave her husband? Would she bring her three kids to Spring Lake to live? Luke stood and grabbed his glass, roughly tossing the ice off the side of the deck. "You fool, she isn't going to leave." Despite this fresh anger, he found himself reaching for his phone and sending a brief text:

Hey

**

Julia felt her phone buzz in the pocket of her khaki shorts. She sat in a folding chair amidst other softball parents. The screen showed the message was from "Lucy" her code name for Luke.

Hey

Hi

What are you doing?

At a ball game

Kelsey was up to bat; Julia ignored the next couple of buzzes. She cheered her daughter's double and her eventual run before she looked at the phone again.

I'm watching the sun set over the lake

Sounds fantastic

Come and see it

Julia looked around, guiltily. *I wish*

Do you? I think I need to visit my sister soon

Now she broke into a sweat. What would she do if Luke came back to town?

Would you see me? Can I call you later?

Yes. I'll text you.

**

By 11:08, the house was quiet. Julia hesitated less than a minute, her conscience losing out on the moral battle. Luke had taken Julia's mind hostage. She could hardly eat, woke up in the middle of the night covered in sweat and guilt. Each morning, Julia would fight her stress headache, and tell herself no more. Then, when the first message rolled in, she responded. Now, her text was met nearly instantaneously with a call. She headed to the living room to answer. "Hello, Jules."

Hearing his voice erased any doubts she had. "How are you?"

He wasted no time with small talk. "I really want to see you this weekend." She sighed, he heard it. "What's wrong?"

"I know I shouldn't."

"I just want to see you, no expectations."

His no-pressure tactic worked, "When will you be in town?"

The grin in his voice was obvious, "Friday, after work."

It was nearly midnight, the locusts hummed outside of the living room windows. Julia had never moved from the chair. Even though she had hung up a half an hour ago, her mind was racing. Luke was going to spend the weekend at Angie's. They were going to see each other privately. Even if it was in the middle of the night again, they planned on meeting. What was going to happen?

Lily came in from saying goodbye to Dylan. She tried to pass the room and head upstairs, but Julia stopped her.

"Come here, Lily."

Lily walked in, already on the defensive. "What?" She stood at the doorway.

Julia had currently lost the battle on Dylan. Ken had gone as far as to say that Lily would be a good influence on him. Imagine her daughter being responsible for that. However, Julia preferred them to be at her house, where she could keep an eye on them. She tried to give herself time to choose her words. This was a conversation she had not had as a parent before. "You really like him."

"Yeah, he's so cute and sweet."

"He's quite a bit older."

Lily groaned, "Not this again, he's only three years older." Now she sat down on the couch, in defeat.

"It's not the number, it's his life experiences." Julia's hands nervously traced the fabric lines in the arms of the chair.

"What do you mean?"

Another deep breath, “You two always look awfully close.”

Lily looked indignant, “You watch us?” Her posture moved from a slouch to sitting up.

“It isn’t hard to miss. Lily, this is your first boyfriend, you don’t have the experience that I’m certain he has.”

“He’s had other girlfriends, so what?”

One more breath, “He’s probably sexually experienced.”

“Mother, that’s not your business.”

“It is when it has to do with you.”

“I’m not having sex with him.” Her mother watched her carefully for a sign of being dishonest.

“But what about the future? Things will progress from where they’ve obviously already started. He expects to do certain things; you don’t want to give your virginity to the first guy who tries.”

“How do you know he’s the first guy who’s tried?” Lily hissed.

Julia sighed, “You know what I mean, and when you think you’re in love it can just happen.” The words were rushing out, she wanted to say just the right thing.

Lily narrowed her eyes at her mother, “Are you talking about me or you?”

That was unexpected. "This is not about me."

"Oh, I see you, can make comments about my sex life, but I can't comment on yours."

"Your sex life, does that mean you have one?" Julia's voice rose slightly.

"No, Mom, I already told you that," Lily began a nervous twist to her hair.

"Lily having sex is a serious thing. It's more than just the act, there are consequences, emotional and physical. Besides giving up your innocence, there are STDs and pregnancy to worry about."

"Mom, I'm not even planning on sleeping with him."

"But what if it just happens? You get caught in the heat of the moment and forget your good sense and have unprotected sex." Lily was quiet for a moment. Julia pressed on. "It happens to so many people, it would change your life forever."

"Mom, I'm not going to be stupid and get pregnant," the indignant tone did not reassure her mother.

Julia snorted, her eyes rolling. She had thought the same thing too. Memories of those moments came back to her; she took on a distant look.

"What?" Lily asked.

Julia shook her head trying to clear the past out, "Lily, I just want you to be careful. Nothing is full proof. You are so young."

"I told you I wasn't having sex. I don't know why you're freaking out about this." She watched her mother closely. Lily was processing the information; a notion hit her, and she leaped up, "You did."

"What?" caught off guard, Julia's expression was guilty.

"Oh my God, Mom it happened to you. Ever since my very first date you've obsessed about safe sex because *you* got pregnant!"

Her mother looked like a deer in the headlights, "Lily."

"Are you telling me you weren't married when you got pregnant with me? You *had* to get married?"

Now Julia sighed and spoke quietly, "This was not supposed to . . . "

"Not supposed to happen? Me?" Lily began to cry.

"Lily, I am happy with my life. Your dad and I were a lot older than you are. He was nearly finished with college," she moved over to the couch, tried to reach for her hand. Lily pulled her own away as if burned.

"I can't believe this, why didn't I ever know?" her daughter asked accusingly.

"It's not something you needed to know."

"Not until I might ruin my life the way you ruined yours?" With that Lily raced out of the room and up the stairs.

Julia did not try to stop her daughter. Instead, she sat on the sofa with her head in hands. Her phone buzzed. At this moment she hated herself because she knew what she would do. She grabbed it from her pocket and looked at it.

**

Being a single mom was not easy. Angie Castile had lived the last nine years like a single parent, she had thought. She had always been responsible for Cody getting up in the morning, getting him ready, taking him to daycare; handling the finances and most maintenance issues around the house. The shopping, the cleaning, and care of Cody's needs during the evenings were all hers. How different could moving alone to a new town with him be?

For some reason, it was a lot different. Marcus had served his purpose as a sounding board. She could toss ideas and problems off him and at least receive feedback if not actions. Now she had no one to discuss things with. Cody was only nine, he did not need to hear the complaints of the office or give suggestions on which trash service to choose.

Angie's new life was hectic, boring, and lonely all at the same time. She said as much to her older sister, Nancy on the phone.

"You need a girlfriend," responded her always outspoken and matter of fact sibling.

Angie laughed into the phone. She could see from her spot in the kitchen that Cody was deep into a racing game on his PlayStation. "I'm not making that drastic of a change."

"I mean a friend, a girl to hang with."

"Oh yeah, easier said than done."

"Don't you work with any women?"

"Yeah, it's just hard to get invited to stuff. I think a single woman is always suspicious."

"Yeah maybe, how about Lukey's little girl?"

"Lukey's little girl?" she snorted, "First off Lukey is nearly forty and it's time to quit calling him that. And do you mean Julia when you say little girl?"

"Mom said she lives there."

"I don't know," Angie frowned.

"Still a bitch?"

"What, she's not a bitch!"

"Well you used to think of her as a summer bitch. I remember her; all long brown hair, tan and skinny, strutting around in a bikini and our little brother not able to keep his hands off her. You said she'd screw him over, and she did, didn't she?"

"I don't know, but she's real nice. She's still pretty but she is not a snob."

"Then call her."

"I don't know, Luke was kind of upset when he left here."

"As Mackenzie says, Uncle Luke can be dramatic." Mackenzie was Nancy's sixteen-year-old daughter.

Angie laughed again, "Maybe. I don't know. He went for a walk that night and the next day when he left he was sad."

"Think he got together with her?"

"I have no idea; she's married to a nice guy, three kids."

"Old flames and all that, you never know. Call her. Take her out; get her drunk, maybe she'll tell you what happened."

"I wouldn't mind hanging out with her. But, I'm not sure I want to hear the juicy details about her and Luke."

"Oh, come on sis, do it for me."

7

The waitress sat a glass of Pinot Grigio and a beer on the table in front of Julia and Angie. Angie picked up the beer and took a long drink, “Just what I needed.”

“It’s been a tough week, huh?” Julia asked her, before she sipped her own drink.

“Yes, between the new job, new town, new house and single parenthood, it’s not exactly the sense of rightness I expected it to be.” Angie shook her head and went for her beer again.

“You know how it is, newness always sucks.”

Her companion laughed at Julia’s bluntness. The waitress returned with fresh guacamole, queso, chips and two small plates. The women each dug into the appetizer.

“How’s Cody doing without his dad?”

“Well, as I told you, Marcus kept to himself most of the time, choosing the gang over us, so I think it may not be as tough on Cody as me. For me, it's the idea that he is essentially not around ever."

"That makes sense." Julia peered at her new friend over her wine glass, "Do you miss him?"

Angie toyed with a chip on her plate, scooping up cheese and guacamole. "I do, actually. It was not as if I quit loving him, it was just that I was so tired of being second or third place in his life."

"Have you guys talked since you moved?"

"Of course, he is sorry, he wants to change, and he wants us home. But that's the point, he wants us home. I am not returning to the way things were. My son and I deserve more than that, don't you think?" When she looked up her eyes were bright with unshed tears, but she kept it together.

Julia patted her hand, "I certainly do. Look, you made this huge step, you can't give up now. Who knows, maybe he will come begging to you."

Angie sniffed in disbelief and finished the last of her beer.

Within an hour, she was nursing a third beer and Julia had switched to Diet Pepsi after a second glass of wine.

"Okay maybe you can give me some good advice."

"About Luke?" her friend raised her eyebrows.

Julia nearly spit her Pepsi across the room, "What?"

Angie giggled, "Sorry. I can't believe I said that. Nancy told me to take you out and get you drunk so we could find out why Luke was so depressed when he left here."

Julia's face reddened, her heart was pounding wildly. She struggled to maintain her composure. She looked across the table at Angie's loose smile and relaxed posture, "I think that's the beer talking."

"Probably, sorry. But do you know why?"

Attempting to avoid a defensive tone she responded, "Why would I know?"

"He went walking that night, Cody found his shoes." When Julie took too long to respond, Angie slapped the table, "I knew it. Did he try to start something up with you?"

"No, we just kind of talked through the end of our relationship, because when we first did it was angry, ugly."

"Oh, okay that makes sense. Not nearly as exciting as I had hoped." Julia smiled a false smile, if Angie only knew that they had started what she was beginning to think of as an emotional affair. She decided to change the subject. Nervously picking up a chip and breaking it into pieces on her plate, she searched for a safer topic. "So how are you on dealing with teenage relationships? My daughter is seeing someone I don't think I approve of."

"What's wrong with him?"

"Three things, she began dating him behind my back. He's nineteen, and he's not the kind of boy I'd like her to date."

"Oooh. She's what, sixteen?" Julia nodded. "That's tricky. I mean three years isn't that big of a difference."

"But," Julia interjected, "he's been out of high school for two years and she just finished her sophomore year. These particular three years seem big. And let me tell you, this guy is persistent, she is constantly on the phone with him, I know he is seeing her at the shop when she works."

"I don't envy you on this one. I guess I would get to know him. Maybe he's a gem other than age or there are more important reasons why she shouldn't see him."

"Nothing makes a boy more desirable than parents not liking him."

Angie nodded, "Don't I know it. Mom and Dad wanted me to move away from Spring Lake and the guys there. They were so disappointed that I was determined to settle with Marcus."

"And maybe parents know best sometimes."

"Maybe. Why don't you make her have the guy over for the first few times?"

"We have. I'm not impressed," she took a drink. "But Ken . . ."

"Big bad scary dad?"

Julia scoffed at the notion, "No, all the kid had to mention was his interest in NASCAR and Ken practically invited him to sleep over."

Angie laughed, "Julia!"

"Well maybe not that extreme, but you know what I mean."

**

Thursday night, Julia could see that her daughter was visibly upset about something. She was moping around and snapping at her siblings at every opportunity.

Julia finally cornered her in her room, "What's wrong Lily?"

Her daughter turned angry eyes on her, "Because *you* won't let me go out with Dylan on a school night, he's out with his friends in the city."

"It's my fault that he's out? Lily, he is nineteen, he's going to do things you can't do."

"Whatever," her daughter looked down at her phone.

"If you don't trust him out, then that means something."

Lily turned on her, "I never said I didn't trust him, it's just so unfair that I can't go out with him."

In the late hours of the night, Julia was awakened by a voice. She lay in her bed and strained her ears to listen; she could hear Lily, obviously on her phone. It was clear that she was upset. Julia could not hear complete sentences, but words like, "What were you doing, lonely, why." She got the gist of the situation; Dylan must have stayed out late with his friends. Would she also have to worry about alcohol with this guy? This needed to end.

**

The next night at dinner, the teenagers were all quiet as they dug into big plates of spaghetti. Julia had one of those moments of serenity as she looked at the family. The kids were growing into wonderful young adults. They had not yet made any progress on the Dylan situation, but Julia was certain that Lily would soon see that he was not a great boyfriend. She glanced across at her husband, he was unaware of her perusal. Such a kind and generous father, Julia felt shame at her own poor choices; the many texts and late-night calls needed to stop.

Ken looked up from his plate and said casually, "I'm going to Chicago on Tuesday and I'll be back on Sunday."

Julia looked at him sharply; most of his trips were one or two nights, not five. She had a suspicion that this one involved a golf outing. This was his third since spring began; she was tired of being the sole parent around the house. She didn't have a problem with his traveling for business, but not extended trips. How was she supposed to stay a loyal wife if he wasn't here? Julia shook her head, who was she kidding, she was planning on seeing another man this weekend. And now Ken wasn't even going to be home. She was moving closer and closer to having an affair. Could she really do it? Julia already knew the answer. The spaghetti on her plate grew cold.

Her calls with Luke grew more intimate every day. The last one was very dangerous because they began reliving their past. Talk of losing their virginity together, skinny dipping in the lake, and having sex in any available spot left them both breathless.

"What do you think it would be like now?" Luke had asked softly.

"Terrifying," Julia had responded. "I don't look the same at all."

"You are beautiful."

"No, but you are just as handsome as always. I'm showing my age."

"I'd like to see where. I mean that." They skated along that line of suggestive flirting. She was flushed when they hung up. Desire infused her in a way she hadn't felt for years.

**

On the day of Ken's departure, Julia brought clean laundry to their room. He was packing with his eye on the television, "Where are my trunks in case I want to swim?"

Julia set her basket down and put her arms around his waist, "I wish I could come too."

He patted her lightly on the shoulder, "Ted and I will be working until late every evening."

She sighed and dropped her arms, "I know, I meant it would be fun if we were going away together."

“Mmm,” Ken responded as he moved to his dresser. A hole in one by the pro golfer on the screen received the excited exclamation she had wanted for herself.

Julia stomped her foot, “I want you to pay attention to me!”

He turned around, “What?”

“I want us to spend some time alone.”

“Look this isn’t a good week.” Ken suddenly leered at her and reached for her, “I have a few minutes now.”

“That’s not what I’m talking about.” She pulled out of his grasp, “I was just saying I wish we could be going away together.”

Ken frowned, “When? Seth’s tournament is coming up, and I have that Indians game with the guys from the office soon.”

“Couldn’t you just say you’d like to?” Julia interrupted.

He shook his head, “I hate it when you get this way. Why don’t you arrange something?”

Now she was too mad to quit. “Because I’d like you to do something for once. You plan a weekend for the two of us. You know make the reservations, make arrangements for the kids, pack our clothes. Not just come along for the ride.”

"What?" Looking annoyed, Ken stared at her, a stack of socks in his hand.

"Last year for our anniversary, all you had to do was get in the car and go. You didn't even bother to buy me a card. I paid for all the meals."

"That's because you went to the bank," he shook his head as if she was being foolish.

"Exactly."

Ken headed for the door, "Whatever, I don't have time for this. I need to get my briefcase packed."

"Which you will do in front of ESPN." Julia moved closer to him, "You're my husband and I wish you'd be more loving."

He stepped over to her and kissed her gingerly on the forehead, "Bad day, hon?" Then he left the room.

Tears welled up in Julia's eyes. He didn't even understand. It amazed her to think that he was satisfied with their relationship as it was. She had wanted more than a man around the house, a provider, and father figure for the children. She had wanted a best friend, a lover, just like Luke would have been. This gave her a small sense of justification. Let him come this weekend, maybe she was ready to see him.

Julia had decided by the time Ken pulled out of the driveway in the morning that she was looking forward to his absence. She had not told Luke that Ken was going to be gone. That seemed to be an invitation for things she wasn't sure she was ready for. But seriously, what did she think Luke was expecting? A married woman had been talking in secret with him for two weeks after they kissed. Now she was planning on seeing him. What was going to happen?

8

On Friday, Julia didn't have a class. She was forcing herself to give the house a thorough cleaning to keep her mind off Luke. He was coming to town this evening after work. Angie had called her on Wednesday and mentioned it in the conversation. Julia already knew, of course. Luke had convinced his sister that they should come to the ball field tonight to see Seth's team play.

Julia was torn. After this time of conversations with Luke, she couldn't wait to see him. But, how was she going to keep her feelings a secret at the ball field? And what about the pure terror she felt at their planned private meeting. Though they had not worked out the details, even if it was in her backyard again in the middle of the night, they had promised to get together when he was in town.

It was a beautiful June night. Julia found herself in the usual spot on the bleachers, surrounded by the other women she socialized with. They were all mothers of boys on Seth's team, most she had known for years, their kids growing up together at the local school. One or two also worked at the college. A few had gotten divorced over the years, there were even new husbands. She eyed these women carefully. How had they found themselves divorced? Had they ever cheated?

The notion seemed ridiculous. Julia certainly didn't consider herself the kind to do such a thing. She had been convinced that wild and adventurous sex was just something you did when you were young. Her love life with Ken was very routine, satisfying to a point. It had seemed fine. Now she was not sure. It was at this moment in her thoughts that she looked up and saw Luke walking across the field with his sister. Her body burned. He looked fantastic in gray shorts, a close fitting black shirt, sunglasses and flip flops. He was tall and lean. Julia chuckled slightly; there was no way that *this* man wanted her. She was fooling herself. Maybe he drunk dialed her at night. As she thought this, he caught her smile and grinned back. It terrified her, that grin told her that he knew exactly what he had been whispering in her ear late at night.

The baseball game was a fog of small talk and a struggle to focus. Afterwards, when Julia finally made it home with her son she could barely recall a single coherent sentence she had uttered. Even at the Dairy Bar, she was in a daze. No one else seemed to notice, including her angry teen daughter who had sent the red pickup careening out of the parking lot when the ball team approached.

Seth staggered to his room, insisting he was too tired to shower off the grime he brought home from the park. Kelsey had left with another family for a sleepover. Lily was already off work and headed to Olivia's. Olivia's mom had been with the group and witnessed the plans. Julia wondered, though, if her daughter would sneak out of the other family's house later to see Dylan.

At the time, she couldn't have argued if she had wanted to. The gang was packed into a wooden picnic table, and Luke's bare knee was scorching a hole into her leg. At one point he had had the nerve to place his hand on her thigh. Now she would sit on the front porch and await his arrival.

Julia headed into her own bathroom, staring at her reflection she said aloud, "And then what?" She brushed her teeth, ran her fingers through her hair to shape it, then a splash of her favorite citrus perfume. As she walked into her room, she tried to tell herself she should get in bed and turn off her phone. This was wrong.

Instead, she headed down to the kitchen and poured herself a glass of wine, a tall glass of wine. Out on the porch, she sunk into the swing, her legs shaky. From the dark side of the porch came a voice, “Did you pour one for me too?”

Julia jumped up, the wine threatened to spill out of the glass. Luke came forward and caught it. “I didn’t mean to scare you.”

“How long have you been here?” She was embarrassed to imagine him seeing all her grooming.

“Just a few minutes.” There was a moment of awkward silence. They looked at each other, the realization that they were strangers.

She looked down at her glass, “Would you like some wine?”

He smiled in relief, “Yes, please.”

Julia led him into the house, to the kitchen. Soon they stood at the island and sipped. He glanced at the steps, “Should we be in here?”

“It’s only Seth tonight and he’s dead to the world.”

**

Luke raised his eyebrows slightly. He knew Ken was absent from the game, but so was Kelsey. He had assumed she must have been playing elsewhere and her father was with her. Julia had never mentioned that her husband was away. Now here he stood in her kitchen with her alone.

Nerves were also bubbling in him, he reached for his drink in hopes of some relief. The bottle of Pinot Noir was more than half empty. He refilled both of their glasses. “This is a bit different than the first bottle of wine we shared.” They both grinned as he held up his glass, “Wasn’t that Boone’s Farm Strawberry Hill?”

She nodded her head in agreement, “As I recall the bouquet of that particular bottle was reminiscent of Kool-Aid.” It felt good to be comfortable. They discussed their jobs. Her love of history and his of architecture bisected one very special weekend after she graduated, they had traveled to Saginaw, Michigan to visit the Castle Museum.

“Do you remember our favorite castle?” they were leaning shoulder to shoulder.

"Of course, Neuschwanstein," Julia's smiling eyes glowed. She turned to him, so close now, "Have you ever gotten to go there?"

Luke suddenly was very glad to say, "Not yet. The closest I have seen was Mont Saint Michel on a trip to Paris, years ago. You?" He could not believe how much he wanted her to say that she had not been to "their" dream castle without him.

"Absolutely not, the biggest castle I have been to was Casa Loma in Toronto. We vacationed there four years ago."

This satisfied Luke. He lightly rested his hand on her hip, the wine bottle was now empty, and he was brave. In a soft voice he spoke, "Maybe someday." Their eyes were meeting now, and lingering. Luke pulled her to him. She leaned in automatically and they kissed for a few minutes. The heat increased, and they wrapped their arms and hands around one another. She finally moved away, he tried gently to pull her back to him.

"I can't risk it," she said softly, and it broke the mood. They crashed back into reality. Here they were in the house she shared with her husband. Her son was upstairs asleep in his room.

"Luke, this between us," she gestured with her hand.

He kissed the top of her head, "Feels like we should never have stopped doing it?"

"Exactly," she whispered, "but you must go. I cannot let it go any further tonight."

**

By the next afternoon, it was a different woman that he spoke to. This one was regretful, ashamed. While Luke had returned to Angie's house, and slept soundly in the guest bed, apparently Julia had surrounded herself with feelings of guilt. The conversation was stilted and awkward. He wanted to express his gratitude and joy. She did not want to talk at all. Luke had no idea how to proceed. As a teen this was when he became obsessed and would have been at her front door, demanding an explanation. Adult Luke knew that this would not work. Despite what he wanted, he allowed her this, and stayed away.

9

Things were strained between Julia and Lily. Her daughter obviously felt betrayed because of the secret she'd learned. When Julia had tried to address the subject, Lily shut down. The secret of her surprise pregnancy nearly eighteen years ago had changed her entire life again, this time with two people. If she hadn't shared it with Luke, then nothing would have happened. She should have respected her husband and not felt the need to explain why they got married so quickly. But no, she blurted it out and that was it. Luke wanted her, and she was afraid that she wanted him too.

What the hell had she done last weekend? Though she thought she was going to throw up, the part of her that was evil relished it. She could still feel his lips and hands on her skin. An image of Lily and herself arguing about Dylan came to mind. Who was she to decide what a good relationship was? She was sabotaging her own marriage. Julia knew this had been a mistake. This situation with Lily was more important than her own needs. What she had done was unforgivable. Things with Ken had to work. He was certainly not helping, she discovered that his business appointments ended on Thursday night and he had spent the entire weekend golfing. He deserved what she had done with Luke. Julia shook her head, no, she must show Lily that she loved her father and that their life together was not a mistake.

Before she could make any more decisions, her phone buzzed. Ashamed at the increase of her own heart rate, she looked at the screen, Julia spoke breathlessly, "Hi Luke."

"Is this a bad time?" he sounded kind and concerned.

Julia wanted someone to be mad at her. He should be, she had ignored his calls for the past four days. She glanced up the stairs where all three of her children were shut into their rooms.

"No, I can talk for a moment."

He was direct as always, "Regret seeing me?"

She sighed, unprepared. "Yes and no."

Damn him, she could hear the smile in his voice as he responded, "I understand."

"I can't see you again, not right now. Maybe never. I don't know. Luke, I never should have done that...." Her voice trailed off, making her words sound unconvincing.

"I'll give you time. I won't expect to see you anytime soon. I'll stay away from Seneca."

He had waited years, decades. But that was exactly why he could give her that. Maybe she would contact him sooner. He whispered sweet words to her and hung up.

**

School ended for the kids, Julia was down to a part time teaching schedule. It looked like a beautiful summer ahead. Lily had not ended it with Dylan, but her mother could always hope. Julia worked very hard on being affectionate with her husband in front of her daughter. Whenever he did something kind, she thanked him profusely, hoping their respect for one another was a good example. Just two nights ago they had gone out to dinner, forcing Lily to keep an eye on her little brother. Though Ken had made an ordeal of recording an "important" Indians game first, Julia held her tongue in front of her daughter. Happily married was what she wanted to represent.

Ken left for a two-day trip, it was his birthday the day after he returned. Julia decided to throw a surprise cookout for him on the evening that he came back. Wouldn't this be a good show of love for Lily to see? And, a reminder to herself that she must end her relationship with Luke? Once Ken got home, she would tell Luke no more exchanges.

Ken had said that they should be back home by three or four on Wednesday. She allowed Lily to invite Dylan and that seemed to help the tension between them. Julia bought burger, dogs, and all the fixings. She cut up fresh fruit in the afternoon and baked strawberry pies and brownies for dessert. By two, with the help of the kids, she was setting up the picnic tables including those brought over by guests the night before. She filled big coolers with ice and added pop, water bottles and one with beer. The grill was cleaned and ready to go.

At three, she had changed into a pair of white bermudas and a bright pink sleeveless top. She put on pink flip flops and headed down to check the progress. Seth and Kelsey were trying to construct the badminton/volleyball net. Lily was setting up her speakers out on the deck.

By four Ken had not yet returned, she tried his cell phone and got only voicemail.

At four forty-five she called Ted's wife, she told Julia that Ken had not yet dropped Ted off.

Shortly after five, Angie and Cody showed up. The women helped each other get the grill lit. Angie added potato salad to the spread of food. The boys jumped right into a game of badminton.

Julia tried her husband's phone again, both calling and texting. Though Ken despised texting back, he would read her message. Guests began to arrive sharply at six. She explained that Ken was apparently delayed but they would eat anyway. The glass-topped table was overloaded with food. Dennis from down the road took over as grill cook and the party moved along nicely.

Dylan had brought another couple with him and the older teens hung out at the farthest table, eating and laughing. Julia watched the boy wrap his arm possessively around Lily and tried not to wince.

She was starting to feel a mixture of annoyance and apprehension. Her first instinct was that Ted and Ken had found a golf course on the road and couldn't resist stopping. This would not be the first time this had happened. But if this were true, he needed to tell her where he was.

Another half an hour had passed, and Julia was enjoying a piece of strawberry pie with some of her favorite friends when Sophie barked letting her know someone else had arrived. She smiled, "Finally."

Julia excused herself and headed around the side of the house to the front. She glanced at the drive expecting Ken's black Chrysler, but instead she saw two uniformed officers getting out of a State Highway Patrol Cruiser flanked by Sophie. Her breath went out of her and Julia began to shake. "Oh no, no, no," she whispered to herself.

They both removed their hats and avoided her eyes. She repeated herself, "No, no, no."

One approached, "Mrs. Darby?" She stared at him and did not respond. He knew that she knew.

"Mrs. Darby, your husband was in an accident this afternoon. We need you to come to the University Hospital in Cleveland."

"Tell me," she said raggedly. Julia had heard from people who had suffered this tragedy that they would direct you to the hospital and then tell you.

"I'm sorry Mrs. Darby; he did not survive the accident."

She began to sob. The other officer glanced back at the drive and all the cars "Are there others here to help you, Mrs. Darby?"

The world faded away right then. Tears blinded her vision, the only sound she could hear were the wails of anguish from her children as they rushed to her looking for protection from this awful truth. Olivia's dad was a local policeman; he pulled the patrolmen aside for details. Ken was driving, Ted in the passenger seat, on the Ohio Turnpike. He was in the left lane and a semi didn't see him. The truck driver attempted to pass a vehicle in the right lane, slamming into Ken's car and smashing it into a guardrail. Neither man survived. Julia stood in one place, clinging to her children as their lives fell apart.

10

The days that followed were a blur to Julia. She did not even have time to face her own sorrow. Seth was hysterical; Kelsey wanted to cling to her. Lily found solace with Dylan. Ken's parents arrived, and Julia' family drove in. She was numb as she moved about making arrangements, holding the children, dealing with the loss of her husband.

It was eleven at night. The calling hours and funeral were over. Julia's phone had been off for days. She glanced at it on the nightstand and turned it on. Message after message from Luke chimed in as it surged on. Julia tossed it to the bed horrified. At that moment, it buzzed again, this was a current message. All it said was, *I'm outside*

Julia flung open her bedroom door. Her parents, sleeping in Seth's room, called out to her, "Honey are you okay?"

"Yes," she forced her voice to be calm, "Sophie needs out, I'm taking her."

"I'll take care of it," her dad spoke in a sleepy tone.

"No, Dad, I've got it." She marched purposely down to the front porch and pushed open the door, making certain that Sophie joined her.

Luke stood in the yard, near the table where they first reconnected. Julia wasted no time to race at him. He held out his arms expectantly and was shocked when she slammed herself at him, not in an embrace, but as a defensive move. "Get the hell out of here!" Julia was outraged. "Ken was a good man. A good husband. His last days on earth I spent talking to you! Get the hell out of my life and don't you ever come back."

Luke tried desperately to calm her and talk sense into her. She could not later recall a single word, only his damnable soothing tone which she would have nothing of. "I regret that I ever even spoke to you again. I can never forgive you or me. If you care about me at all you will get out of my life and stay away!" With those words, Julia stumbled back to the porch, up the steps and slammed the door. Luke heard the locks click shut.

**

Julia's world had changed permanently in such a short time. It was more of a nightmare than a reality in her mind; the calling hours, the funeral, the children's grief, facing relatives and friends from all over. She felt physically drained.

Her mother came out to the porch swing where Julia sat. She handed her daughter a mug of coffee. "You look exhausted hon, why don't you take a nap."

"Thanks Mom, but I can't just sleep through the next six months."

"You're right," her mother said quietly.

They sat for a few moments in silence. Julia stared unseeingly at the beautiful trees in her yard. She could not imagine the days, weeks, months and years that lay ahead of her. What was she going to do? She was a widow and single mother of three.

"I need to get a full teaching schedule," she mumbled to herself.

"What's that about teaching, dear?" asked her mother.

"I said I need to work full time."

"Oh honey, you don't need to worry about that right now."

Julia turned to her mom, “Yes, I do, I want the kids’ lives to go on with the things they have been used to. I’ll be raising three kids alone from now on.”

Tears sprang to her mother’s eyes, “It’s just not fair.”

“Please, Mom; I’m trying to keep a clear head. I have a lot of decisions to make.”

“What kind of decisions?” Julia’s father walked out on the porch.

“The insurance money allows me to give the children time to adjust to the loss of their father, but I need to earn a full salary.” Julia gazed out on the corn fields surrounding their two acres of land, “I don’t even know if I’ll stay in this house.”

“Julia,” her father said gently, “You take one step at a time, there’s no need to hurry. Financially you’ll be okay for quite a while.”

“I know, Dad, thank God.”

Lily came to the screen door, “Mom, can I go over to Dylan’s?” Dylan had been a great support for Lily during the past week. Despite her previous concerns, as Julia had struggled with her own shock and grief it had been good for her daughter to have someone who was concerned about her feelings. She had even seen Dylan crying at the cemetery. He had been in and out of the house nearly every day and when they had begun to go places together, Julia had let it happen.

"Okay, keep in touch if you leave his house at all."

Lily leaned down and hugged her mom, "Thanks, love you."

"Love you too."

Seth came out of the house and climbed on his mother's lap. Julia stroked his hair. This is how he had been, constantly needing to be near her. He was at a difficult age where crying came easy, but it was embarrassing. Just clinging to her seemed to give him comfort.

11

Luke had been patient at first, waiting to hear from Julia. Days had turned into weeks, and then months. Angie had kept him informed of how she was doing, though it was tricky trying not to ask too often and give anything away. He realized she had meant what she said; she never wanted to see him again. It hurt nearly as much as it had twenty years ago.

Thinking of Ken's death made Luke ashamed of himself. This man had died, only 42 years old. He'd had a great life, three kids and the best wife anyone could have. The wife Luke wanted. Things were only getting worse as he sat at the lake.

A change of scenery was just what he needed.

**

The country was beautiful. Looking at the sunset from the other side of the world was amazing. Luke had no regrets coming to China to do a job. Time was flying between meetings, dinners with local builders and sightseeing. He had planned on sending two others from his office to make the bid in China. It had been wise to go instead.

His work would take more than a month, he was excited to experience the process. Everyone was very nice and for the first week he would find himself returning to his small apartment late at night, falling right to sleep. It was during the second week that things slowed a bit in the evening. He had begged off some of the lengthy dinners to stay in the apartment to work on his computer.

It was while he was working so diligently that his Pandora channel began playing an old classic from his phone. When he heard Richard Marx singing *Endless Summer Nights* his mind went to Julia. He felt a pang in his gut; he really didn't want to give himself over to the thoughts.

Luke caved by the second verse, he leaned back in the seventies style orange chair and closed his eyes. He recalled that final conversation in the moonlight. Damn, had he done the right thing letting her go back in? Her words were like a knife in his chest, but he knew where they came from. He had felt responsible when he heard the news of Ken's accident. Not that he had ever believed in karma, but it was eerie. As every moment had been for them since he was 19, their brief moments of happiness had swiftly gone downhill. She didn't run to his arms for support and comfort. She turned on him. It really tore him up to remember the complete agony she was in. He knew that it was the right thing to step away. Was that how it was going to be forever? Luke rubbed his eyes; he really didn't want to think about this.

"Aargh," he groaned out loud and stood up. In the fridge, he found a bottle of water, put it to his lips and drank half of it. He twisted the cap back on and carried it back to the desk where he was working. At the keyboard, he clicked on his iTunes, finding current music to play as he resumed his work.

12

Five months moved past. Julia watched the first snowflakes of winter stick to her bedroom window. There was no joy in this lovely sight. The trees, silver with frost, did not please her as they usually did. She didn't have the sudden urge to put her Christmas music on. In fact, she hardly noticed the snow at all. Her eyes stared unseeing at the beautiful scene before her. Her mind was spinning. It had taken these five months for her frozen heart to melt. The time following Ken's death had been one of her moving in a robotic manner. She was loving and understanding as the children struggled with their grief. She had handled Ken's parents and brother smoothly. Julia was working a full load at the college.

Only Angie questioned her emotional strength. This woman was her constant friend. Her own newness as a single parent made her available for whenever Julia needed anything; a conversation, company or the need to vent. True loneliness was a new burden. She despised the constant responsibility of serving as a single parent.

Today Julia was alone, and this had allowed thoughts that she'd kept hidden bubble up to the surface. The kids had all gone to Ken's parents, Lily grudgingly. They had picked them up as soon as school let out. Now it was six p.m. on Friday and Julia was alone. Her last class had ended at eleven, so she had run errands and packed for the kids before they got home. Now a long empty evening lay ahead of her. She poured herself a glass of wine and glanced in the fridge uninterestedly. Julia had lost nearly ten pounds since Ken's death. Food, like everything else in life, had lost its pleasure.

She moved into the living room and settled on the couch, flipping on the remote and looking through the channels aimlessly. Her wine disappeared as she continued to find nothing of worth to watch. Out the window, a flash of red on the road caught her eye. Was it Dylan? Shortly after the family had driven away, he had pulled into the driveway and she had informed him that Lily was gone. She'd called Lily's cell and her daughter confirmed that he knew she was gone.

Back in the kitchen she topped off her glass and this time grabbed some crackers.

With nothing to watch on television, she settled on the stool at the island and turned on some music. An old Buckcherry song was on, “Sorry”. Julia let the words fill the room. Sorry, that was her. Sorry that she had lost her husband, sorry that her world was permanently changed. Sorry that she had not appreciated and enjoyed Ken and their marriage like she should have. Sorry about Luke.

Luke. His name rolled itself around and tore through her heart. Painful tears spilled down her cheeks. “Luke,” this time she spoke aloud.

“It was my fault that Ken died,” she choked on a sob. “Ken, I’m so sorry. It was wrong of me. I loved another man.” Julia cried hard racking sobs. Her heart ached, her head throbbed, and her body shook uncontrollably. Finally, Julia was admitting what had been eating away inside of her.

She spent the weekend suffering. Friday turned into Saturday and she didn’t turn a light on. She never changed her clothes or ate. Julia’s only actual function was to let Sophie out and feed her. She wandered the gray rooms of the house in agony. "I'm sorry," she would whisper repeatedly.

Late Sunday afternoon, the doorbell rang. Julia decided to ignore it. She wasn't capable of a conversation. It was Angie. Julia had not answered her calls. She knocked and rang until Julia was forced to answer. Angie gasped as she looked at her friend. Her face was pale and swollen, red from continual crying. Her hair and clothes had obviously not been touched for days. Angie grabbed her friend and threw her arms around her, "Honey, what's going on?"

Julia collapsed against her embrace, her body trembling, allowing herself to be led to the couch. "Have you been like this all weekend? It's time you let loose and felt your own loss," Angie pressed her friend's head against her shoulder. "You've been so strong, you needed to let go."

Julia's voice was a ragged whisper, "I've been avoiding the truth and it was time to face it."

"He's gone, hon." Angie let her cry some more before she spoke, "You haven't eaten for days, have you?" She glanced at two empty wine bottles on the coffee table and stood up, "Let's get some coffee started."

Over the sounds of the water and cupboard doors she spoke, "I wish I'd known that you were alone. I could've stayed here. Cody is with his dad at the lake. They competed in a fishing tournament with Luke." She heard a strangled wail from the living room and raced in. Julia was slumped over on the couch, her face in her hands, sobs racking her body.

Angie knelt beside her. "What's wrong?" Julia continued to cry out loud. "Are you sick? Did I say something?" She thought about what she said and whispered, "Luke?"

Julia shook her head violently, "Please don't talk about him, please."

"Julia, what about Luke is upsetting you?"

"Don't," her cry was desperate.

Angie wrapped her arms around her friend and rocked her. Julia was so silent that she thought she may have fallen asleep, but Julia's eyes were open. Finally, she pushed back slightly and holding Julia's hands said quietly, "I think you need to explain what's going on."

Julia attempted to take a deep breath, but it shuddered in her chest. "It's my fault." The words came out as a whisper.

"What is?"

"Ken's gone... because of me."

Angie was quiet, trying to put together what Julia was talking about. Ken died in a car crash, that wasn't her fault. Luke's name made her lose control. It was her fault. The truth dawned on her. "You're involved with my brother?"

"No," she paused a moment, "not anymore."

The realization shocked Angie. "You were?"

Julia moaned but nodded in agreement.

"Did Ken know?" Negative shake.

Angie hugged Julia, using this as a chance to absorb it all. She spoke her thoughts out loud, "You feel that your unfaithfulness caused your husband to die?"

Julia's arms dropped, "You make it sound ridiculous."

Angie looked Julia in the eyes, "Because it is."

Julia was silent for a moment, "I feel so horrible and guilty. I deserved to lose Ken."

"No, you didn't. You want to tell me about it?"

It took Julia quite a few minutes to collect her words. Once she started to talk, she couldn't stop. She told about the first night in the yard, the texts, the phone calls, the night in her house and even the last conversation.

"Damn him, he knew better."

"So, did I."

"Shame on him for trying to get you back."

"But Angie, he didn't have to try very hard."

"Still."

"Look, I'm not innocent, he never would've said any of those things to me, if I hadn't been out on my porch in the middle of the night when he walked by. And I was out there not sleeping because I was thinking about him. That's not his fault. And everything afterward was both our doing."

Angie grabbed her friend's hands again, "Do you see that as bad as you think that is, it has absolutely nothing to do with your husband's death?"

Julia's eyes became clear for the first time, "Thank you, Angie. I still feel guilty as hell; I spent part of Ken's last months thinking of another man." Fresh tears rolled down her cheeks.

Angie joined her in tears too, "I'm so sorry. I've been so proud of how you have handled yourself and the kids. I'm glad that you have finally let loose some of the emotion."

Julia leaned over the kitchen sink and splashed cold water over her face. Next, she took a long swallow of coffee. “I must look like hell.”

Angie shrugged, “You may want to shower before the kids come home. When will they be here?”

Julia glanced at the clock on the microwave, “Not until this evening.”

“Why don’t you shower while I get you some lunch?”

Julia started to head out of the kitchen, “Angie, thanks for being so kind. I don’t deserve it. I’m ashamed of what I did. I want you to know my friendship with you is authentic. I wasn’t using you to get to him. And nothing will ever, ever happen between us again.”

Angie responded, “You’re my friend too, no matter what. This doesn’t change that.”

Later as they walked out on the porch, a red truck drove past the house. Julia frowned, “That wasn’t Dylan was it?” She shook her head, “I’ve got enough on my mind without worrying about a paranoid teen aged boy.” She hugged Angie, “You were meant to move here when you did, I couldn’t have gotten through this without you.”

**

Julia had recovered from her nightmarish weekend. By the time her in laws had arrived she appeared to be her normal self. She was so grateful to Ken's parents. They had kept the kids busy all weekend with movies, shopping and bought new clothes for each. Their grandparents had taken them out to eat and ice-skating. It sounded as if even Lily had enjoyed herself though Ken's mom was a little perturbed about the constant phone calls from Dylan. Things got emotional as Julia hugged Ken's mother. Somehow her loss seemed even worse as Julia considered her own son.

Now the three were in their rooms, headed to bed before returning to school tomorrow. Julia had made the rounds downstairs locking doors and shutting off lights.

13

Angie watched Julia's life move on. She saw her new friend tackle her role as a single parent with a dedication that was inspiring. Angie's own personal response was what surprised her. Julia took on full time work; managed two teenagers and a pre-teen. She continued to be involved in the school organizations and church activities; handling a big country house and the responsibilities of maintaining it. Just yesterday, when Angie had dropped Seth off from an overnighter, a truck had been there, someone was hired to repair the rain gutters.

Angie watched it all and realized this was exactly not the way she wanted to be. She wanted to be a couple; she missed a man being there to call the cable company when the bedroom cable box wasn't working. When Cody needed practice with the soccer ball she wanted his dad to go out and do it. Marcus hadn't been perfect;

Julia had felt the same about Ken. No man is! Had Angie been mistreated? Abused? Absolutely not.

The best surprise was that she was not alone in her thoughts about her family; Marcus had begun taking Cody on weekends. The day of the funeral had been so devastating, it meant the world to her that Marcus had come and stayed in the guest room. He had been with the two of them at the cemetery standing between them with an arm around each as they cried. He had met her halfway every other weekend to take Cody back to the lake. It had been great; the guys had spent a lot of time together and Cody had gotten to see both sets of grandparents.

Angie was considering what sacrifice she had made to her husband and son for the sake of making a point. Was what Marcus offered, being there most of the time, good enough? Six months ago, she would have said no, but watching Julia bravely struggle through life alone without a choice made Angie begin to waver.

Just yesterday she had been on the company website looking at positions available near Spring Lake. Maybe she would just have to find hobbies and organizations that she would like to be involved in alone to keep her active when Marcus was busy with the guys. The tragedy of Julia had really done her in. Marcus was her first and only true love, which was a lot. She thought maybe she should go to the lake next weekend and see how things went. Cody loved the lake; she might broach the subject with Marcus when he called about Cody's upcoming visit.

Angie looked out in the backyard from the kitchen window, Cody was playing ball with the dog they had picked up at the Humane Society last month. Bart had turned out to be just the companion he had needed. A two-year-old mix with a heart of gold, perfect for the two of them, he was already housebroken and could be alone in the house during the day without accidents. Bart also had a great bark when anyone came over which made Angie, a woman alone, feel better. As she thought this, Bart in fact barked at the driveway. She heard the slam of a car door and moved toward the side kitchen door which led to the driveway as Cody called eagerly to their visitor.

Angie opened the screen door just as Cody catapulted into his father's arms. She was shocked to see him. Marcus turned to her with a cautious smile. "Hi."

"This is a surprise."

Still with an arm around his son, Marcus moved towards the back porch, "I hope a good one?"

"Of course, what are you doing here on a Sunday evening?"

He took a deep breath, "Cody, there's something in the backseat for you, why don't you get it?" The boy moved toward the car and Marcus came up the first of three steps on the porch.

"Well Angie, I decided to take a week's vacation."

Still unsure she answered, "Where are you going?"

"I thought I'd spend the week in sunny Seneca."

Her eyes widened, "You want to spend the week here?"

He nodded, "Yes, I can spend the days with Cody while you're at work and I thought that maybe I'd also look around."

She tried to be cautious, "Around for what?"

"A job?" he looked for her approval.

"Are you serious?" she put her hands to her chest.

"I miss you, babe."

Her voice cracked, "I miss you too."

He took the last two steps in one stride and grabbed his wife for a kiss.

14

Julia was so tired of this life. She felt like it was one of those bad summers when a child is dragged to camp and just waits each day for it to pass so he can get back to his normal routine life. She felt she had had enough of the drudgery of this life alone. Hectic mornings, work, after dinner with the kids, then the stand still of time during the evenings. Another Netflix movie? Read another novel? Sitting at Kelsey or Seth's ball games with the other couples acting as if it didn't matter?

Then there was the blossoming of Lily and Dylan's relationship. Julia knew that she had allowed this relationship to grow, it had made it easier for both she and Lily. How was it going?

Julia felt as if she had become two people, the self-sufficient, strong woman that everyone could count on and marvel at her strength and inside the person who wanted to be whiny and nasty and feel sorry for herself.

Single women invited her to do things. She had gone to a couple of happy hours with them, but the manhunt part of it was not for her. The reality that one day she may want to date seemed absurd. The men who had looked at her that way repulsed her. Julia didn't mind an occasional chick flick with the girls. Her best friend without question was Angie. She knew Angie also didn't want to be the single mom that she was, and if Julia spoke the truth she would say that it was only a matter of time before she and Marcus were permanently reunited.

By ten, Kelsey was in her room chatting on her phone to her classmates. Seth was tucked in for the night. Lily's curfew was in thirty minutes, which was the rule on a school night. Julia heard the front door slam, before ten thirty, that was a surprise. She looked up from the television as Lily's shadow crossed the doorway.

"You're home early."

"Yeah," Lily seemed to hesitate between coming in and heading to her room.

"Nice date?"

Her daughter paused then said quietly, "We broke up."

Julia patted the couch next to her, "I'm sorry Lily, come here. Want to talk about it?"

Lily did not respond or sit by her mother, but she did settle on the recliner. "Guys are jerks. He's always saying I'm everything to him, but when I was gone over the weekend he went out with his friends every night. Then when I get home he acts like it's my fault and says I don't show him how much I love him. Guys are idiots."

"Don't I know it, what did he do?"

"I think he might have hooked up with another girl. He says he didn't."

Julia tried not to gasp; hoping she had the vocabulary wrong, "Hooked up with another girl? You mean slept with another girl, like he has with you?"

Lily smoothed her face quickly, "No Mom, just kissed." Instantly she realized that she had taken the bait and looked down.

Julia felt her heart pound, they were headed into territory she did not want to be in. Trying to recall her own experience and what she would have wanted her mom to do, she spoke, "Lily, are you having sex with Dylan?" The teen was quiet for a long moment, which Julia felt confirmed her suspicions, but she remained silent forcing her daughter to answer.

Finally, Lily spoke softly, "That's personal, Mom."

"Not when you're sixteen and I'm your mother."

Another long stretch of silence, and then, "We're being careful."

Julia detested being a single parent at this moment. "How?"

"Mom!"

"I mean it, how?"

"He uses. . ." Lily trailed off.

"Well, that's, well." Julia could not bring herself to congratulate her sixteen-year-old daughter because her nineteen-year-old boyfriend was using condoms. "Lily, you said he'd been with girls before you."

"Mom he's had tests, he doesn't have anything."

Though she had her doubts about that, she addressed a safer issue, "Lily I'm going to make you an appointment with my OB-GYN."

Lily looked horrified, "Why?"

"Well, to make certain you're healthy and maybe to take birth control pills."

Lily thought for a moment and nodded, "Okay."

Julia stood up shakily, "I don't want you to be having sex, you're only sixteen."

"I will be seventeen this month."

"That's not any different. But, I'm going to schedule an appointment for you."

Lily rose from the chair awkwardly and headed for the door, her mother spoke to her back, "Lily, I worry about you. There's seems to be more fighting than fun in your relationship. That's not normal."

Lily smiled, "Oh, Mom, Dylan has a rough life with his parents' split. His mom has a new baby with his stepdad and isn't interested in Dylan. His dad is a drunk who brings home a new woman every night. Dylan has a sad life, I make him really happy."

"Does he make you really happy?"

"Yes, Mom, don't freak out," she paused and swallowed, "Until he acts like an asshole." She looked at her mom.

Julia could only agree, "He was an asshole."

Uncharacteristically Lily hugged her mom, "Thanks, night."

Julia gave her daughter a tight squeeze and let go, "I love you, babe."

"Love you too, Mom," she heard from her daughter's retreating back.

**

Lily was barely in her room before the phone began to buzz. Dylan was sending a barrage of text messages to her. His words went from “love you” to every name in the book. She was a whore, a bitch, then she was the best thing that ever happened to him and then a complete waste of time. The next set were that she was his entire life and the only reason for living.

It had been difficult these last months. When her dad had first died, Dylan had been so understanding. She could always count on him to hold her. That had been enough for a while.

As they got closer, he was more demanding of his needs. Lily was now accustomed to being alone with him, naked. She was initially terrified of actual having intercourse, her parents’ predicament haunted her. They had gotten pregnant, married and now her mom was alone. It was scary. Dylan had taken care of the issue. One afternoon, last summer, they were alone at the quarry, swimming. Afterward they lay on the blanket kissing and touching. He had his hands in her bikini bottom and she was unaware that he had opened his trunks. Lily was shocked when she felt herself being filled with a part of him that was not his fingers. Her virginity had been lost without her even giving permission.

15

Julia was amazed just how much she liked Marcus. She had called Angie on Monday hoping she and Cody would come the next night for dinner. Angie had told her about Marcus' surprise visit. She had immediately tried to take back her offer. Angie insisted that all three of them would love to come over. She convinced Julia that it was important that her best friend meet Marcus. Julia agreed finally. They had met each other in passing many years ago at Luke's house. According to Angie, he was also at Ken's funeral, but Julia could recall no one who had offered her condolences on that day.

It turned out to be a good time. Julia led Angie into the kitchen on the pretense of needing help with food to ask her friend for details. Her friend could not quit smiling, "He just showed up and said he wants to consider getting a job here."

Julia hugged her, "Is this it? Are you back together?"

"We have a lot to talk about. The past two nights have been like it's all new and we are sort of starting over, but we're not. I did leave for a reason and we must talk about that before the week's over. It's been six months and I want to be certain about what changed his mind."

Julia pulled a salad out of the fridge and handed it to Angie as she talked, "I really think this is going to work, and I really like him."

Angie grinned, "Me too, thanks."

The two boys had wolfed down plates of food and headed out to the television to play with the PlayStation. Kelsey went out to the driveway to practice basketball. Lily lingered in the kitchen at the table with the adults. Marcus watched Kelsey through the window, then joined the women in the kitchen, "She's quite an athlete."

"Yes," Julia agreed, "her father's dream girl. He was such a sports nut."

"Not you?"

Julia laughed, "Good heavens no. Not a single sport."

Marcus said, "Not even water skiing, after all those summers at the lake?"

"No, I made a good lookout and could pull one behind the boat, but my skiing performance was pretty weak."

Lily looked interested, "You can drive a boat and ski?"

"Of course," Julia nodded at her daughter, "everyone at the lake could do that."

"Did you have a boat?"

"Oh, your grandpa just had a dinky little speed boat but ....," Julia hesitated a moment, "but the Thomas's," she motioned toward Angie, "had a nice boat."

"Did you drive that one?"

"Occasionally."

Angie laughed, "I think you were in that boat more than me, it wasn't exactly considered mine."

Lily looked puzzled then her eyes brightened, "Oh, your brother's?"

Marcus spoke up, "Man, Luke was such a good skier. I'm sure he taught you a thing or two." He laughed at his own innuendo.

"He was too good, I couldn't keep up with the slalom and barefoot skiing that everyone was doing," Julia answered, pointedly ignoring the joke.

Lily looked at Marcus, "Did you know my mom then?"

Marcus shrugged, "Not really, Angie and I were older. We both worked full time, we didn't get to play around all day like her and Luke."

Lily's eyes widened, "Mom and Luke?"

Angie had not shared the recent past with him, so he thought nothing of saying, "Luke was your mom's boyfriend."

Determined to stop that line of conversation, Julia watched her daughter glance at her phone for the tenth time, "Is there something you want to ask, Lily?"

"Can I go out with Dylan to the movies?"

Julia frowned, "I thought you were broken up."

"We got back together. He felt terrible for everything; he even left flowers in my car," the smile on Lily's face made her mother feel nauseous.

The women shared knowing looks. Julia tried to be subtle, "But Lily, there were problems."

Her daughter stood up and shook her head, "No Mom, everything is fine, we worked out *everything*. Please, I'll be home right after the movie."

Julia considered the nice time everyone else was having, "Okay, no later than ten thirty."

When Dylan picked up her daughter a very short ten minutes later, Julia had trouble letting her smile reach her eyes as he said his typical, “Hey.”

Angie looked at her as they left, “Things not going so well?”

“He has her convinced that he’s the perfect boyfriend, but from where I stand it’s not that great.”

**

Lily zipped her jacket as the first chill of winter assailed her. Dylan, next to her seemed unaware of the temperature, wearing only a flannel shirt open over a t-shirt. In the truck, he pulled Lily close, “Oh baby, I was dying.” He grabbed her for a long kiss, his hands all over her back. “Don’t ever leave me again,” he said when he pulled away, “It sucked without you. My life without you is hell. My old man threatened to throw me out.”

Lily was instantly concerned for him, “Oh, honey, why?”

He shook his head, looking miserable, “I cramp his style. He brings in all these bitches and if I’m there it messes up his plans.”

“Oooh, that’s awful. How embarrassing for you. I’m sorry Dylan.”

He looked at her, “You think your mom won’t bring home guys now that your dad is dead?”

Hurt, Lily pouted, “Dylan, that’s mean, my dad hasn’t even been gone long.”

He gave a cold laugh, “You just wait.”

The truck turned onto his street as they talked. “I thought we were really going to the movies,” Lily frowned as she realized his plans.

Glancing sideways, Dylan saw her reaction. “Baby, I want to make this up to you and I know just how to do it.” He ran his hand along her thigh.

“But I told my mom. . .”

Dylan was already climbing out of the vehicle, “Let’s just come inside for a little bit, then we’ll go to the movies.” Lily sighed, knowing the movies were out.

16

Packing up Ken's possessions was difficult. Julia knew that half a year was more than enough time. She took the empty boxes she had gotten from the office up to her room. Opening Ken's side of the closet she stood back and looked at all his clothes, touching them gingerly, all his favorite golf shirts mixed in with his collection of dress shirts. "Oh, Ken," Julia ignored the tears streaming and began to take them down one by one, folding them and putting them in the boxes. She had room for more clothes and moved to the dresser.

Lily walked in as she was adding shorts to the current box. "What are you doing, Mom?"

"Packing up Dad's stuff."

Lily moved to an open box and picked up an Ohio State sweatshirt, "I want this."

"Okay." Julia kept working.

"Why are you doing this?"

"Because its time."

Her daughter acted hurt, "But what are you going to do with them?"

"Give them to charity, someone could use them. They're not getting used here."

Pressing her face to the sweatshirt, Lily cried a bit. She looked as if she wanted to protest, then to Julia's surprise spoke quietly, "I'll help."

"Okay." While Julia worked at the dresser, Lily went to the closet which had only shoes, belts and ties left. She began adding ties to an empty box. She pulled over the desk chair and stood on it, collecting shoe boxes.

"How do I know which are Dad's and which are yours?"

"Most are obvious; men's boxes should all be on his side, the left side."

Julia was now sitting on the floor, emptying the bottom of his dresser filled with sweaters, she was not watching Lily.

Lily had emptied her father's side of the closet. She examined the boxes on the side of her mother's. In the far-right corner looked to be a large man-sized box with the brand Nike on it. Maybe his tennis shoes had gotten mixed into her mom's shoes. Lily pushed her chair closer to the right and pulled the box to the front of the shelf. She lifted the lid to check the shoes out. There were no shoes in it. It was filled with notes, pictures and things. Was this her mom's box of romantic stuff from Dad? Her mom would love to have this now, Lily bet. Lifting the first envelope, she saw the slanted scrawl of a boy, and the letter was addressed to Julia Gordon. On the back were two hearts, one said "I love you" on it and the other had initials "L.T. loves J.G."

Lily dropped the letter back in as if it had burned her, L.T. that was Angie's brother. She quickly stuffed the lid back on and put the box back in its nearly hidden spot. Her mom still had this stuff? Lily decided she would look at this some other time, when her mother wasn't home. She got down from the chair and looked at her father's empty closet side. Somehow finding that box while packing up her dad's things made her angry.

Julia stood up just then and walked over to her daughter, giving her a hug, "All done? Thanks for helping, honey. This was hard, but it was better with you." Lily slipped out of her mom's arms and left the room without a word.

**

Julia would love to move, she was not a country girl. This two-acre lot was more than she wanted. Getting the kids to take turns mowing it, trying to get the trimming done had been such a burden. How was she going to deal with the driveway now that winter was here? The ancient pick up that Ken kept in the old barn had a plow on it, but she had never used it. She dreaded the need to get the thing out and learn to plow snow. Julia would have loved to move to a house in town with a small yard. Actually, she would not mind moving to an entirely new city and start over. She hated running into people at the grocery store or school and have them give that sad look and say, "How *are* you doing?"

But, she knew that any of that would be entirely unfair to the kids, especially the girls. Both were in high school and deserved the chance to graduate from Seneca High. As for the house, the kids were accustomed to the yard and space. They had their bedrooms just as they wanted, it would be selfish of her to change.

**

Her current schedule was teaching a three to six-thirty class on Tuesdays and Thursdays. Lily didn't mind overseeing her brother and sister on those nights. They were capable of taking care of themselves and they both had solemnly promised not to mention that Dylan came over.

It was her job to see where they were, take care of Sophie and make sure everyone ate. The ice cream shop was closed for the season and her mom paid her well for this. It covered her gas and spending money. Before Dylan arrived from work, Lily pretended to be the dutiful big sister and looked in the living room at Seth playing PlayStation on the TV, "Don't forget to do your homework. Do you want me to cook for you?"

Without taking his eyes from the screen, Seth replied, "I'm done with homework and I'll zap something later."

"Okay" one down. She moved up to her sister's room, Kelsey was on the phone, her math in front of her. "What are you doing?"

Kelsey held the phone away, "Natalie is grounded so we're studying for math together over the phone." In front of her also sat a sandwich and glass of milk.

"Okay, study hard. I've got a paper to write." She walked away smiling to herself. They were not going to need her; she had over an hour to do what she wanted.

Dylan strode into the front door without knocking. He came up to Lily at the kitchen counter and grabbed the back of her jeans. "Nice," he whispered huskily in her ear. Lily gave a surprised laugh and turned around, allowing him to kiss her and put his hands under her t-shirt. She pretended to smack at his hands, "Seth is just in the other room."

He kissed her neck, "Then let's go to your room."

"Dylan," she protested smiling. Her eyes got bright, "Actually there is somewhere I would like to go." She grabbed his hand and led him up the stairs. Lily moved into her mother's room, shut the door and locked it. Ignoring Dylan's crude comments, she took the desk chair and moved it to the closet. Soon she had the Nike box on the bed with her. It was bulging with all sorts of things.

Dylan reached for it, "What's in the box? Booze? Pot? Sex toys?"

Lily gave him an irritated look, "No, I don't think so, it's my mother's secret memory box from her old boyfriend." Dylan looked bored and plopped himself on Julia's bed, kicking off his shoes and lying down.

The box smelled faintly of men's cologne and she wondered if *he* sprayed her mom's letters. There must have been fifty letters along with dried daisies, and a lock of dark brown hair. Was that his? It was long and wavy. Lily tried to remember what the guy looked like.

Rolling across the bottom of the box was a boy's silver class ring with a blue stone. She looked at it *Spring Lake HS* with the year *1997* on it. The initials inside were *LST*. Why did her mom still have Luke's class ring? Wouldn't she have given it back when they broke up?

There were also movie tickets, miniature golf score cards, a comb and some cassette tapes of old bands like Def Leppard, Bon Jovi and INXS. Lily thumbed through the letters; she would read some later; maybe sneak them out of the box. At the bottom of the box was an old photo album creased from being bent to fit. She opened it, "Well, well, well." This got Dylan's attention and he sat next to her, looking over her shoulder.

There they stood. This thin handsome guy with long brown hair and an earring wore nothing but jean shorts and a chain with a ring around his neck. He had both arms wrapped around a tan, skinny girl in a bikini. She had her arms around his. This was her mom? Yes, if Lily really looked she recognized her. Boy, they were close in that picture; his hands were on her bare skin. Dylan commented, "Is that your mom? She's hot."

The next picture must have been her mom's prom. Once again, they were wrapped around each other. He had driven to her mom's school for dances? Sure enough, there were pictures of her proms, his proms and homecoming dances. There were a lot more casual photos, some he took of her, some she took of him. Usually they were wearing the same thing, her in a bikini, him in jean shorts.

There was a photo of a hill on a sandy beach by the lake. Under it, her mother had written, "The future home of Mr. and Mrs. Lucas Thomas." Lily felt a stab; her mother had wanted to marry someone else. Wonder what happened?

Lily knew the truth; her mom married her dad when she was pregnant with Lily. When had she broke up with this guy and had sex with her dad? Dylan lay back down on the bed. She returned to the letters looking for a clue. They were postmarked so she began to look for the newest ones. She found some marked two years before she was born.

Lily noticed these did not have the hearts and love notes on the front. She opened one.

Jules,

Baby, please forgive me. I know I screwed up. I was such an ass to make that mistake. If I could take it back I would. Please, Jules, let me see you. Let me explain. I know I should never have gone out. I should never have had anything to drink.

I should have quit my job and moved to Ashland. Please, I'll do anything. Whatever it takes to get you back. To hell with my scholarship. To hell with school. I'll just move there and work. I must be with you. I can't live without you. I love you so much, you're my life. I can't live without you. There's nothing but you that matters.

Julia, tell me what I must do, and I will do it to be with you. Please, please.

I am so sorry. I will never ever give you a reason to not trust me again. I know I'm not worthy of you, but I have got to have you. I miss everything about you. If I never get to touch you again, I think I'd rather die. Please, please call me.

I'll be there the second you tell me to. Please call, Jules.

I love you,

Luke

Lily folded the note up. It was pretty desperate, in fact it reminded her of how desperate Dylan had sounded when she broke up with him last week.

It was obvious that Luke must have cheated on her when he was drunk. But still, he was willing to quit school and move to where she was. Wow, her mom was cold hearted to not take him back.

Lily had a moment of regret reading the letter. It was too strange to think of this man thinking her mom was all he could live for. Certainly, he had married someone else too. She tried to remember that night that she had met him. Did he have a ring on? Maybe she could get some info from Angie without her knowing.

Lily carefully replaced everything in her mother's closet. When she stepped over to the bed Dylan pulled her on top of him. His hands reached for the waistband of her jeans, she did not push them away.

17

Marcus Castile was discouraged, there didn't seem to be work available in Seneca or any of the towns surrounding it. He knew that he'd have to be back in the plant by Monday. This week had been amazing. He and Angie had really gotten along. Being around Cody, getting to see his school, taking him to basketball practice, it was great. Even last night when they had sat down together and really talked about why she left, he felt Angie wanted them to be back together too.

He had been an idiot risking the loss of his family to hang with the guys. He hoped if he moved here, he could find new places to hunt and fish, but he was not going to mess this up. It would be easier around new people, Joe and Gary had both been divorced a couple of times and could not understand what Angie wanted from him. He hadn't understood either, but now he did. Marcus closed the laptop and looked around. Maybe he would whip up his famous chili for supper and surprise Angie when she got home from work. He had to make the most of this weekend since he was going to have to go back to the lake.

**

Angie was thrilled to walk into a delicious smelling kitchen with her husband and son waiting for her. This was what she could get used to. It had been a fabulous five days with Marcus. He was interested in everything she and Cody had been doing. He had also taken care of anything in the house that she had needed. Last night their talk had gone better than she could imagine. She almost regretted leaving him but knew that was what it had taken to open his eyes and decide to come to her. Angie felt she was living a fairy tale. The magic ended when Marcus informed them over dinner that he did not have any leads on jobs and would have to be heading back on Sunday. Cody looked as devastated as she felt. Marcus assured them that he would continue looking and making calls, that this was only temporary.

The phone rang as she was cleaning the kitchen up, it was Julia. "Hey, Lily is on her way into town to pick up a pizza. I thought it would be a great idea if she came and got Cody for the night."

Angie hesitated, “I don’t know he’s pretty upset, Marcus just told him that he couldn’t find a job and has to return to the lake on Sunday.”

Julia sounded sympathetic, “Nothing? He has to head back in two days?”

“Yes.”

“Then that is exactly why you need to send your son to my house for the night and spend the time alone with your husband.”

Angie smiled into the phone, “That *would* be terrific. In fact, I will talk him into it, tell Lily to come on by. Julia, you’re absolutely the best, thank you.”

“No problem, I’m so happy for the two of you.”

Angie felt a pang of guilt, “Thanks, look I know . . .”

“Shut up,” Julia cut it in, “Listen, you pick him up when you want tomorrow, no surprise visits. Enjoy yourself. Goodbye.” She left Angie smiling and hung up.

**

The parents of Kelsey’s freshman basketball team were slightly obsessed. They wanted the girls to have a small gift for each home game and they wanted the parents to take turns providing a nice meal before each away game on Thursday. Julia found herself, on a Monday night, headed to the parents’ meeting to sign up for her night of meal prep and to write some outlandish check for Kelsey's gifts. Her only concession was that Kelsey loved the game. She imagined some of this was tough for parents who had to watch their child sit the bench for most of the games. Her daughter was a strong point guard, always out on the court during a game.

It was amazing to watch her middle child zoom up to five feet eight during the first half of her freshman year. Ken would have loved this so much, a child in high school sports. It was so unfair that he was not here to enjoy it.

She added her name to the food schedule and wrote out her check. As the meeting ended, the coach and also the town's eye doctor, Eric Saddler, approached her. "I'm Eric, your Kelsey's mom, right?"

Accepting the hand shake, she nodded, "Yes, I'm Julia."

"I hope your daughter is still on our team when it's your turn to bring food. She's doing so well," he looked around to make certain others weren't listening, "It would be an advantage to the JV team to take her from us. I'd hate to lose her, but she could be ready for varsity by next season."

A mix of pride and surprise crossed her face, "That's great to hear. Thank you, I guess all of those hours in the driveway have paid off."

"Has she attended a lot of camps and traveling teams?"

She shook her head, "No, my husband took her to a couple of camps, but no other teams."

He looked slightly embarrassed. "Oh hey, yes I'm sorry . . ."

"Thank you. Also, thanks for letting me know how well she's doing." Julia was slowly getting used to saving people from making awkward comments.

**

The next evening, she had just put popcorn in the microwave for Seth. when Lily walked into the kitchen and opened the fridge. With her head still in it, she spoke, "Cory Saddler asked me for your phone number today, Mom."

Kelsey who was at the table, typing on the laptop, responded, "Ooh Lily, he's cute."

Lily frowned, "No, not my number, I've got Dylan. He freaked out when he saw me talking to Cory in the parking lot." She popped the top of a can of Diet Coke.

Kelsey made an ugly face, "He always freaks out after school."

Julia was lifting the steaming bag of popcorn, and froze the motion mid-air, "What do you mean *always after school*?" she asked sharply.

Lily glared at Kelsey, "Thanks a lot, big mouth." She started to make a hasty retreat out of the kitchen, but her mother's words stopped her.

"Why is Dylan at school?"

Deciding she was already in trouble with her sister, Kelsey answered, "He's there to check on Lily and make sure she's not flirting with anyone else."

"Is this true, Lily?"

"No," Lily denied, "he gets off work at 3:30 and knows I'm coming out of school then." Kelsey harrumphed at her laptop. Her sister shot her a look, "Shut up."

"All you guys do is fight." The sibling battle had begun.

Lily slammed her can on the table, "You don't know anything."

"You're right, that's not all you do." The girls stared daggers at each other waiting for the next one to say something damaging.

Julia poured the corn into a large plastic bowl, “That’s enough both of you.” She looked at her oldest, “I will talk to you later. Now what is this about Cory Saddler and my phone number?”

“His dad wanted it. I think he’s going to ask you out.” All three of her kids looked at her.

Seth was the first to speak up, “Are you going to date Kelsey’s coach?”

Julia shook her head, “No, I must’ve left it off the form.” Over the past months she had come to terms with the fact that she was done with love. As a young girl she had a beautiful young love; then she had married a good loving man. She had ruined both the memory of the first and the marriage to the second. No more.

Kelsey eyed her, “You will someday, Mom.”

“Exactly,” intoned Lily.

“Girls, please. I’m not interested in dating.” This was too much, Julia crossed the room to another cupboard and lifted out a wine glass. She went to the fridge to get a chilled bottle of Pinot Gris from the shelf.

Seth seemed to consider, “Mom, you might as well. Lots of kids have step dads.”

“Oh, please,” Julia protested, “I can’t even think about that.” She took a sip of her drink, letting the wine chill her.

“We’re not trying to marry her off, Seth,” Lily scolded her brother, “We’re talking about dating. You will at some point Mom, you know you will.”

“Coach Saddler is really nice,” added Kelsey.

“Kids, this is very nice, you guys trying to make this decision for me. I loved your dad; no one can ever mean to me what he did.”

Lily gave her a look she didn’t understand. Kelsey spoke, “Mom, you’re not even forty you can’t quit now.”

“Just don’t marry anyone with kids,” Seth suggested, stuffing his mouth.

Julia took a bigger swig. “Seth, I am not considering remarrying.”

Kelsey shrugged, “Maybe it’s time to date, Mom.”

“Really Mom, what better things do you have to do on the weekend?” Lily agreed, thinking if her mom had her own life maybe she would stay out of Lily’s.

18

After the game on Thursday, Coach Saddler approached Julia. She felt a moment of dread, but he seemed to just want to talk about Kelsey's performance. "See what I mean, she is a level above. Our sweep in the second half was due to her good eye and instincts. She's a killer on the court."

Julia could not help but glow, "She really was terrific. Thank you."

"Would you like to have dinner with me on Saturday night?" he caught her unexpected.

She took a moment trying to come up with an excuse. Finally, she rushed through the words, "I'm sorry I have plans with a friend."

He grinned, "I'll try again."

Reluctantly she nodded, "Okay."

He patted her shoulder and turned toward the locker room, "See you at the next game."

Julia felt her face go hot, did it sound like she had agreed to go at another time? A date with a man? She didn't want to do this.

**

Angie was not sympathetic. "It's dinner, you'll survive."

"But I don't want to."

"Why not, Lily says he's good looking."

"Since when have you been talking to Lily?" Julia lay on her bed, later that night, complaining to her friend on her phone.

"She babysat for me last night, remember? She told me he was probably going to ask you out."

"I told him I was busy, and he just said he'd ask again. I'm completely rusty on how to firmly say that I'm not interested."

Angie laughed, "That I understand, when I was single I had to deal with that a bit at the office."

Now it was Julia's turn to laugh, "Listen to you 'when I was single' how many months was that?"

"Hey, I moved here as a single woman."

"That was just a power play."

"A successful power play, I might add," said Angie. "Anyway, maybe you should go out."

Julia's voice was serious, "No, not interested. I'm up to my eyebrows in motherhood. Dylan is obsessed with Lily and seems to control her. First, I found out that he has been showing up in the parking lot at the end of the school day, to see who she is talking to. Then last night he was over, I heard her complaining, when I peeked in, he was going through *her* phone."

"Ooh, I don't like that at all. He checks up on her at school and on her phone?"

"Yes, and I took her to the doctor, as if I gave her permission to have sex with him."

"Julia, she never asked your permission, remember? How would you feel if this guy got her pregnant?"

"Thank you, Angie, I needed that. See, there is just too much going on for me to even think about going out on a date."

"That's where you're wrong, going out is just what you need. Take your mind off your troubles. If it turns out to be dreadful make him bring you home. You don't have to stay out, but you do have to go at this point. Maybe you will like him, Julia."

"I don't want to start over," whined Julia.

"I know hon, that's the part that's not fair." They were both silent for a moment.

"Hey, I know, text me if it's bad and I'll call pretending to be a sick kid."

19

Winter was here, and the Darby family was barely thriving. They had gotten through Christmas which was difficult. Those were the moments when Julia realized what an important part Ken had played as a father and husband. Putting up the tree and hanging the lights was a monumental task for her. Many of the ornaments held special memories for them. The children each had a Disney one, these were precious souvenirs from a family trip. Julia couldn't help but laugh as she recalled Seth, only five at the time, being afraid of the costumed characters. Ken had taken on a pretend battle with Buzz Lightyear so that Seth would laugh and then pose next to his favorite movie character. This year, her son was not interested in helping her trim the tree. On the couch nearby, he was engrossed in *Elf*, the movie that they always played while decorating.

Lily, in one of her moods, had chosen to stay out of the moment. In fact, she was barricaded in her room, writing a paper on *Macbeth*. Kelsey had helped to get the tree situated but was now shoulder to shoulder with her brother in front of the television. Truth be told, Julia would have preferred to pick up a small table top tree that held only a few ornaments. She felt, though, that these things must be done just as he had, to help the children with the transition. Christmas cards were out of the question, Julia had gone to the card store on Black Friday. Each heartfelt message was nauseating. "From our family to yours," couldn't convey the heartaches and misery that the Baker family was living through. Julia decided that tradition was permanently wiped away. Social media allowed her to keep in touch with most anyways.

She also changed the Christmas day tradition. As the kids were older, they had started spending the actual day alone. The next day, they would travel to celebrate with extended family. This way the kids could enjoy their gifts and she loved making a big holiday meal for just the five of them. Now, Julia realized the house would be full of sorrow on that day. The night after the tree went up, Julia broached the subject.

Lily was the first to give a strong opinion. "It will suck with just us." She knew her mother would never allow Dylan to come over. Lately, the last thing she wanted to do was spend time with her own family. Going to Grandma's would keep her mother's attention off her.

Kelsey looked a bit forlorn, "We've been having Christmas morning here forever."

"What about snowman pancakes?" Seth inquired, his father always cooked up chocolate chip pancakes in the three small circles and covered them in powdered sugar to look like snowmen.

Taking a deep breath, and blinking rapidly to hide her emotion, Julia answered, "I promise that we can make those in Grandma's kitchen." It was decided that she would take the kids to her parents on Christmas Eve. Her entire family had been supportive and her brother, his wife and kids had also crowded into Grandma and Grandpa's house for an overnight Christmas Eve. It had been the right choice. The kids had done just fine with the crowd. She had been so proud of the girls' mature attitudes. They had taken it upon themselves to go out and buy her a few small gifts. Normally this was a task they shared with Ken. She was unbelievably touched by their effort.

Dylan and Lily had another big fight because she went away overnight. Julia tried very hard to be supportive when Lily was upset, but she desperately wanted to force her daughter to stay away from him, her instincts told her he was trouble. The week between Christmas and New Year's had Lily on her phone constantly; texting or talking. One morning when Lily was in the shower, Julia picked up her daughter's phone and checked it. According to the history, Dylan called every two minutes, and his texts were nonstop. Julia placed the phone back on her daughter's dresser and went to her own room. What was she going to do? Lily was young enough that she could refuse to let her see him; she could take her cell phone. Is this what she should do? Everything she saw told her this was an extremely unhealthy relationship. She knew from the start that he was too old for Lily. It was when Ken died, that she had allowed Dylan into Lily's life because it seemed to help. Now Julia saw the error of her ways.

She went back into her daughter's room and picked up the cell phone. A new message was already blinking, she read it. His use of the "F" word was shocking.

Just as she was headed out, Lily walked into her room, a towel wrapped around her body. "What are you doing with my phone?"

"I'm taking it." Julia grasped it tightly in her hands.

"What?" Lily reached desperately for it.

"Lily, you can't seem to be able to stay away from Dylan, I'm going to get involved. You're my daughter; he's not good for you. The relationship needs to end." She tucked the phone into her jeans pocket.

"You can't do this mother!" screamed Lily.

"I can, and I am going to," her mother turned to leave the room indicating that the conversation was closed but she grabbed her elbow.

"Mom, we're broken up."

Julia lightly put her hands on her daughter's shoulder. They were immediately shrugged off. "Yes, but how many times will he call before you give in again?"

"You don't understand. He's got no one else. His Christmas was horrible; I'm the only one who truly cares about him."

"That's what he tells you to keep you."

Lily was crying now, "It's true. You don't know him, you don't understand." She flopped down on the bed.

Julia sat down beside her daughter, not touching her. “If he’s so wonderful why are you broken up with him?”

Not looking at her mom, Lily spoke quietly, “He cheated on me, when I was at Grandma’s.”

“Then why are you defending him?”

“He’s so sorry, it was a dumb mistake.” Was she trying to convince her mom or herself?

Julia rolled her eyes, “Please.”

Icy eyes glared at her, “I’m not like you, Mom. I can forgive when someone makes a mistake. I don’t think *I’m* perfect.”

Julia looked at her daughter in surprise, “What are you talking about?”

“Never mind. Just give me my phone back.” Once again, she held out a pleading hand.

“What did you mean by that?” she continued to probe.

“I just know you.” Lily built a lie; “You think everyone has to be perfect and if they’re not, they’re not good enough. Please give me my phone back.”

“Lily, I’m doing this because I love you.” Julia stood up and left her daughter. She heard the door slam at her back. She was shaking as she closed her own door and looked for a place to hide her daughter's phone. She chose a drawer in her bathroom which held her flat iron that she rarely used.

Julia had also taken her iPad for the week. She knew that the internet left a wide-open opportunity for the two to communicate. The next afternoon she was dusting when her own cell phone beeped in her pocket. She looked at the screen; it wasn't a number she recognized.

She slid it open, "Hello?"

"Why won't you let Lily talk to me?" It was Dylan.

"How did you get my number?"

He ignored the question and took on a pleading tone, "I love her, and she loves me. Why can't we see each other?"

His nerve was appalling, "Dylan, you spend your time fighting. I see the words you use. Lily is only seventeen, I'm her mother and I have decided that she is done with this relationship."

"But why? Please, give us a chance. We love each other."

Julia was amazed, "Dylan, I am done with this conversation, it's time for you to move on with your life." She clicked the END button. Less than a minute later her phone buzzed again, and she powered it off. Why didn't she have Ken here to help with this, then again, he had always been soft hearted, Julia knew he would have felt pity for the young man. However, Lily was his little girl. Julia liked to think that his physical presence alone could have kept Dylan at bay. What good was she? From the sound of it, he learned from his father's knee to have no respect for women. Wouldn't a man around make this situation easier?

20

By New Year's Eve, Lily seemed to have lightened up a bit. In fact, Julia was thrilled to see a bit of her happier self-emerge. She noticed her daughter's wardrobe choices improving. When going out with Dylan, she rarely dressed up. Sweats and t-shirts were her uniform, and Julia always felt this was an indication of how they spent their time. Watching her with her slim jeans and stylish tops encouraged her.

She had asked if she could spend the night at Olivia's family, this was a tradition. Her parents always had a big family party and Lily had been a part of it for years. Julia had agreed but informed Lily that she would be talking to Olivia's mom letting her know that Lily was to have no phone or computer privileges. A few of the girls' mothers had years ago made a pact to keep each other informed of anything their teenagers were doing. They based it on "I would want someone to tell me if my child was doing something wrong." It worked very well. Liz

Barnett was more than reassuring that she would make certain that there was no contact with Dylan on New Year's Eve. Julia had to admit it was a relief to have that burden off her shoulders for a night.

Cody was staying over with Seth. Angie was headed to the lake to celebrate with Marcus. Kelsey had a sleepover with the church youth group. It was a lonely night, not that she and Ken had ever done much for the holiday, but it felt different. Julia would be glad to get back to the everyday world instead of the holidays.

She was waiting for the day when Angie would tell her that she was moving back to Spring Lake. Marcus was still unable to find a job in Seneca. She knew the couple wanted to desperately be together. Julia felt that Angie was biding her time for the school year to be out. After that, the job would not be nearly as important as being with her husband. Julia agreed with that, marriage was too important to take for granted. She had certainly learned that the hard way. What would she do when she lost Angie? Angie had been one of the main reasons that she had survived after Ken's death. Her friendship had been invaluable. She seemed to know when Julia needed someone to hang out with or to call at just the loneliest of moments.

On this night of the year's end, Julia felt self-reflection was called for. As she sat in the kitchen, hearing gaming sounds from the boys in the other room, she considered if she wanted a warm coffee or a glass of wine. Her thoughts of Angie lead to the lake and she compromised. Her new Keurig, a gift from her parents, brewed her a quick cup of coffee. Reaching above the stove to her highest cupboard, she pulled out a bottle of Baileys. A couple splashes added a nice zing to her mug.

There was a battle in her heart to not include Luke in her ruminations. The guilt was pushed back, and she was left with a sad loneliness. A mental shake tamped down thoughts of him. As for her current love life, Julia was operating on the theory that it simply was not necessary. The one date with Eric Saddler could only be described as awkward. They were able to talk about school and kids, but nothing more. When he did not even walk her to the door, she knew her disinterest had been obvious.

The staff Christmas dinner, where a professor from the accounting department desperately tried to get close to her, wasn't any better. She thought she'd politely turned him down, until he stopped her under the mistletoe and tried to put his tongue down her throat.

The companionship of marriage was gone, and solitude was devastating. She could now be completely honest without feeling like a traitor and admit that deep conversations and heartfelt talks were not shared with Ken. However, she was missing another form of closeness, a strong, lonely ache when sexual thoughts crossed her mind. This, she acknowledged, was something she was going to have to struggle with. Still in her thirties, and though she had made the decision herself, at times was bitter about the fact that her options for a healthy sex life were nil.

On New Year's morning, Julia was alone watching NBC's best of the year show at the kitchen table. The boys had managed to stay up until one the night before; she had gotten engrossed in a new novel and lasted a bit longer. The phone rang, catching her off guard. Perhaps her mom was calling to say, "Happy New Year". It was a tearful Lily, "Mom?"

She was surprised, "Lily, where are you?"

"I'm still at Olivia's; my tires were slashed last night." She heard her daughter's sobs.

Julie sat down with the phone in her hand, "Do you think it was Dylan?"

Lily's voice was broken, "I don't know, probably. Mr. Barnett called the police, and they came and took my statement. Now he's got AAA coming over to replace them."

"Oh Lily. Let me talk to Terry." No one had noticed Lily's car when the other guests had left after midnight, they could have been done by then. The police said New Year's pranks happen, but even after the guests left there were three cars out and only Lily's had been slashed.

Terry assured Julia that Lily had willingly given Dylan's name to the officer saying that he was an ex-boyfriend who had been bothering her. He also said that he would make certain that the new tires were on and that Julia could worry about the bill later. She thanked him, asked him to send Lily home as soon as possible. This was beginning to feel like more than she could handle.

Her own parents were on a cruise and she didn't want to bother them. She decided to call her brother, Tim. Tim was just two years behind her in age. He lived near Indianapolis with his wife and two sons; seven and nine. "Have you considered phoning his parents?" Tim was home and listened to her situation.

"Well, I thought of that. He's twenty and Lily says he really doesn't have a definite home between either place. Mom is remarried with a new family and Dad is an alcoholic with a string of girlfriends."

"How did Lily meet this guy?" his voice emphasizing the word *this*.

"At her job last summer at the ice cream shop."

"Too bad." His response was quick, the followed silence let her know he was considering solutions. "Well, one thing I think I would do is not let Lily drive her own car. He obviously was looking for it last night."

"That's a good idea; I could trade her cars for a while."

"Julia, I hate you driving it either."

"Well Tim, I'm the man of the house now, remember?" she sounded nearly defensive.

"I know Sis, I'm sorry. I've seen teen girls in bad relationships, they don't always walk away when they should." Tim taught high school.

"No one in our family has ever modeled this behavior, why would she accept this bad relationship?" her voice rose slightly.

"Don't blame yourself. Girls are gullible, and don't forget Dylan's timing was perfect. Just when she lost her dad, he was there to rescue her."

Julia felt tears forming, "You're right."

"I know you thought taking her a phone was a good idea, but you don't want her out on the streets without a phone, she may run into him. Why don't you block his number?"

"I can do that?"

"Yes, and she can't unblock it without your code." They discussed the details of this. Tim turned it back to Lily, "The main thing is to encourage her to want to stay away from him. Maybe she could talk to the school counselor?" Julia found herself appreciating his business-like tone, it calmed her emotions.

"I can check on that."

"I'm so sorry this is going on. If you want me to come over this weekend, I can."

"Thanks Tim, you've given me some great suggestions. I think I'll be okay."

21

Fortunately for Julia, it was a mild winter with little snowfall. She had kept a handle on clearing the drive. Kelsey had her learners permit, she would be sixteen in May. Part of her driving practice became driving the old pickup with the blade. Whenever snow piled up, she loved to climb into the truck and clear it off their property. Kelsey's freedom behind the wheel at the end of spring would help with the many different directions the family of four were constantly headed. After New Year's, Julia had briefly traded cars with her daughter, but despised being cramped in the little blue Honda. Instead, she had taken her SUV, that had well over 100,00 miles on it, and traded it for a new Ford Fusion. Her saleswoman had shown her an older Hyundai that would be a perfect third car. Buying the two vehicles together was an excellent deal. Lily was now driving a car that her ex-boyfriend was unfamiliar with. The

Honda was moved to the barn and would one day be Kelsey's vehicle.

Lily appeared to be functioning without Dylan. The high school was doing a production of *South Pacific*, Lily joined the chorus. It was a relief to see her busy every evening with rehearsal, and on the weekends, spending her time with her friends and castmates. Julia felt her daughter was glowing without the shadow of Dylan around her.

The university kept Julia busy, she was teaching three on campus classes and one online. She discovered that she enjoyed the online work. In the evening when the loneliness wanted to creep in, she would get online and work on her class.

One night, the two younger kids were home from practice, had dinner and were both working on school work in their rooms. Lily was still at rehearsal. Julia was sitting at the desk in the study paying bills online. She opened the electric bill, no surprise it was a bit higher in the winter. She checked the cell phone bill. Now the four of them each had a phone. As a working single parent, she felt the need to have all her kids accessible. Out of curiosity, she wondered which of her teenagers was making all the calls and texts; it was unlimited, but still.

Lily's seemed to be exorbitant. Scrolling down she could see that it was all focused on one number, an unfamiliar one. Julia felt a twist in her stomach, the owner of the number was obvious. Dylan must have gotten a new number.

What was wrong with Lily? Had she ever quit seeing him? Julia walked to Kelsey's room and pushed the door which was slightly closed. The teen girl was stretched out on her bed, textbook in front of her. Her calculator and cell phone lay next to her. "Kelsey I'm going to ask you a question and I need an honest answer."

Kelsey looked up at her mother, pushing her glasses up on her nose. She normally wore contacts when she left the house. "What?" she was hesitant.

"Did you know that Lily was still with Dylan?"

Kelsey looked down at her homework, "No," she replied in barely a whisper.

"I want the truth."

Her daughter sighed, "Yeah."

"For how long?" Julia crossed her arms, the standard angry parent stance.

Now her daughter sat up, "I don't know, a while. She's such an idiot. He's a total loser."

"Has he been over here?"

Again, a look down, “A couple of times.”

“Why didn’t you tell me?”

Kelsey shrugged, “She made me promise. She’s blind to him, Mom.”

“Why would you lie to me all this time?” Julia’s hand moved to her hips.

Kelsey raised her voice, slightly, “I didn’t, you never asked.”

Julia raised her hands, “Okay fair enough I didn’t. But from now on I need you to let me know what’s going on. Kelsey, I don’t think this relationship is safe. I think that Dylan has some serious issues.”

“Obviously,” Kelsey agreed.

With her forehead on the door frame she spoke more to herself, “What am I going to do?”

“Mom, she’s never going to listen to you.”

Julia went to her own room and sat down on the bed. What was she going to do? She absolutely dreaded the confrontation. And where was Lily now? Was there even musical practice? She decided to drive to the school and see for herself. She would lock up the house behind her, but not tell Kelsey that she was leaving. She didn’t want her to forewarn her sister.

Julia made her way down the frozen driveway and headed to the country highway toward the city limits. The high school was just at the edge of town. Julia pulled into the parking lot; relieved to see a dozen or so cars in the lot. At least there did seem to be practice going on.

Lily's Hyundai was there, so she parked and moved toward the sidewalk. Walking through the rows of cars, she realized that also among the other vehicles was Dylan's red truck. What was he doing here at school during rehearsal? Inside the building, the auditorium was directly across from the lobby. The spotlights were bright and student actors were on the stage. A piano sounded from the orchestra pit. Scattered in the dark seats of the auditorium were various groups of students not needed on stage. Julia strained her eyes, searching for her daughter and Dylan. It did not take long to find the farthest corner and see a couple alone. She slid into a row ahead and scooted along past the seats, making her way toward them. Julia recognized her daughter's long wavy hair and his ever-present ball cap on his head.

Naturally, it looked as if they were fighting. She realized that if she sat where she currently was, a row ahead and six or seven seats away, that she could hear their words unnoticed. Her face angled toward the stage, but her head was slightly turned in their direction to listen.

"Just drop out of this dumbass musical," were the first audible words.

"Dylan, I like this, it's fun."

He groaned, "Come on, think about it. Your mom thinks you're here and we could have so much time alone."

There were sounds like he was kissing her. Lily spoke, "That's all you think about."

"Bullshit," he growled. There was a moment of silence and then it was as if Dylan's personality had suddenly switched gears. His voice took on a childish, needy tone, "Come on Lily, you know that's not true. I love you, baby. You're my whole life."

"You just say that."

"I mean it; my life is worthless without you." He was quiet and then Julia heard, "You don't respect me, Lily. I devote all my time to you, and you," the way he said it came out like a hiss, "do shit like this show. Your bitch of a mom keeps us apart enough, then you do this. I never get to see you."

"Dylan, I'm sorry. But, we couldn't be together if I wasn't here." There was a pause, her voice was pleading, "Come on sweetie, don't be upset."

Julia was feeling nauseous. Her daughter was cooing to the monster that was her boyfriend. This was too much for her to deal with here, a confrontation was pointless. She decided she needed time to think. Back in the car, she found herself headed to Angie's, with a quick text letting Kelsey know that she had run over to visit her friend.

Angie took one look at her and spoke, "Coffee?"

"I could really use something stronger, but that will do."

"Cody's already asleep, come into the kitchen." They moved through the house.

As Angie poured and handed it to her friend, Julia shared all that she had discovered that evening. Her friend shook her head in amazement. "This is a big problem."

"And I have absolutely no idea of what to do," Julia's hand shook as she poured creamer in her mug.

"Yeah, she's seventeen, you can't lock her up in the house, drive her to school, and keep her with you 24/7."

Privately, Angie considered that she was blessed to only have a son.

Now, Julia felt angry tears threatening to spill, "If I wasn't a single parent of three kids I could be at her side, but I have others to take care of, not just her."

"Exactly, I think Lily is going to have to make this mistake on her own."

"But I'm not kidding; I think he might be dangerous. He seems like the kind of guy who would hurt her, physically."

"I know, he does," Angie thought of everything she had heard and seen. His control of her time, wanting to check her phone, his driving by to see if she was where she said she would be.

"But I must punish her, she has broken all the rules, he's been over when I was at work, she's been sneaking around with him. And I guarantee that when she is under my watchful eyes at night that he's probably out drinking and being with other girls. That's what he does every time they break up. How can she be so dumb? She was not raised to think so little of herself," Julia toyed with a chocolate chip cookie that she had taken off the plate that Angie sat out.

"Tell her the truth; tell her everything you've discovered. Let her know you'll be watching her and keeping them apart as much as you can. Let her know what your concerns are. Just keep reminding her that it's her you care about," even as she spoke, Angie knew this was neither new or helpful advice.

Julia thought about it. "Yeah, at least let her know that I'm not blind to what she's doing. Let her know I'm only doing all this because I love her."

**

Lily was on the defensive the moment Julia walked into the kitchen and hung up her keys. Her daughter was fixing herself a bowl of cereal and didn't turn to greet her. She guessed that Kelsey had told her sister about her discovery. She took a deep breath, her voice full of tears when she spoke, "Lily, six weeks ago Dylan snuck to your friend's house in the middle of the night, took a knife and slashed all your tires, he called you every insulting name possible. What are you thinking?"

Lily looked up, "We don't know that he slashed the tires, he denies it."

"Bullshit." Lily looked surprised at her mother's language. "We both know he did, you were the first one to think it was him. Don't you dare deny it now!"

"Mom, he loves me, I love him."

"Being obsessed and controlling is not real love, Lily. Sex is also not real love."

"You don't understand," her focus was on her bowl.

Julia sat on the stool opposite her daughter, "You're right, I don't understand. There is absolutely no reason for you to think that this is what real love is like. You're not missing love in your life; you should not be accepting this poor excuse for a relationship. Lily, I love you so much," at this her voice broke, "I 've been looking out for you, keeping an eye on what's going on because I'm the one who really loves you. Not him. I want to protect you. If I just ignored all of this and allowed you to do what you want, I'm afraid something bad would happen. I would never forgive myself if something happened to you."

Lily sighed, feeling a bit tearful herself, "Mom it's not that serious. He does stupid stuff, but he's not going to hurt me."

"Lily, slashing your tires, and speaking to you the way he does is just not 'stupid stuff' it's very serious."

"Mom, I can't talk to you about this right now. You don't understand how it is for me. You're not going to listen to how I feel." Lily stood to leave, and Julia realized she was out of words. Nothing had been settled, but she would have to wait until morning, she was too wiped out to handle this responsibly.

She watched as her daughter left the room, then laid her head in her arms and sobbed. When she had cried enough, she looked up at the ceiling, "How dare you leave me, Ken."

**

The next couple of weeks were very difficult. Julia had made it clear that Dylan was not ever welcome in their home. Kelsey's basketball team had made the playoffs and Julia knew she must be there to support her daughter. Perhaps she should have forced Lily to quit the musical and attend every game with her, but she didn't think isolating her from school activities and friends was the wisest choice. Julia went nowhere but work without her daughter. She also began taking and picking Lily up from musical practice, who knew if this was keeping them apart. Twice a week she didn't arrive home until six and none of the kids would admit whether Dylan was at the house or not.

The week of the musical rolled around, and Lily was busy at practice every night. Julia had bought tickets for both shows. Her parents would be coming in for opening night and Ken's parents for the final show. On opening night, Julia sat in the auditorium surrounded by her family. She was proud of her daughter, so animated on the stage, singing and dancing to "*I'm gonna wash that man right out of my hair*." This was the sweet girl she had raised.

After the curtain call, she picked up the small bouquet of flowers at her feet to give Lily when she came down to see them. When the curtain lifted the cast made their way to the steps. Lily saw her family and waved, but just as she got to the stairs, Dylan appeared with a monstrous bouquet of roses and a teddy bear. She swung around in his hug as he lifted her off the ground. When she came to see her family, she was still hand in hand with him. He greeted her grandparents with a friendly shake. Julia chose not to acknowledge him.

The cast party was after the show. She could not forbid this celebration. At home, she said good-bye to her parents, then paced the floor. Kelsey wandered into the kitchen where Julia was once again looking at the time on her phone. She reached into the fridge to pull out a container of yogurt. Setting it on the island and peeling off the top she spoke, "Mom, no matter what you do, Lily is going to keep seeing him. You need to let her make her mistakes."

Julia didn't answer. Kelsey continued, "Come on Mom, you seem so unhappy and lonely. Maybe you need a hobby or a boyfriend."

Julia laughed at her daughter, "The last thing I want right now is my own boyfriend."

"Okay, how about a hobby? Emily's mom knits all these blankets for orphans."

"I don't really see myself knitting," she patted her daughter on the head as she moved past her, "but thanks for your concern, honey."

22

Spring rolled into Seneca, Julia was happy to open curtains and look at the sun. One day as she was raising the living room blinds, she realized that it had been years since she had purchased them. A glance around the room showed her that the paint was fading and there were some marks and scratches from the years gone by. With a smile, she decided it was time to do some remodeling.

When they bought the century old farmhouse, they spent the first six months remodeling from floor to ceiling. After that long process, Ken had despised household projects and she could not get him to make any changes. Hopefully, she could get her kids to be a bit more enthusiastic about it. It turned out that Kelsey had a real knack for interior design. The two of them spent hours watching HGTV and pouring over Pinterest. Soon they had chosen to cover the practical cream with a soft shade of gray and a white chair rail across the middle. The black leather furniture still worked but they added bright pillows and replaced the heavy blinds.

Even Lily admitted that the new room was fantastic. The kids began to speculate how they could change their own rooms. Julia, herself, had spent some time staring at her four walls. Suddenly she felt she was spending her nights in a man and woman's room; maybe it was time to make it her own comfort haven.

**

Julia knew her weak attempts at keeping Lily away from Dylan were probably not working, but she remained vigilant. At the end of March, Lily came to her devastated that he had been seeing another girl. He had convinced her that it was her fault since her mother wouldn't allow her to spend time with him. Once again Lily announced she was permanently through with him. It was not more than a week however that Lily was shutting herself in her room in the evening. Julia knew she had once again taken him back.

The Junior/Senior prom was just a month away. Julia was dreading the moment when Lily asked her if she could go with Dylan. As much as she felt defeated in keeping them entirely apart, Julia felt like she would be going against everything she knew was wrong if she allowed it. It was a battle when they had the discussion, but Julia had remained firm.

Lily shocked her when she came home one day and said she was asked to the prom by Coach Saddler's son, Cory. From what Julia knew of him he seemed to be a nice boy. She was thrilled and gave her permission instantly. Together they drove to the big city and found a lovely pale pink dress at Macy's. Lily chose silver sandals and convinced Julia to make her an appointment at the salon for an updo.

When Cory picked her up on prom night, he gave her a wrist corsage of pink roses and daisies, Julia took pictures of the couple. Lily said they weren't going to get their pictures with a large group, because Cory had to stop at both his parents' houses for pictures. There was an after-prom party at the local recreation center and then breakfast at the Saddler's, so Julia had agreed to allow Lily to be gone for the night.

Kelsey had couple of freshmen girls over to watch movies, Julia had spent the evening painting her bedroom. She'd left the windows open because of the paint smell and snuggled under an extra quilt to sleep. The room was an oasis for her. She had chosen a soft blue shade called Raindrop for the walls. The bedding was a mix of the same color blended with pale gray. Everything about it was relaxing.

A car pulling out of the drive woke her, she glanced at the clock it was five thirty in the morning. The prom activities must be over. She listened for Lily's footsteps up to her bedroom. She considered calling out to her and asking about the night but decided to wait until her daughter had slept. Julia dozed off for another hour and a half. She awoke, freezing and quickly closed her windows. After pulling on her robe, she headed out of her room. She saw that Lily had left the bathroom light on. She reached in to turn it off and noticed her daughter's sparkling earrings, rings and her corsage lying on the counter.

In the kitchen, she was making coffee when a thought struck her, Lily's corsage in the bathroom; there was something wrong with it. Julia headed upstairs to get another look. In the bathroom she picked up the already withering corsage. Her mind was confused, this was made of pink, red and white roses, there were no daisies. Had she picked up someone else's? Julia didn't understand, but decided it wasn't important.

Lily did not appear until after one. She said the prom was wonderful, the music great, the after prom an absolute blast. As for Cory, she made a dismissive face and said she didn't like him like that. Julia had hoped that she could get her mind on someone new and off Dylan. But at least she had gone on a date and made a step in the right direction.

On Monday, Julia was in her room, finishing painting the trim. She heard the slam of doors as her daughters arrived home from school. It sounded as if they were arguing as they went in to the kitchen. She moved to her door and listened. Kelsey was the one doing the yelling and Julia heard words such as, "My coach", "Embarrassing" and ended spitting out the word "whore".

Lily responded with her own profanity and Julia yelled down the stairs, "Girls, what is going on?"

She heard harsh angry whispers as she came to the first level of the house. In the kitchen the girls shot daggers at each other, but when Julia repeated her questions she was greeted with mumbled "nothing's."

Throughout dinner the silence continued but she could see that Kelsey was visibly upset and it was aimed toward Lily. Finally, in the evening, both girls had shut themselves into their rooms. Julia had an idea. Alone in the kitchen, she opened her phone and clicked on Instagram. As she knew the case would be, both girls had their names locked in a password. She knew Lily's would be impossible to crack, she had secrets to keep. Kelsey was as predictable as Julia expected her to be. Her password was SHS for Seneca High School and her basketball jersey number. Soon Julia was looking at her daughter's photos of her friends, her team, and even the dog. Continuing to scroll she found her oldest child's photos with Dylan. They were kissing in some, or it was just him with his tongue hanging out. There was a picture of them that looked like they might both be topless, but the picture stopped at bare shoulders.

Her heart dropped as she glanced at the photo of Lily in her prom dress, the boy holding onto her was not Cory, but Dylan! There was another of the two of them kissing on the dance floor and another of them dancing with him pressed against her backside. Julia almost shut it off at that but decided to look at the messages from people.

Dylan had sent many, one had said "You know how to do more than dance!"

Another message was from Olivia, her best friend, it was angry. “I thought we were friends.”

Julia covered her mouth with her hands. Dylan had been her prom date? Cory had just picked her up to fool Julia? That explained the different corsage. And what had happened at Sadler's house? She scanned further and saw comments indicating that Dylan and Lily had been caught by Coach Saddler in his bed, during the breakfast.

Julia flew up the stairs and confronted her daughter. She did not even attempt to hide her fury as she accused her of what she had discovered. Lily looked appalled and her first response was, “I knew Kelsey couldn’t keep her mouth shut.”

Julia continued to yell, letting her know that her sister did not say a thing. All her patience was gone. She knew that the entire household was hearing what she had to say but at the moment she did not care.

Lily broke into angry tears and screamed back, “Why don’t you just say it Mom, that you think I’m a slut?”

“No, I don’t think you are, but it sounds as if you’re making everyone else think it. You ended up in Cory’s dad’s bed with Dylan and got caught?”

"Mother, it was embarrassing enough, I don't need you rubbing my face in it."

"How do you think I feel?"

"It's not about you."

Were these words really coming out of her daughter's mouth? "This is your sister's basketball coach, no wonder she's upset. You've embarrassed her."

With a dismissive wave of her hand, "I know I'm ruining the family. Why don't you just send me away?"

Julia was tempted to say she wished she could, but she struggled to calm down. "Lily, you think you've been grounded up to this point? You don't even know."

It was after one when Sophie's growl at the window woke up Julia. The air was warm on this April night and she had cracked open the window. The dog was watching, her nose at the screen. Julia did not turn on the light but pushed Sophie out of the way and cautiously peered out of her second-floor window. She had left the security light on the back porch on and could make out the shadowy figure of someone standing in the yard. It looked as if the person was yelling and she strained to hear. Suddenly, she saw the person lean down and pick up something off the ground and throw it at the house. Julia realized this was Dylan and he was trying to wake up Lily.

Throwing jeans over her pajamas, she ran down the stairs with Sophie at her heels. Julia knew that if she simply let the dog out she would be no help. The young man outside was not actually dangerous, but Julia felt nervous as she opened the back door. His shouts of "Lily" were beginning to increase and she decided that none of her children had their windows open. As she pushed her head through the small opening in the glass door she watched him sway a bit, he was obviously intoxicated, "Dylan."

He looked around trying to locate the sound. He spotted her. "I need to see Lily," he spoke as he moved toward the deck.

"Don't come any closer. You're not going to see her or talk to her tonight."

He stepped up onto the first step of the deck, "I need to see her."

"Go home Dylan. You will not see her. If you come any closer, I'll call the police."

That stopped him, but his voice became insistent, "I have to see her! She's ignoring my calls and texts."

"Dylan I will not allow you to speak to her, now go home. I mean it, no more, go home." Julia decided that any more conversation was pointless. She closed the glass door, placed the security bar on it, and closed the curtains. She then snuck into the study and peered out the curtains where she could get a full view of the deck.

Dylan yelled in the direction of the door again, "I need to see Lily."

He then stepped down and moved back to the place below Lily's window. He began picking up more rocks and hurtling them in the direction of her window. Fortunately, he had no aim because of his drunkenness and most fell three feet ahead of him.

Julia realized that this was going nowhere. She wished she had his parents' names and numbers. His last name was too common in Seneca, when she checked online there were half a dozen. Finally, she sighed and did the very last thing she wanted to do. Julia dialed 911.

The police came quietly and escorted him off the property. Julia told the officer who came to the door that she didn't wish to press charges; she just needed help getting him to leave. By this time Lily had heard the commotion and was screaming at her mother to let her go out and see him. He was taken home in the patrol car and the next day a man looking like an older, more haggard version of Dylan picked up his truck and drove off without coming to the door to apologize or explain.

23

School was nearly out, one more week to go. Angie had been working hard to convince the Darby's to join Cody and her on a trip to Spring Lake for the weekend. Julia had adamantly refused to return to Luke's place of residence. Angie insisted that Luke would not spend time with them. Julia tried to suggest that they would be intruding on a few days of romance. Angie had countered that with a suggestion that her parents were out of town and Julia's family could stay at their house just two doors down from Angie and Marcus.

All three of her kids were eager to take a trip out of town and especially to visit a lake. Julia decided it would be a welcome change for all of them and as they headed onto the highway wondered why she hadn't thought about going away sooner. She fought to ignore the other side of her brain that was considering being at Spring Lake, right in Luke's world

Her discomfort increased as they approached the lake. She found herself traveling back in time to her teen years and all the feelings surrounding her time at the lake. She especially felt unsure about staying in the home of the Thomas'; she had spent a lot of time in that house. Angie insisted that she had been in touch with Luke, and he knew to stay away from her this weekend. There was a fleeting sense of guilt when she thought about not allowing him family time. What should she do?

**

In the backseat of the car, Lily watched the lake come into view and thought of Dylan. She'd like to take Dylan on an out of town trip. Maybe if they were away from his horrible family and his obnoxious friends he would be that wonderful guy she was seeing less and less of. To make matters worse, Dylan blamed her for it. It was so sad when he broke down. He constantly reminded Lily that his life was useless without her and if she would just handle her mom then they could both be happy. Other times, he said he hated her, she ruined everything. Just when she decided to give up on the relationship, Dylan would beg her to save him or threaten suicide. Lily sighed and closed her eyes.

**

The old road was lined with a mixture of cabins built as early as the 1960s and newer permanent homes. A rough, whitewashed, square bungalow could be nestled next to a comfortable, split level with brick and siding. The land surrounding the lake was sloped at different heights. Most places had a hill into which steps were built to reach the shore. Just a few places were water level. From between the row of houses, Julia could glimpse the lake, serene in the afternoon sun.

Now as they rolled down the familiar gravel lane, nostalgia was taking over, and she felt uncertain. She had been through so much; Julia was amazed that Ken had died nearly a year ago. Her loneliness combined with memories might make her an emotional wreck. Walking into the pale blue one story home of Angie's parents did not help. She placed her bags in the master bedroom, a place which held no memories for her. The girls would bunk in Nancy and Angie's old room. Seth headed to the first bedroom on the left of the hall. Julia stepped slowly into the room. This had been Luke's room and she nearly blushed thinking about some of the moments she had spent in here, afternoons when the Thomas' were both gone, with the curtains covering the screen and the midday sun. Her hand lightly trailed over the twin bed, still covered with the blue chintz bedspread that had draped it more than twenty years ago. Julia couldn't help herself as she scanned the top of the dresser and the cork board looking for traces of herself. She saw none.

Seth was off to the lake before she had even turned around. Together with the girls, and Sophie at her heels, she headed down the six steps to the dock. Angie's parents had a small row boat and a paddle boat; the girls were delighted to get to take a spin around the lake using their legs for power.

The full expanse of the lake brought a smile to Julia's face. It was such a beautiful place. Spring Lake was a relatively small body of water, no more than a mile long and half a mile across. She remembered all the lovely years she had spent growing up here. Her parents had owned various boats over the years; an old wooden speed boat, an upgrade of a small outboard boat and eventually a pontoon so that her parents could take slow cruises around the lake each morning and evening. Days were filled with swimming, boating, and sunbathing. The nights were filled with hiking behind the houses to one friend or another, bonfires or late-night swims.

Maybe she and Ken should have done the same for their children.

Cody had jogged over from his front yard, already in trunks, the boys were soon splashing in the water. Julia pulled two life vests from the row boat then tossed them into the back of the paddle boat. The girls had run up to put on bikinis. When they returned she gave them brief instructions on how to steer the boat and what direction to travel. Soon they were making their way away from the dock.

She was excited to also go around the lake and see all the old places, she hoped her friend would be ready to take out the gorgeous inboard parked at their dock. As if they read her thoughts, Marcus and Angie had appeared. Marcus was removing the cover from his boat. Angie was wearing her bathing suit and shorts. "Get your suit on and we'll go for a spin around the lake," she called.

Julia fastened a dog chain to a tree and tied up Sophie, the dog, who gave her a look that said, 'How could you?' Julia scratched her head, "It's okay girl, you'll be able to see us from here." Then she jogged up and put on her suit. She had never felt better in her coral and brown tankini. Though the ten pounds she had lost last year was from stress, the new look was appealing. Over the suit she threw on a white cotton cover-up and grabbed her sunglasses.

The lake water was clear and smooth. Only about a half a dozen boats were out pulling skiers and tubes. There were quite a few jet skis. “Cody wants one of those as soon as he’s fourteen.”

“I bet he does.”

As they made their way around the sandy point, Julia’s breath caught. Up on the hill sat the house from her imagination. She looked at it; each detail was what she had planned with Luke. The house stood apart, a good acre between it and neighbors. Its structure included a multi-leveled roof, and the windows were all tall and wide. There was an immense deck that stretched down to the dock. On the second floor was a matching balcony.

Marcus spoke, “That’s Luke’s house. Isn’t it a beauty? He spent three years on it.”

Angie shot her husband a look; he continued unaware, “You should see the inside, big open rooms, and so many windows.”

Julia nodded in agreement. She knew exactly what it would look like. She glanced at the dock. There was a large red ski boat, covered up. A jet ski was locked up on a rack. No sign of life. Perhaps he had gone out of town because of her demands that he stay away.

The evening rolled on and they built a bonfire in the back of the Castile yard. Even the teenagers had a great time making S'mores. At one point, Julia's marshmallow caught fire and sizzled to black ash. Lily met her mother's eyes and they both laughed. This felt good, almost therapeutic.

The sound of the waves woke Julia of in the morning. She felt refreshed from a night of cool lake breeze blowing in and a sense of freedom being away from her home and all its responsibilities. Making a pot of coffee, she decided to jump in the shower and wash the smell of bonfire off her skin before she went out to the lake. A bit of mascara on and some gel to her damp hair was all the cosmetics she wore. Next, she threw on khaki shorts and a plain cornflower blue tee.

With coffee cup in hand, she padded barefoot out to the yard. At the dock, dropping her feet in the still chilly water, she sipped her coffee and took in the morning view. Despite the many memories that had been occupying her mind yesterday, she felt peaceful. The water always did that to her. The sound of a slow engine was nearby, and she turned to look at the early fisherman. It was a red ski boat moving close to the shoreline. A red boat? The driver's brown hair blew slightly in the wind. Her heart began to pound. It was certainly not him, Angie had promised. Julia's emotions went in all directions; betrayal, fear, and, shamefully, excitement.

**

Luke had his eye on his sister's place, though he had promised to stay away, he could not help hoping to catch another glimpse of Julia. Last night he had been at the window in his room, with binoculars, watching their progress around the lake. Now as he got closer to his parents, he saw a lone figure on the dock. Strange, he knew they had left town for the weekend. It was not unusual for a young fisherman to walk dock to dock and along the shore. This however, was obviously a woman. It looked like Julia, why was she on his parents' dock? It was clear she had seen him, he steered the boat toward her.

At first it looked as if she was preparing to bolt. Before she could, Luke pulled to the front of the dock, out of habit, Julia grabbed the side of the boat. For a moment neither spoke as he shut off the engine. “Hi,” he said with a quiet smile.

“You aren’t supposed to come over.” Julia’s expression told him that she did not trust his motivation.

Luke sighed, “I know. I thought you were staying at Angie’s. I saw someone on Dad’s dock and was just checking to see who was here.” Her response was a skeptical frown. He gave her a weak smile, “I promise.”

Julia looked at him; he had on navy and green trunks and a plain white T. He was as she most remembered him barefoot. His hair was windblown, and he took her breath away. His eyes told her he was scrutinizing her also.

“Why are you staying at my folks’ house?”

“They’re gone.”

He grinned, “I know.”

Determined not to fall for that smile, she looked down at the water, “I wanted to give Marcus and Angie some time to themselves.” There was a moment of silence, “Your house is beautiful.”

“Does it look like you thought it would?”

**

Julia felt her heart pound. The house looked like the drawings he had made, the lists they constructed. The magazine photos they had pasted to paper. “Exactly.” He held onto the post of the dock. she was holding the windshield frame of his boat. They were very close, Julia felt if she leaned in their foreheads would touch.

There was a moment of silence, both lost in their thoughts. Luke finally looked at her carefully and spoke, “Jules, how are you doing?”

She moved her head away for a moment, “I’m doing okay. We all are.”

“The kids are here with you,” this was a statement not a question.

“Yes.”

“Luke, I’m not here because of you.”

The smile disappeared, “I know. I truly didn’t come out here to find you.” After a glance away, he confessed, “I was, perhaps, hoping for a glimpse of you.” She looked at the lake, past his face. He watched her closely. “I can’t believe you’re sitting here.”

“I can’t. . .” He didn’t give her time to answer, before he placed his hand over hers.

"Julia, I'm sorry. Sorry for last year. I'm not here at this moment to force anything on you."

Before she could respond, she felt weight on the opposite end of the dock and turned to look over her shoulder.

Lily had been looking for her mother and come out into the yard, at first it looked like her mother was holding onto an empty boat and then she realized that her mom was leaning extremely close to the driver. Who was it? As her mom turned, she could see Luke Thomas.

"No way!" she hissed.

Julia looked at her daughter in surprise, "Hi Lily. Do you remember Angie's brother?"

"I remember who *he* is." Julia was shocked at the venom in her daughter's voice.

Luke reached out and squeezed Julia's hand. "Maybe I better get moving. I'll see you later," he said quietly. She continued to focus on her daughter.

Turning, she stood up and faced her. "Lily, what's wrong?"

"Is he why we're here?" her daughter demanded.

"No, what do you mean?" Julia's breathing was shallow; did Lily know what happened between them last year? How would she know?

Lily responded by rolling her eyes, "I bet. Has this been your plan all along? I can't be with the person I love, but you get what you want." Her voice had been getting louder with each word.

Julia looked shocked, "What I want?"

"Oh, I know all about him!" with those words, Lily raced back up the hill and into the house.

**

From the middle of the lake Luke could not hear the words but saw that something was going wrong for Julia. He grabbed his cell phone from his shorts pocket and hit a number. Angie answered on the first ring. "Angie, I think Julia could use your help. Could you go over there right now?"

She was quiet for a beat, "You went over there? I promised her that you wouldn't."

"No, I just went by on the boat and saw her," he sighed impatiently, "she's having some trouble with her oldest, could you go over?"

**

Angie gave a half knock on the front door of her parent's home. "Hello," she called into the screen.

"Come in," came a muffled response from Julia. She was at the kitchen table staring into an empty mug.

Angie came to her and smoothed hair, “Hon, what happened, Luke just called.”

“Ugh,” Julia pressed her hands over her face. She sighed deeply and put her hands down.

Angie sat down next to her friend. Julia spoke in a low whisper. “I was sitting on the dock and Luke pulled in on his boat. We were just talking, and Lily came down. She blew up. She said she knew all about me and Luke.”

Angie raised her eyebrows at this information but kept silent. Julia’s voice became ragged, “She said I was probably glad Ken was dead, so I could be with Luke.”

Lily charged into the front room and pointed at her mother, “You have two, two pictures of you and dad before you were married. You have an entire box of things with him.” Tears poured down Lily’s cheeks.

Julia appeared caught off guard. “What are you talking about?”

“I saw the house on the hill, the home of the future Mr. and Mrs. Luke Thomas.”

Relief washed over Julia’s face. This wasn’t about last summer, this was about the box. “Oh honey, I’m so sorry. You found the box.”

Lily nodded, “Why would you still have that?”

"I didn't realize that I did. It's been up there since we bought the house when you were a baby. I promise I haven't looked at it once since I put it there."

Angie slowly backed up; this was not a conversation that she needed to be part of. Silently she opened the screen door and went out. As she headed back through the yards to her own home, Angie thought about the box. Why did Julia still have it?

**

Julia finally got Lily to sit across from her, "Honey, I'm not here for Luke, in fact I made it clear to Angie that I didn't want to see him."

She had hoped this would be reassuring; instead it aroused suspicion in her daughter. "Why? Why didn't you want to see him?"

Feeling backed into a corner, Julia struggled with a new level of lies, "I guess I thought it would be weird. When we broke up, just barely older than you, I never came back here. I'm here as Angie's friend, but since I no longer have a husband, I didn't want anyone to think that's why I came back."

"For real, Mom?"

Grasping both her daughter's shoulders, Julia spoke, "I promise."

**

Lily had gone back to bed after the confrontation. It was nearly noon when she awoke. There was a note on the table, telling her the family was on the beach at the Castile's. Her first instinct was to check her phone. As usual, it was flooded with messages from Dylan. Lily began to respond when she was distracted by screams of laughter from the shore. She joined the gang and was surprised to see her brother and sister in life vests climbing on a tube. Her surprise continued when she saw her mother, in her swimsuit and sunglasses, expertly giving instructions to them on when to hold on and when to let go. Marcus was behind the wheel of the boat; Cody was in the water helping Kelsey get her balance.

**

Julia looked up mid-sentence at her oldest daughter. Lily smiled and then gave her the thumbs up signal trying to let her know everything was okay. She smiled widely in response and the boat took off. Seth and Kelsey were having the times of their lives keeping the tubes inside of the wake and bouncing along the surface of the water. As the boat rounded the bend, she could not help but glance at the house on the point, there were no signs of life, so she turned back to watching her kids calling to each other.

After a round they were ready to go in. They both let go and let the water pull them down. Angie was standing at the dock with Lily. After a moment they hugged. Then Lily joined Cody at the shore, taking the life vests from the others for their own turn. "My turn to be lookout?" Angie asked. She jumped into the boat next to her husband, as Julia climbed out. Seth and Kelsey were scrambling onto the dock, then jumped into the boat. The next group of tubers took off with a shrill scream of delight from Lily.

Julia down to watch alone. Just as earlier that day, she felt a footstep at the opposite end of the dock. She looked over her shoulder, it was Luke. Her first reaction was to nervously look out toward the boat.

He was now down to just swim trunks. Holding up his hands in surrender, Luke spoke, "Julia, I got a text from Angie that Lily is okay with me here, but it is your decision," there was a question in his voice.

"I can't keep you from your family. Of course, you can be here." He sat down next to her, his feet also dangling in the icy lake water.

Julia felt the heat of having his arm pressed next to hers. "I'm sorry for the way things went this morning. I thought she knew about last year, but she didn't." It was easier to sit side by side with him, facing the water and not looking at him. She sighed, "I've not been doing the best job as a single parent."

He touched her leg as a gesture of support but let go quickly because it was bare, "That's exactly the opposite of what my sister says."

"Luke, I don't want to talk about anything dealing with the past year."

"Of course not, I'm sorry. You're here for a vacation."

Just then the boat made its way in. The kids flew off their tubes close to Luke, who was assaulted with a spray of water. Julia laughed as he pushed his hair off his face and wiped water from his eyes. Cody saw it was his uncle in the water and threw himself at Luke. They went down together. As soon as he surfaced, Cody confronted Luke, "Can we go jet skiing? I told Seth it's the best thing ever."

Luke picked Cody up, "Have you grown a foot in Seneca? Sure, we can go jet skiing," he tossed his nephew off the dock.

**

It had been a fun filled day full of water sports, sunshine and an ended with a cookout. Luke had insisted that they come to his house for the dinner; he had a huge deck and state of the art grill. He also boasted the only real sandy beach on the lake and the girls wanted to see if they could still build a sandcastle. Not wanting to see the house or willingly spend time there, Julia had tried to hold the party at her house and was outnumbered on votes. She and Luke had kept a cautious distance from one another but whenever she found herself watching him, she would catch him doing the same.

The girls had thrown shorts over their bikinis, just as she had every evening as a teenager and grabbed hoodies in case it cooled down. Seth was, of course, not changing out of his trunks until he fell into bed that night.

Julia saw Luke standing at the dock as they approached by boat; he was wearing khaki shorts and a yellow golf shirt. The feelings that shot through her body horrified her. Maybe she should have claimed being ill. Would Marcus take her back across the lake? Before she could make her excuse, Luke held out his hand to her. She took it and joined him on the dock as the others made their way to the house. Lily and Kelsey settled themselves into cushioned chaise lounges, playing music on their phones with ear buds.

Angie was already in the kitchen; Marcus had taken it upon himself to work the grill. Luke and Julia headed into the glass door that led to the kitchen. His sister looked up from the large marble island, "I've got it under control."

Luke smiled graciously, "Then I'm going to show Julia my house."

It was exactly as she knew it would be. He had not forgotten any details from the high ceiling in the great room to the small balcony off the master suite. She was pleased, yet almost uncomfortable. Had he thought she would live here? How long ago did he build it? She voiced this question.

It was complete about nine years ago. Okay, that was over a decade after they had split up. Julia was confused, if not concerned. Luke seemed to sense her unease. "Julia, I built this house exactly this way because this was my very first and favorite design."

As they stood on the balcony overlooking another corner of the lake, he turned to her, "I'm not going to lie and say that I never imagined you here. But I did not live in some crazy fantasy world that you would show up at my door someday." In a near whisper he added, "Yet here you are." Julia did not respond.

After dinner, the kids decided they had had enough of the water and gathered in front of Luke's flat screen to watch Netflix. The adults sat on the deck, a fire in the stone fire pit, enjoying the quiet, sharing a bottle of wine. "Well sis, when are you coming back, or Marcus are you leaving?"

Angie spoke up, "School's out in a week. I've been working on being allowed to do my job at home. That would mean that Cody and I will probably be heading back here." She looked apologetically at Julia, "It's not final."

"Angie, that's wonderful, that is exactly what you should be doing. I'm so happy for all three of you."

Luke looked across the deck to where Julia was stretched out in a lounger. "What are you doing all summer?"

She shrugged, "School's out next week. Lily starts at the ice cream shop on Wednesday. Kelsey has basketball camp and will be doing some babysitting. Seth has little league. I'm teaching one class at the college and one online class, summer will just fly by."

Luke nodded, "Any vacations planned?"

She shook her head, "No, haven't quite got the nerve to do that alone yet."

The reminder of her widowed status settled in the air. The group was quiet for a moment. Angie jumped in, "But when I'm back here, she'll be visiting every chance she gets."

Luke grinned, "I'm amazed how old your kids are."

"I can't believe that Lily is going to be a senior in the fall," Angie added.

"I know this is the summer we start looking at colleges."

Marcus yawned. Angie smacked his leg, "Come on old man, let's get everyone on the boat, you better get us back before you fall asleep at the wheel." She opened the door and called down to the kids. There were protests that the movie was not yet over.

Luke stood up, "Look Ang, why don't you and Marcus take the boat back, I can bring everyone else back in the Range Rover, when the movie's over."

Marcus stood up and stretched, "Sounds good to me."

Angie murmured "Are you sure?" and turned to go. At the top of the steps Marcus turned, "Ready Julia?"

Julia jumped to go, but Luke stepped in, "Do you mind waiting for the kids?" She struggled with the decision, but it seemed rude to ask him to sit alone and wait for her three kids to finish a movie before driving them home.

They stood waving as the boat disappeared in the dark and sat almost simultaneously on the step. The fire was nearly out. For a moment it was peacefully silent. Julia breathed deeply; it felt so good for once to be thinking away from home and the troubles and memories that surrounded it.

"I can't believe a year's gone by since I last saw you," Luke said quietly.

She didn't look at him. "I know, it was a million years ago, it seems."

"I'm sorry about coming over that night." He too must regret what they had done. "I meant well, but it was wrong of me to try to talk to you."

He didn't mean the night they kissed, he meant after the funeral. "I'm sorry, I nearly attacked you that night."

"Don't apologize. I can't even imagine what you were going through. And I have felt like hell ever since for adding to your grief."

"It's my own fault, Luke."

"I played my part in it. I behaved badly from the moment you walked into Angie's house that day. I never wanted to be that man."

"A few months after Ken died, I went crazy one weekend. I had myself convinced for a long time after the accident that what we did had caused his death. I know that sounds ridiculous."

Luke put his arm around her, "I know exactly what you mean."

She didn't move away, but instead said what she thought was the truth, "We ruined our past by what we did."

"No, Julia don't say that. Those memories shouldn't be destroyed because of our behavior last year," Luke dropped his arm from her, but angled his body so that their heads were closer.

They were silent for a moment. Julia felt she had to put the rest out there, "Luke, I can't ever be with you."

His expression was one of extreme sadness, "I was afraid you'd say that. And I know why you're saying it.

Jules, I won't do anything to go against your wishes. But can we at least be friends?"

"I don't know. I really hate myself, because I was so weak."

"Can we try? Maybe you could text me or call me if you wanted." He looked at her, it was time to change the subject, "So tomorrow, you go back home." She nodded, self-consciously straightening her hair as the kids approached. They both stood.

"Do you know what time?"

"The kids have school on Monday, but I'm sure that Angie doesn't want to leave too early."

"Can I hang out again?" he asked hopefully.

She smiled weakly, but didn't get to answer, soon they were surrounded by the kids. Lily and Kelsey eyed their mom carefully. *When had Angie and Marcus left? What had their mom been doing out here in the dark?*

As the kids tumbled out of his car, Luke spoke softly, "How about we meet on the dock in the morning at sun up. Maybe tomorrow it will go better."

Julia stood at the car door and leaned in, "Maybe," chastising herself for immediately going against her own strong words. Why couldn't she have any self-control when it came to Luke?

Later in bed, she realized sleep wasn't going to happen. She was feeling a complete contradiction of heart and body. Her body was relaxed from the day in the sun and water, but her heart was in turmoil. *Could they be friends? Should they be friends*?

She thought about the house she was in, and all the times she had been in it before. In her mind. she imagined how things might have turned out if she had been forgiving of Luke's mistake and waited for him to come to Ashland. Julia knew it was unfair to do this. Her life had been incredibly lousy these twelve months, so it was so easy to make the "what if" life seem wonderful.

She had loved him so much, and he had been such an unbelievable boyfriend, lover, and friend. Julia felt tingles just remembering his body. Then her memory recalled that night last year when he had held her and kissed her. It had been incredibly passionate. Soon this all dissolved into shame, and like so many nights before, Julia cried herself to sleep.

**

The weather had taken a slight turn as is common in the Midwest in early June. At sunup, Julia slipped out of the house and headed to the dock in jeans and a jacket, with two mugs of coffee in her hands. She told herself that she was going to tell him that seeing him was like backtracking. If she was going to survive the rest of her life, she needed to make a break with all things Luke forever.

She stepped onto the dock when Luke coasted in, engine off. He tied up the boat and helped her in. Handing him a mug, she sat in the passenger seat.

"Thank you," damn him, every time she saw him she decided he was even more handsome than the time before. He looked down into his mug and his hair swung over his forehead. Her fingers itched to return to their longtime habit of pushing the hair back up, away from his eyes.

When he looked up he caught her expression and gave her a devastating smile, "What?"

She blushed, "What, what?"

"What were you going to say or do?"

"Nothing."

"Come on, Jules," he thought a moment, "were you going to fix my hair?" This was not going the way she had planned. "I don't care if you touch me." He meant it lightly, but they both felt the heat of the moment and simultaneously took a deep breath.

He spoke "What are we going to do?"

"Drink coffee?"

Luke frowned, "No, that's not what I mean." He gazed at her, "You know that's not what I mean."

"Luke, what do you mean?" she asked him.

He gave a merciless laugh, "Julia, I know you. You probably beat yourself up again last night. You came down here this morning with the intention of telling me we should never speak again. Am I right?"

She was amazed at his straightforward words, "Yes."

Luke gave her a soft look, "But then this happens."

"What's this?"

"I know you feel it too, we get together and it's like we're returning to normal. I know we destroyed it all last year. But, this weekend means something."

"Oh," she whispered.

"And it's more than that," he was serious. "Come on Jules, you know as well as I do that if I pulled you to me right now and kissed you like I want to, that without thinking, I'd probably say 'I love you' afterward." He looked right into her eyes, always aware of what was on her mind, "What would you say if I did?"

She didn't need to reply. Instead she made a move as if to leave, "Luke, please don't say these things. You just told me last night you wouldn't do this."

Touching her arm to stop her departure, he sighed deeply, "Yep, then I went home and thought about us being together."

"Me too," she nearly whispered. "I hate myself. I have for a year."

"Don't say that. Hate me, but don't hate yourself."

Finally, she had the courage to look at him, "That's the problem, Luke. Seeing you, I can't hate you. I know I should, I'm so weak."

"You weak? I've heard exactly the opposite. Raising three kids, taking care of a house, handling the finances. Dealing with problems with your daughter. Weak is the last word I would use to describe you. You want to punish yourself for what happened between us. I get that, I thought I was willing to accept it. I just didn't know I would see you again."

Julia was quiet for some time. Finally, she spoke, "You're right. I didn't think we would see each other again. But we did, and I'm powerless around you. I may be headed for hell, but I can't run away again."

Luke gave a miserable laugh, "Not quite the sentiment I hoped to hear, but it's a good start. There is something between us."

"So, this is a problem."

He took her chin and lifted it, “It doesn’t have to be. Besides we still live hours away, we can go slowly.”

It was her turn to be realistic, “As if we will. Luke, I don’t know how my kids are going to handle this.”

“Can we try?” He put his hands on top of hers. “The one thing we didn’t do all those years ago was try when things were tough. When it was good, we were perfect; as soon as it got difficult we both gave up.”

She nodded and turned her hands, so they were holding his, “That’s exactly what we did. I must tell you what Lily was upset about. I’m embarrassed to say that I used to collect all our things; pictures, movie tickets, letters. I kept them in a big shoebox. I never threw it out and somehow it ended up in the top of my closet.”

“You still had it?” Luke was processing this.

“I didn’t even remember it, but somehow Lily found it. When she saw us together yesterday she accused me of coming here to get you back. She knows the truth is that I brought her here to keep her from Dylan. I promised her that this was not going to happen, that you and I would never even be friends.”

“You kept the box,” he said again.

“Please, quit focusing on that. I may have a situation with Lily if suddenly today we are friends.”

"You tell me what to say or do, I'll trust you on how to deal with that."

"It's not like we can go on dates or anything," she said more to herself than him.

"I am allowed to take out of town trips on the weekends now," he joked.

She smiled finding herself caught up in the moment, "And I might really need to visit with Angie a lot this summer."

Luke leaned close, "Don't talk yourself out of it again the second you leave. Both of us being here this weekend means something."

24

Julia's cell phone buzzed as she walked into the house. *Are you home yet?* It was Luke.

Just got in.

She was carrying her bag up to her room, and felt it signal again in her pocket. *Angie said that the boyfriend has shown some aggressive behavior. Is your house okay?* Julia hadn't considered this. Would Dylan come in when they were gone? Without responding, she peeked into the kids' rooms, all was intact. Downstairs there was nothing out of order.

She sat at the bar, the mail in front of her, and picked up her phone, *Everything is fine. I don't think he's an intruder.*

Good. He's really shown up in the middle of the night?

She tried to lighten the conversation, *He's not the only one.* That changed the mood and the next few texts were just friendly exchanges. At last she said good-bye and laid down the phone. So, she was going to engage in this? Her heart so desperately wanted to.

What was on Lily's mind about the weekend? Perhaps she was too full of the Dylan issue to pay attention. Julia was concerned about allowing her to go back to her job, that was where they met, and he was certain to return to last summer's habit of stopping in. Had that really been a year ago? She had known then that it was a poor choice. What had she done wrong?

**

By Friday, they had survived a week of final exams for the girls and field day for Seth. Julia had to finalize some things at the college, when she returned home, she found the girls on chaise lounges in the backyard working hard not to lose the tans they had begun at the lake last weekend. Seth was out front shooting hoops.

"Hey girls," she called coming out on the back deck. Julia had to call louder a second time and saw two pairs of headphones come down.

Kelsey squinted in her direction, "What?" Lily also looked up, shading her eyes with her hand.

"What do you guys want to do tonight? Dinner out to celebrate the end of the school year or maybe a movie?"

Lily spoke first, “Mom, I was hoping to go shopping with Olivia.” Her mom looked at her a long time. “You can check with her mom and Rachel’s too, it’s just girls.”

“I will.”

Kelsey spoke up, “Emily, Mandy and I are going to go see the new Adam Sandler movie.”

Julia’s shoulders slumped, “Oh, okay.” She turned back into the house.

Lily looked over at her sister, “I feel kind of bad. Mom needs a social life.”

“Maybe a boyfriend,” Kelsey added, laying her head back down.

“You think?”

“I think she really likes Angie’s brother.”

Lily turned, “She does, remember he’s her old boyfriend. It was a big-time thing when she was young.”

“So? It’s kind of cool if they get back together.”

Lily opened her eyes again and looked at her sister, “Yeah, but I mean if she does it's going to be serious.”

“You think?”

“Did you not pay any attention to the way she acted last weekend?”

“I heard you screaming at her about him.”

“Whatever.”

"What's the big deal?"

"Do you want her to marry this guy?"

It was Kelsey's turn to roll on her back and close her eyes, "It's weird I know, but Mom isn't even forty, I want her to be happy. You're freaking out; they haven't even been on a date yet."

"Yeah, well if they do, you'll see."

"Whatever, Lily."

**

Julia did indeed check with the other mothers, as she knew it would be, they were both aware of the situation with Dylan. It was a small town. Julia was happy to let her daughter go, at seventeen she knew how important those social contacts were. Who was she kidding; they were important to her too. Marcus was home for the weekend, so Angie was occupied. Julia faced another weekend of loneliness.

**

Three weeks had gone by. Luke had not pressed Julia to get together. He had made it very clear that all she needed was to say the word and he would be in town. The busy days of summer were flying by. There were ball games nearly every night. This was also the first summer that she had worked. When she climbed into bed with the windows open, Julia always fell into a sound sleep. Now it was almost the weekend again and time for the annual Darby family reunion. They had traveled to Ken's parents every summer for the past fifteen years. He had a large extended family and they always got together overnight at a resort. The kids had cousins they saw rarely more than that one weekend in the summer. Last year the entire event had been cancelled because the family was together at the funeral. All the relatives were especially enthusiastic to return to happy circumstances.

Julia heard the girls discussing it this morning as she was leaving for the college. This was something they needed. Last week had been the anniversary of Ken's death. It was a sad afternoon when she and the kids went to the cemetery and planted flowers at his headstone. It was the first time that she had seen Seth break down since last year. At home, they watched old family videos. This had been the best possible way to honor his memory. Watching Ken playing a prank on the kids; hiding in a closet when they got home, brought hoots of laughter. Seeing him on the dance floor with Kelsey at a father/daughter dance tore them up. But in the end, watching the life they had with him was cathartic.

This was when the reunion had first come up in conversation. Julia didn't want to go. Now that she was dabbling in this relationship with Luke, possibly moving on from her marriage to Ken, she didn't want to be a part of it. She simply could not bring herself to explain this to her mother-in-law. Unfortunately, all three kids were looking forward to the event. She was beginning to feel boxed in.

Her mother-in-law called that Tuesday and Julia knew she was going to have to commit. Ann Darby's words surprised her.

"Julia, why don't you let the kids come without you?"

"What?"

Ann hesitated, "I would imagine that you're not looking forward to this. I know it's hard to see all of Ken's family. The kids really want to come; Jim and I would be thrilled to take responsibility of them. Why don't you let them come alone?"

Julia was shocked, "Really? "

Ann was quiet for a moment, "I want you to know that we will always consider you our daughter-in-law and the mother of our precious grandchildren. We will always love you as one of our own."

"Thank you, Ann."

"But, you are a beautiful young woman; we know that someday you will move on to another man."

"What?!" Julia had never suggested this to her mother-in-law.

"I mean it, I would've wanted Ken to find someone if the tables were turned. I trust your judgment in regard to the children."

"Thank you," Julia said quietly.

"So, what I really want to say is, you may feel funny about attending the family reunion, but please promise me that nothing is ever going to come between us and the children."

"Ann, you have my solemn promise that you will *always* be their grandmother and an integral part of their lives and mine. I love you and Jim."

**

Julia had to admit that long distance was exactly the right way to start a relationship after being out of practice for so many years. She felt like they covered so much more in their nightly phone conversations than they would have in person. For one thing, there was not the distraction of physical contact. Luke's voice was irresistible enough; she didn't need that handsome face and lean body around when she was trying to take things slow.

He truly loved his work. She could hear the tone of pride as he described the latest home that he had designed. He was thrilled when she asked him to send photos of the project.

On her end, she tried not to sound too boring as she discussed her days as a mother. Luke, however, was interested in how the baseball and softball games went. He always was concerned about Lily's situation.

They also spent a lot of time reminiscing. It was fun to have him update her on all the people they'd known as a couple and what they were now doing at the lake. It seemed they never ran out of things to say. They nearly always ended discussing how they missed one another and wanted to spend time together. She decided she would really like the opportunity to visit him and see how it went.

**

Lily was seeing Dylan every day. Her mom was pretty controlling about the evening, but thanks to friends she had managed to have some time away. Just a few nights ago they had been able to sneak in a camp out overnight.

That was the first night that Lily had ever drunk alcohol. It was not unusual for Dylan to have beers with the guys. Lily usually avoided it. She knew her mom would ground her permanently for that. But that night in the tent, she drank a couple beers.

Lily had liked the loose feeling at first. They had sex, and she had felt more reckless than ever. But after a while, when Dylan had gotten grouchy and tried to tell her what to do, Lily found the alcohol gave her a voice. She spoke right back to him and it had gotten ugly. The next thing she knew, he had her pinned to the tent wall. The fury in his eyes and painful grip he had on her upper arms terrified her. With soft apologetic words, she calmed him down, but for the rest of the night he blamed her for his bad mood.

When she got to work the next afternoon, there were flowers waiting for her. Sometimes Dylan was exhausting, but Lily knew no one else would ever love her as much. He needed her to survive.

25

Julia's grand opportunity to see Luke presented itself. She was headed to Cambridge to deliver her three children to their grandparents. She was not headed home after she dropped them off, she would be halfway to Spring Lake. Her heartbeat sped up as she contemplated what she was doing. The idea had come to her the moment she had hung up with her mother-in-law. Was this her chance to spend some time alone with Luke?

Was she ready to spend time with him? This was a big step. If she went to his house or he came to hers and they were alone, was it inevitable that they would be intimate? Julia was afraid that she would fall apart if they tried. They'd not even kissed for over a year; would the first kiss immediately evolve into that? After all, they had slept together more times than she could count when they were young.

Now her heart was jumping again. The kids were safely with their grandparents and she was alone with her dog, in the car headed toward the lake. Julia flipped on the radio trying to relax. K-Ci and JoJo were singing "All My Life" on her 90s station, it carried her back to the girls' dorm bathroom on campus, the window looking out onto the highway. Those were lonely nights watching the cars speeding by, wishing she had one to jump in and go see Luke. Oh, how she wanted the freedom to be with him.

Life had made a crazy circle, now here she was feeling as if she was headed out on one of those illicit weekends. Instead of not telling her parents where she was headed, she was not telling her kids. Now she was sneaking back to Spring Lake, back to Luke.

The hour and a half flew, soon she was pulling off the familiar exit and following the direction of the signs which pointed to "boat access" and "fishing". Instead of turning at the first lake drive which would have taken her to her old cabin or Angie's house, she went another mile down the road and took the drive which led across the lake to the sandy point on the hill. Julia's hands were nearly shaking as she steered her car into the driveway and parked next to the Range Rover. She climbed out of the driver's seat and he appeared at the door.

Julia turned to Luke; he stood there in jeans and a black pullover shirt, barefoot, she was in white skinny capris and a sleeveless black blouse. He was still, in her eyes, the boy in the swim trunks and messy hair. Was she still the bikini clad girl?

He gave her his most devastating grin and spoke, "Come here." Without hesitation she fell into his arms. Their kiss was long and passionate, fueled by the adrenaline of waiting for the moment together. Luke wrapped his fingers in her hair, his other hand tight around her waist.

Julia felt all the desire and emotion come bubbling up to the surface. When they stepped back she looked at him, not veiling her feelings, "Hi." Her indecision about him faded away. He grabbed her and pulled her close again.

Luke carried Julia's bag into the house and sat it at the bottom of the steps. She walked to the front windows and looked out. "The lake is so beautiful. I 've missed it so much."

He came up behind her, "Let's go out on it."

She nodded, "Will Sophie be okay in here? If you're worried, I can tie her out."

Luke laughed, "I know she's harmless, let her stay in, does that mean you're ready for a ride?"

"I would love to."

As they headed through the kitchen, Luke glanced at the counter, "Are you hungry, do you want to eat first?" Julia shook her head no, already removing her sandals. He stood back and let her walk through the deck door, "Let's go."

Julia loved his boat, it was so quick and sleek. When Luke took off at full throttle she felt her hair fly behind her. She loved a speeding boat, laughing out loud as they skimmed over the waves. After two fast rounds, Luke slowed down. The sun was beginning to set, and Julia lifted her sunglasses up onto the top of her head. "How long have you had this boat?"

"It's two years old. You know me, I can't resist boats," He rubbed the dash proudly.

"I know, for some guys its cars, for you boats," she looked at the line of cabins on the shore, "It looks as if everyone is still taking good care of their places."

Luke pointed to a large new log structure, "Mr. Fisher died, I think he was 92. His great grandkids tore down the old place and are building that to live in."

"Wow, that's going to be nice. Good that it stayed in the family."

They passed her old cabin. "I noticed last time that my family's place looks great. New dock, even."

"Yes, that's the second family to own it since you did."

"I was shocked that my parents sold it, but they took their boat to a reservoir close to their home."

Luke stared at her old summer cottage, "That seemed so final when it was no longer your family's."

She tapped his knee, "Guess it wasn't."

He smiled at her, "Here you are in my boat, again. I guess it wasn't."

They were floating past Angie's place. "The kids had such a great time here."

Turning to her, not the scenes on shore, Luke inquired, "How are they doing?"

"Oh, they're just fine; believe it or not we've not had any major drama for nearly a month. Now they're with their extended family," she looked off, her mind on the reunion.

"Let's go back to the house; I'm going to cook for you." Luke kissed her forehead and sped up the boat.

Her joy left for a moment, replaced by guilt. *Who did she think she was? Did she have the right to this selfish pleasure?*

Across the boat, Luke glanced at her, recognizing the war of emotions on her face. "Julia." She turned, not smiling. "You can enjoy yourself."

She looked at the man next to her, grateful for his concern. "Thank you," she responded quietly.

**

Back at the house, Luke soon had placed sliced potatoes in foil and two beautiful steaks on the grill. Julia was pouring two glasses of Malbec, the dark red wine sparkled. She walked out on the deck and handed him one. He touched the rim of his to hers, "Here's to us." She let the rich liquid pour down her throat. Now that they were back at the house she was once again nervous, this should help.

**

The moon had taken over the chore of lighting the deck. Luke lit the torches to keep away the bugs. Julia stood and felt herself sway slightly, realizing she had taken no more than three or four bites of food but that her third glass of wine was only half full. She giggled out loud.

Luke turned to her as he finished lighting the last flame. "What?"

"Nothing, it's so nice out tonight." Julia walked to the railing and looked toward the lake.

"I still can't believe that you're standing here with me. It's like a million fantasies come true," he spoke as he came up beside her. They kissed. She rubbed her hands along his neck and snuggled closer against his chest. Luke let his hands wander down her back and rest on her hips. When she did the same, he said in a husky voice, "Ready to go inside?"

Julia allowed him to take her hand and lead her up to his room. Though her heart began to pound at a dangerous speed, she did not resist.

**

The cherry sleigh bed, which had looked so lovely when Julia had first visited the house a month ago, now appeared intimidating. Luke flipped on a small lamp beside it, then turned off the overhead. Her confidence grew in this dimmer atmosphere. Together they sat on the bed. Without hesitation, Luke pulled off his shirt. Julia stared at his trim but firm chest, she remembered it. Deciding to fake her own confidence, she began unbuttoning her blouse. As the first glimpse of her black bra was revealed, he reached over and traced her collar bone. “May I?” he whispered. His fingers gently unfastened each button until her blouse fell completely open. Luke moved his fingertips over the swell of her breasts. With a shrug, she let the blouse fall to the bed and lifted her arms out of it. Then she reached behind her and unclasp the bra. As her breasts were revealed, Luke whispered, “I guess you have changed!” Before she could cover herself or do anything else to distract him, he pulled her down on the bed with him.

**

It was late in the night when Julia awoke to the sounds of locusts outside the window. She slowly sat up. On the other side of the bed, Luke was on his back, his beautiful hair fanned out on the pillow. She grabbed the sheet for a moment and covered herself. She couldn’t believe where she was. The sex had felt comfortable, not awkward, familiar and incredibly satisfying. All the bad emotions; shame, embarrassment and guilt, had stayed away while they kissed, explored one another’s bodies and made love. Now with painstakingly slow movements she climbed out of his bed. Grabbing her short nightgown out of her suitcase, she tried not to make a sound.

As she tiptoed past the den she saw a fleece blanket thrown over a leather recliner and grabbed it. Out on the deck, Julia wrapped herself in the blanket and settled into a lounge chair. The moon was the only light, its beam flowed with the waves. A small breeze moved the leaves on the trees and caused a stray curl to move across her face. She could hear the waves slowly beating against the shore and smiled. She had come back to Spring Lake and spent the night with Luke. Her eyes drifted shut.

When she next opened them, the sun was breaking across the lake. Julia sat up suddenly; she had been asleep for a few hours. The wooden deck was chilly under her bare feet as she stood. Standing near the rail was Luke; he had on only his jeans. His hair was tousled from sleep. She felt momentarily breathless. "You slept out here?" he asked with a look of concern.

She self-consciously touched her unruly hair, "Just a couple of hours, I didn't intend to."

"You couldn't sleep with me?" his voice was a mixture of sorrow and disappointment.

Julia gave a slow smile, then got up and boldly moved to him to stroke his cheek, “I was a little too keyed up to sleep.”

Luke was reassured, “That’s a good thing.” He reached down and touched her arm, “You’re like ice, Jules. Come here.” He pulled her against his warm chest and she let the blanket drop as she wrapped her arms around his ribs.

He kissed her, “Let’s get you warmed up.”

**

The sun was shining full force in the bedroom window when Julia woke up, this time alone. She headed into the bathroom, turning on the shower. After she dressed, she fastened a thin silver chain around her neck. As a habit, Julia reached for her rings; her wedding ring, engagement ring and the mother’s ring she wore on her right hand. She suddenly became aware of the jewelry. Taking a deep breath, she placed the mother’s ring on her left hand and zipped the other two back into her jewelry bag.

The smell of coffee assailed her nose as she headed down the steps. In the kitchen, with his back to her stood Luke, intent on buttering toast. Julia walked up and put her hands on his hips. “Good morning,” she said in his ear.

The knife clattered to the counter as he turned and grabbed her. “You scared me.” He smiled and pulled her close, “Good morning to you.”

“Breakfast ready?” She looked over his shoulder at the toast now face down on the counter.

He turned and looked, laughing. “I thought maybe you were going to sleep until lunch. Since you’re up, showered and beautiful, how about we go out for brunch?”

“Sounds great.”

The afternoon was incredible. The couple slipped into their comfortable habits with ease. They conversed about everything, sharing details of their jobs, places they had vacationed at. When Luke held her hand or put his arm around her it felt natural.

Back at the lake they put on their suits and floated around on rafts at the beach. It seemed natural to end up in the shower together afterward to wash off the sand.

**

It was late Sunday morning, Luke and Julia were out in the boat, engine off just floating and talking. "I'm so glad I came here this weekend."

Luke stroked her hair, "Me too. It's been even better than I thought it could be."

She silently nodded her agreement, turning her face to the sun and closing her eyes.

"Now what?" Luke spoke quietly.

Julia opened her eyes and turned to him, "Now what? I don't know."

"Can I come see you in Seneca?"

Julia thought about it, tried to imagine a weekend with Luke at the house. Slowly she nodded, "Yes, I think so."

"You think so? Are you planning on keeping me a secret?"

"No Luke, I didn't mean that. It's just hard to imagine introducing us to my family, my life."

He sat up straight and looked at her, an annoyed spark in his eyes, "I know that this is new. This is the first weekend we've spent together. But dammit, Julia we have a history. We love each other; at least that's how it seems to me." The word love, so soon, threw her off but she didn't acknowledge it. "I'm not going to play games with you. This isn't a normal situation. I understand we need to take things slowly, but not that slowly. I want to see you again, soon. God, I can't live without you now that I've found you again." She was silent. He spoke softly, "Did I just scare the hell out of you? Do I sound like Lily's guy?"

"A little."

He ran his hands through his hair in a frustrated gesture, "Is this one sided?"

She sat up straight and put her hands on his shoulders, "No, no that's not it at all. Truth is I feel the same way about you, and in a perfect world that's all we would need to know. We found each other again and we live happily ever after. But Luke, this is far from a perfect world. I have three kids, and not young children who will do what I want and go anywhere I want them to. I have a house, a job and responsibility that is unbelievable. I can't act as if you and I are all that matters." To her surprise Luke grinned at her, "What?"

He continued to smile. "I understand what you said."

"What's good about that?"

"It's what you didn't say. You're stressed because you want to be with me, like I want to be with you." Luke pulled her close and kissed her. “That’s a good thing, Jules.”

She smiled weakly, “It is?”

“We’ll work the rest out, it’s not going to be easy and it could take a long time. I hate the thought of that, but if we both want the same thing it will be okay.”

Julia pulled him close, “I like the way you look at things, Lucas.”

26

At the weekend's end, Julia had stood at her car, looking at the water, then the beautiful house behind her, finally at the man putting her luggage in the back of her car. This was a dream that she had told herself she'd never have come true. In no time, she would arrive at her mother in law's house to pick up her kids. Was she ready to take on the conversation, the kids, the relatives?

A half an hour from Cambridge, she squeezed the steering wheel and the glint on her finger caught her eye. Oh no, she wasn't wearing her wedding rings, she couldn't risk the girls noticing, not yet. Julia pulled over at the next rest stop and pulled them out and slid them back onto her left hand. How was any of this possibly going to work out?

The kids were happy to see her and chatted excitedly as she headed back to the highway. They thought nothing of the dog being in the car with her; lately

Sophie was her constant companion. The reunion had been a success. They had lots of updates on how everyone had grown and what cousins were engaged and who was going to have a baby. Their cheeks were pink from time in the sun. Julia was pleased that the time with Ken's family had been good for them.

Lily sat in the passenger seat and glanced at her mother. "Mom, you look really tan, have you been out in the sun?"

"Yes. "

Her daughter raised an eyebrow, "In our backyard?"

Julia took a deep breath; this came up sooner than she wanted it to. "No, actually I was at the lake."

"What lake?" this came from Kelsey in the backseat.

"Spring Lake."

Lily opened her mouth to respond but from the back seat came a whine from Seth, "You went to the lake without us?"

"With Angie?" it was clear that her eldest was quickly figuring it out.

"*Ugh*," thought Julia, but said aloud, "No."

"Ohhh," this was from Kelsey.

The daughters exchanged glances, Seth picked up on it. "What?"

"Nothing," Lily dismissed him.

Kelsey however responded, "Mom saw *Luke*."

Seth was quiet a moment and then looked at his mom, "Do you like him?"

Julia felt one hundred years old, she did not want this conversation. She sighed, "Well, yes I do."

That satisfied Seth. "Cool," he responded as he pulled his phone out of his bag and settled back in his seat to play a game.

Lily eyed her mom, "Where did you stay?"

Kelsey moved closer to the front seat, anticipating her mother's answer.

"Girls, we're not having this discussion. Let's talk about something else."

"That's so unfair," Lily threw back at her, "you think you have to know every detail about my love life."

"I'm your mother and you're seventeen, that is entirely different."

"Whatever," Lily slumped in her seat and put in her headphones, Kelsey followed suit.

Within twenty minutes both girls were asleep, and Julia relaxed.

**

On the porch swing late that night, she was on the phone with Luke. Julia couldn't believe she already missed him or how she'd behaved with him.

"I have an idea," his voice warmed her.

"Yes?" Julia waited to hear it.

"What if I come for the weekend?"

"Here?" her voice squeaked.

He was silent a moment, "Of course there, where else?"

"I'd like to see you," she conceded.

Her answer was too short, "But what?"

"I didn't say but anything."

"Things come up with the girls?"

"Lily got a little pushy." She thought a moment, "Hey, Angie could use some help getting ready to move back there."

He sighed, "I need an excuse."

"No, it would just make it easier."

"Okay."

They were silent. "Jules, I had the best weekend of my life."

"It was amazing." As she spoke, Julia watched a truck approaching the house. She was glad the porch light was off. It slowed to nearly a crawl. Dylan was checking on them, how many times had he been by today, waiting? She saw a light flicker in the cab of the truck and realized it was his cell phone. Was he calling Lily?

In her own ear she heard, "Julia, did I lose you?"

Without meaning to, she whispered her response, "No, just watching some activity on the road."

"What's happening?" Luke's voice was full of concern.

"Dylan is crawling by the house in his truck, he's on the phone. I'm wondering if Lily is going to try to sneak out." She watched him move just past the house, his brake lights flared on. "Well hell, I think he's waiting for her."

Luke's sigh was audible, "I despise you dealing with this alone."

Her focus was on the situation, her response vague, "I know," she'd barely gotten the word out when she heard the creak of the side garage door. There was her eldest daughter, barefoot, holding flip flops, moving onto the driveway. "Shit, here's Lily, I've got to go." Without waiting for a response, she disconnected.

Trying to move without making a sound, edging off the swing, Julia headed slowly down the porch steps. Her daughter was about to pass in front of her, not six feet away. Just as Lily got close, Julia intoned, "Where the hell do you think you're going?"

After a scream of surprise, Lily looked up at the sky and gave a dramatic sigh, "Mom, just let me go. I've been gone all weekend."

Julia was not proud of the angry bark of a laugh that emitted from her mouth, "Absolutely not, is this a regular habit of yours?" With her head she gestured toward the truck, "Is that the meeting spot?"

Her daughter's expression was nearly desperate, "Just let me go tell him that I have to stay here."

Was this really happening? "No, give me your phone and head back into the house."

Her daughter turned from the truck but attempted to shove her phone into her pocket. Julia could feel the vibration of her own phone, receiving multiple calls. "Give it, or I promise you, the next phone you have is one you buy yourself at eighteen."

Her daughter turned dark, tear stained eyes toward her, "I hate you." She tossed her phone in the grass and ran back to the house. Julia reached down and picked it up. Dylan was calling. Her initial reaction was to ignore it, but how long would he sit out here, and would he eventually try to come to the house?

Julia swiped it open, his voice began an angry string of words, speaking firmly she said, "Dylan, I see you out here. I have the phone and Lily will not be joining you. Stay away from her or I will seek legal means to keep you apart." She powered off the phone and watched the tires of the truck squeal as he disappeared into the night.

**

Three hours later, Julia was sitting up against her pillow. She had dismissed Luke's request for a call, telling him that everything was fine, but she didn't want to talk. One difficult man at a time. She had spent the next hours sitting in bed, searching Google for advice on what to do, how to end her daughter's relationship. After reading what felt like hundreds of articles, blogs and posts, she could agree that the relationship was toxic, and that Dylan was controlling. There didn't seem to be a cut and dried answer. Exhausted and discouraged, Julia lay back on the pillow and fell into a troubled sleep.

**

It was lunchtime the next day, Lily had not appeared from her room, but Julia had checked to make certain that she was there. The rest of the family was in the kitchen together making sandwiches. Julia was slicing an apple for Seth. "I talked to Angie this morning, Cody's moving next week."

"I know, who am I going to hang out with all summer?" Seth complained.

"You have lots of friends, but I'm sure we can visit him some," Julia suggested, both of her younger children agreed enthusiastically.

Kelsey grinned at her mother, "Just him?" Julia looked at her daughter to gauge her feelings on the subject. She continued, "Are you two dating?"

"Well, he lives hundreds of miles away, so dating is kind of tough. But I like spending time with him. In fact, I think he may come here this weekend to help his sister get ready to move."

**

Lily sat on the merry-go-round at the park; she was leaning into the arms of Dylan. It was her break at the Dairy Bar. Her mother couldn't stop her from going to work.

"I've missed you so much, Lily," Dylan was holding tight to her hips.

"I'm here now," she wasn't sure why he wasn't at work, but she decided to let it drop. He had been mad enough when he showed up at the Dairy Bar because of last night's mess.

"You can't let her keep us apart again, okay?" his voice was fierce in her ear.

"I know, I'm trying to work it out," attempting to keep the peace was exhausting.

"Why can't she just get over it and let us be?"

Lily hesitated, "She did have to call the cops on you when you wouldn't leave last month."

"Are you on her side?" Dylan moved as if to push her away.

Lily snuggled closer, "Of course not."

"I can't stand sneaking around, I need to spend more time with you," he pushed his hips against her to emphasize his point.

"Dylan, we're at the park."

"It's not my fault we can't be alone," now his voice was accusing.

"Well her new boyfriend is coming to visit this weekend, maybe she'll be too busy to notice what I'm doing." The thought made Lily feel even more justified in sneaking around, if her mom could have a boyfriend, so could she.

"Is he an asshole?" Dylan had pulled out his phone and asked disinterestedly.

"No, it's just weird. He's that guy from the box."

"Oh, her high school boyfriend? Does he have a bunch of kids?"

Lily shook her head, "No, he doesn't have any."

"Will they have any?"

That was easy to answer, "No, definitely not."

Dylan laughed. "Hey, I've got two stepsisters and now a baby brother. Marry your mom off to this guy, if there won't be any new kids he's a good deal."

"I've got to get back, my break is over," he wasn't giving her the responses she wanted, she pushed his hands to stand up.

Dylan grabbed her and gave her a long kiss, "Lily, I have to be alone with you. I'm dying." Lily laughed at her boyfriend and climbed into her car.

27

Luke arrived at the Darby house on Friday just after eight. As his car rolled into the driveway, Julia's heart did a little leap. She got outside just ahead of Seth. Though she had an urge to race across the drive and throw herself at him, she restrained herself in front of her son. He gave Luke a wave and headed to the barn to retrieve his bicycle. Now, Luke moved toward Julia and gave her a strong hug. He pulled her back a bit and looked at her, "Hi. I've missed you."

She smiled, "Me too." She saw he wanted to kiss her badly, but she wasn't ready to let her son see her like that with someone other than his father. "We'll find a moment alone."

Soon they were sitting on the back deck; Kelsey had returned from a babysitting job and had joined them. Julia heard another car pull up. Lily soon came out to the backyard. She was on her best behavior and smiled politely at Luke.

Julia looked at her daughters, "Do you guys have any plans tomorrow?" When both girls shook their heads, she went on, "Angie is headed to the lake tonight to get unpacked. Cody is going to stay and will leave with his uncle on Sunday. I thought we'd take Cody and Luke to Cedar Point. Cody has never been there." Cedar Point was Ohio's biggest amusement park.

"Great idea," enthused Lily.

Kelsey interjected, "Can I ask Emily to come?"

Julia hesitated, "I thought you'd hang out with your sister."

Lily smiled, "That's okay, I like Emily." Julia was pleased with how agreeable Lily was being.

**

Angie closed the trunk. When she turned to Julia, tears were already rolling down her cheeks. A sob escaped Julia's throat and she grabbed her friend. She never imagined how much this would hurt. The squeezing ache in her heart was reminiscent to the day Ken died. In a choked voice she spoke, "I wouldn't have survived this year without you."

Pulling back and looking at her dear friend with matched grief, Angie nodded. "I feel the same way. I'm going to miss you so much. Thank you for being there when I showed up as a stranger in Seneca."

"How can you thank me? You saved my life. Every time I needed to talk, cry or scream, you've been there." The two friends collapsed into a hug again. Finally gaining composure, Julia spoke, "I'm so happy for you. You're heading back to your home. Back to your husband. That's exactly where you should be."

"Thanks for that," Angie looked at her friend, how could someone go through so much in twelve months? "I will be in touch every single day. And please promise me that you will visit as often as possible." Now she mustered a smile, "I can thank my brother for guaranteeing that."

Final farewells were said, then Julia headed back to her home. Luke had been kind enough to take the boys home earlier.

**

The family made plans for the park; how early to leave and what to bring. The boys were relegated to Seth's room, the campout they had hoped for would certainly lead to late night hours and sleep was needed. The girls had disappeared in their own rooms as Julia shut off Seth's light. She had gathered a pillow, sheet and blanket for Luke and headed back to the family room. When she arrived, he was in the half bath changing into shorts and brushing his teeth.

He came out as she placed a pillow on the couch for him. "That doesn't look big enough for two," he grinned.

"Sorry." After a glance at his shirtless self, she kept her eyes on the couch as she stretched a fitted sheet on the cushions.

He came across the room and pulled her into an embrace. They kissed hungrily, the evening had not given them a chance for even a chaste peck. As they sat down together on the couch, they locked lips for a longer, yet softer moment. Just as they began, they heard voices at the top of the stairs, "Mom, we're thirsty."

"One drink then off you go," she called back and quickly turned on the TV.

The boys didn't even come into the room.

Luke laughed as he pulled her close when the boys were heard trudging back upstairs, "I haven't made out in front of the TV for a long time."

"Me either. We were so spoiled last weekend." She leaned into him, their lips meeting.

Luke stopped for a breath and groaned, "I'd love to sleep with you."

"Me too," she whispered against his lips.

He pushed slightly away from her, "This is only going to lead to frustration."

She sat up and straightened her hair, "You're right."

He smiled, "I like your house."

"Thanks, it needed a lot of work when we bought it, but it was the most space for the money, so Ken did a lot of renovating." She hesitated, "Is that weird for you?"

Luke shook his head, "No it's a fact of life. I understand that he's always going to be a part of your family."

She leaned on his shoulder, "Thank you."

**

As it turned out, Luke and Julia couldn't have chosen better for alone time. On Saturday, they arrived at Cedar Point and everyone scattered in groups. Except when the kids text them for money or food, they were alone to ride the rides. Luke loved fast roller coasters and Julia had some terrifying moments. She got him back by forcing him to watch the Rock and Roll oldies show in the theater.

Late in the afternoon, they had just finished a spin on the Ferris wheel when they came upon Kelsey and Emily. Lily was not with them, and Julia asked them about it. Both girls looked uncomfortable and Julia's radar went off instantly. She looked sternly at her middle child, "Where is your sister?"

"She's here in the park, somewhere," Kelsey answered evasively.

Julia was exasperated, "Kelsey Anne, tell me."

Emily looked at her friend and nodded, urging her. Reluctantly, her daughter drew in a deep breath, "Dylan is here."

"What? Dylan is here? He met her here?" Julia was beginning to raise her voice.

Luke stepped in, placing his hand on the small of her back. He turned to the two girls, "Thank you for being honest. Do you need anything, money?"

The girls shook their heads but took the twenty he proffered. Julia gave her daughter a quick squeeze, "Sorry to put you on the spot."

The teens walked away. Luke pulled Julia into his arms. "Wow, this is bad. This is the kind of deceit you're dealing with?"

"Constantly, we need to find them, how dare they!" she marched down the causeway.

Luke quickened his pace and spoke carefully, "Julia, if we hunt them down now, then what?"

"We'll make him leave the park and we'll. . ." she didn't have an answer.

He grabbed her hand, "Exactly, you can't make the other kids leave the park early."

She could see his point, "Okay, I'm not going to ruin my day with you, looking for her. I'm certain she's keeping her eye out for us. When the day is over, we will deal with this. Kelsey, Cody and Seth deserve a good day." She looked at Luke, "And so do you, I'm so sorry this had to happen this weekend." Luke had never had kids or family responsibility. He had wandered into her life at the worst possible time. She knew this drama would chase him right away.

They were stopping for ice cream when Julia's cell phone rang, and it was Seth and Cody. The boys wanted to meet Julia and Luke for a round of miniature golf. After a sound defeat of them all by Cody, the boys wanted to get back in line for the Top Thrill Dragster, the fastest Coaster in the park. Luke and Julia strolled past the midway, hand in hand, watching people try to win stuffed animals. As they glanced over at the ring toss, a young man in a black tank top caught Julia's eye. His arms, covered in tattoos, were wrapped around a thin girl. With her wedged in front of him, he was trying to throw the rings over the bottles. With the position of the girl, the motion seemed vulgar. With a sinking heart, Julia realized why he had caught her eye, it was Dylan and Lily. Julia drew in her breath quickly and Luke followed her gaze.

He pulled her to him, not letting go of her hand. "Don't do it Jules, I know you want to confront them, but don't do it here."

Julia struggled, her first instinct was to march up there and grab her daughter out of that monster's grip. But, Luke was right, what then? If they didn't leave the park immediately, Lily would make the day unbearable for everyone else.

"Let's both turn completely around in case they look this way and walk back the way we came," Luke whispered in her ear, gently.

Julia took a deep breath and did just that. With his arm around her shoulders, she forced herself to trace her steps away from the Midway. Together they sat on a bench near a duck pond. She stared unseeingly at the water in front of them. "He took her virginity, and then he drinks, and smokes weed, has slept with numerous girls behind her back, called her every name in the book, slashed her tires and harassed our house until I had to call the cops. He has convinced her to break every rule and she continues to do it," she leaned on Luke's shoulder, "I have no idea what to do."

He leaned his head on top of hers. "You've done everything within your power, getting involved, trying to keep them apart. She's simply not going to see it clearly until she's ready."

"She has once again openly defied me, what do I do?"

He was quiet, thinking. Julia took his silence to mean something else. She sat up and looked at him, "I'm sorry, this is way more than you bargained for isn't it? This is a mess. Luke, I completely understand if you want to leave now."

He got up and turned his back to her. A duck waddled near him and he knelt giving it a chunk of bread deserted on the grass. In that position he turned and looked at her sharply, "Julia, do you think so little of me?" He got up and went to her, he sat down next to her, taking her hands, "I'm upset about this because I can't take it over and fix it for you."

This time she reached for him, she placed her hand on his jaw and pulled him close, without a word she kissed him.

**

By closing, the four younger kids were dragging. Julia had asked Kelsey on their last trip to the ladies' room if her sister knew that Julia was aware of Dylan being at the park. Kelsey promised that she hadn't seen or heard from her sister. As they came out of the restroom, Lily walked up smiling innocently. "Kelsey, there you are, I can't believe I lost you. Hi Mom, did you have fun?"

Julia moved away from the women milling in and out of the bathroom and motioned to her oldest daughter to come to her. She voice was icy calm as she spoke. "Two hours ago, I saw you. You were with Dylan; I know he met you here today. I know you planned it that way. I want no lies. I will not ruin this night for the rest of the family. We will deal with this later. I just want you to know, you didn't get away with anything." With that Julia walked away from her daughter and joined the rest of the family. She forced a smile on her face and herded them toward the car.

They were barely out of the parking lot when all the kids were asleep.

Julia looked over at Luke, driving an SUV full of kids. "You look pretty natural in this role."

He grinned, "Is that an offer?"

Julia was quiet for a moment then in a near whisper she spoke, "Luke, I'm done having children. It is no longer possible. I thought you should know this, you've never had any of your own."

He squeezed her hand, "I don't want to be a new dad at forty."

She turned to look at the night sky, willing her mind to enjoy her time with Luke and not let the situation with Lily ruin it. She was unaware that she'd fallen asleep until Luke had to nudge her awake to get directions home. When everyone was in bed, Julia walked into the pitch-dark family room with Luke. He sat on the couch and pulled her down with him. This time they did not stop at kisses. In time, she haphazardly pulled back on her clothes, kissed him tenderly and headed up to her lonely room.

Sunday it was pouring rain. Julia was drying Sophie off with an old beach towel when Luke wandered into the kitchen. He was still wearing only shorts and she couldn't resist. She wrapped her arms around his bare waist, enjoying the feel of his skin next to her cheek. He lifted her chin and kissed her.

At the doorway they heard giggles. The boys stood at the kitchen door. Luke groaned into her hair, before she pulled away. "Hello boys, what would you like for breakfast?"

She was relieved that Seth saw nothing but humor in catching his mom kissing a man. Soon she was caught up in making chocolate chip pancakes and scrambled eggs.

Luke returned to the kitchen after a shower, more appropriately dressed in jeans and a Great Lakes sailing T-shirt. Cody looked up from his plate, "Hey Uncle Luke, if you married Seth's mom would we be cousins?"

The adults had mirrored shocked expressions on their face. Seth looked interested in the answer. Luke shook his head and smiled, "Yes, you would be."

"That'd be awesome!" Cody announced. The couple exchanged looks and did not respond.

Kelsey and Emily made their way down lured by the smell of breakfast cooking. Lily was either sleeping in or avoiding the confrontation. The boys began to complain that the rain meant nothing to do, Kelsey joined in moaning about canceled softball practice. Finally, the four of them started a movie. Julia offered to go to the store and pick up food. The two of them headed out in his Range Rover. She took this opportunity to show him her town.

"Luke, you jumped right into the fire this weekend. Yesterday, we spent the day at Cedar Point, now we're trapped inside for a rainy day with five kids."

He smiled at her, "It's perfect, I mean it."

In the driveway, they sat in the quiet of the car, enjoying the rain. She looked over at him, "You know you can head home whenever you want."

He pulled her close, "I don't want to go home, period." They kissed in the car, fogging up the windows like they'd done dozens of times as teenagers. Soon her phone beeped, it was Seth wondering if they were ever going to be home.

Luke groaned, "It used to be we had to sneak around our parents, now we have to sneak around the kids."

She smiled her mouth at his neck, "It's a killer. Come on, we have to go in, before they find us out here."

He gave her one more kiss before grabbing the groceries.

When the kids were on the second movie of the afternoon, Luke and Julia sat on the front porch swing watching the rain. Earlier when Angie had called to talk to her son, the boys cooked up the plan that Cody could stay for the week. His return home would either be done by Julia or Luke.

"I don't want to ruin this moment, but can I ask for your advice?" Julia was staring into her mug of coffee, not seeing. He nodded. "Any idea what I should say when I sit down with my daughter tonight?"

Luke was quiet for a while. "Besides outwardly defying your wishes, what else is she doing wrong?"

Julia considered this, "Besides lying, attempting to sneak out and being involved in something that's only going to cause her pain in the future?"

"Right, is she doing anything else she's not supposed to? School is out so she's not skipping classes, is she working when she says she is?"

"Yes, she is, and she is home most evenings, at least for now.

"Can he get her pregnant?"

"No, I took care of that. Who knows what he might give her, I wonder if she's thought about that?"

"I think you're going to have to let her find out the hard way. You seem to be doing everything that you can control. But Julia, be careful and keep a close eye. From what I've heard this guy is not level headed."

They were quiet as she considered it all. "I'm better off having to tolerate him where I can keep an eye on them than to have her sneaking around."

"It sounds like a lousy solution, but it may be the only one. She'll eventually make the right decision."

Julia turned and put her arms around his neck, "Luke, thank you so much. I just wanted you here because I wanted to see you again. I feel like you're being here has been so much more. I don't feel so alone."

It was nearly ten when he prepared to leave. She smiled, "You were standing at my car door last year when I was leaving Angie's. You took my breath away that day. "

"Oh, I didn't want to let you go. It was so devastating to meet Seth; I realized that you really had built a life without me." He looked down and then back into her eyes, "I'm sorry."

"No, it's just that when I think about that weekend I feel guilty." Julia spoke seriously, "Luke, I never wanted to lose Ken. I don't know if I'm telling you or me, but I just feel the need to say it."

He frowned, "Being happy with me doesn't mean you wanted him to be gone. Quit beating yourself up, Jules."

She hugged him, "Thanks, that's what I needed to hear." Julia pushed his hair from his eyes as he leaned out the car window. "Go home; you have to work in the morning."

He kissed her, "I'll see you in five days."

28

Angie called the next night. Cody gave her a thirty second hello and passed the phone back to Julia. “I can see I’m missed terribly,” Angie joked.

“Sorry, it’s so difficult for him. How was your weekend alone?” Julia was in her room, hanging up clean laundry.

“Pretty terrific, we even went on a date on Saturday. How was your weekend?”

Holding a hanger in one hand and a blouse in another, Julia smiled at the memory, “Well, your brother is crazy to have spent all that time with four kids.”

“Hey, it’s about time he got to see what we live with. Besides Julia, he’d do anything for you.”

“I guess he proved that.” She filled Angie in on the Cedar Point dilemma and how helpful he had been.

“How’s it going?”

"The deal is that I know exactly when she sees him, and if she sneaks around again, I will take unbelievable measures," as she said it, she wondered if Lily was in her room, having her own phone conversation with the first person that sometimes Julia felt she had ever hated.

"Sounds like a good step. Do you know what those drastic measures are?"

Julia shook off the angry feelings and forced a laugh, "Don't you have a spare room?"

"Very funny. Glad Luke was there."

"Me too."

"So, what happens this weekend?" Julia had been asking herself the same thing. If she went to the lake, she figured that Luke would want them to stay with him. How would that go over with the girls?

"I don't know."

"How do the kids feel about their mom having a boyfriend?"

"Kelsey seems fine. Seth and Cody asked Luke and me if they would be cousins if we got married."

Angie laughed, "They did? I bet they thought that was a great idea."

"I think so."

Angie got serious, "Me too, Julia."

"Whoa slow down, this is only technically our second weekend."

**

Dylan was sitting on Julia's couch, his arm around Lily. It made her sick to her stomach. She was really struggling with her decision. Part of her felt as if she had rewarded the two for the sneaky plans at Cedar Point. Instead of trying to pry them apart again, she was allowing him into her home. Why was this better?

Julia had to remind herself that having them here in front of her was the best choice right now. Kelsey was also in the room, watching television with them. This was good, though she was not sure the couple cared who was around. Twice when she had walked in on the pretense of bringing a snack or getting a magazine they had been kissing. Both times she had spoken up that public displays like that were not okay.

Her cell phone buzzed, it was Luke. Julia was in the kitchen and headed out the back door. She liked to talk to him in private.

"Hi Jules, what are you doing?"

She laughed, "Sneaking outside to talk to my boyfriend."

He joined her laugh, "Boyfriend, I can't remember when I was last called that. How was your day?"

"Oh, you know, another exhausting summer Tuesday. How about you, boss man?"

"It was pretty hectic. We have two new clients coming in on Thursday and it's crazy getting everything ready. I haven't seen the sunset on the water for a week."

"Are there gorgeous women at your office who I should be jealous of?"

He laughed, "No there are not, I only have eyes for you. Speaking of which, I found some of our old pictures. It was fun looking at those. I was thinking of framing the one of you in that purple bikini and putting it on my desk."

"Don't you dare," she protested," if I ever meet the people at the office they will feel sorry for you when they see me now."

"No way, you're still just as hot."

"I'm not, in case you haven't looked in the mirror, you are the hot one."

"Ugh, I hate being apart. What are the plans for the weekend?"

Julia sighed, "I don't know, Lily's having trouble getting off work because we kept her off last week to go to the park. I certainly can't leave her here with the Dylan issue. I don't want to make her friends' parents responsible for my unruly daughter. I haven't ironed this out yet."

"It's never simple, huh?" They were both silent a moment, considering possibilities. "I could always come back and get Cody."

"I know and that would be sweet of you, but I really wanted the kids to get to enjoy the lake again." She had wandered into the garage, leaning on the trunk of the car.

"You guys will just have to come back here when Lily can."

"I know, give me a day or two to see what I can work out. I'd love to get Lily with me and away from here."

They talked for another fifteen minutes. Julia heard a yawn on the other line and laughed, "Okay old man, you're tired. Hang up with me and go to bed."

Luke made a suggestion of what he would rather do, and she snickered. "Don't tease, Lucas. Alone time for me and you seems to be in the very distant future."

"I can wait. I miss you."

"I can't wait to see you in a few days. Good night." She ended the call and sat for a few minutes more in the dark garage watching the stars. Soon she heard the front door open, apparently Dylan was leaving. Julia decided to sit and wait. They came down the front steps and out on the walk. It sounded as if they were arguing, again.

Lily was whining, "Why are you leaving, my mother didn't say you had to go."

"Christ, Lily it sucks sitting in your house with your sister chaperoning us."

"You're the one who screwed things up for us; at least we get to be together."

Dylan grabbed her arm, "Don't be a bitch." Julia fought the urge to step in.

Lily turned as if to go.

He caressed the arm he was holding, "I'm sorry baby. That was mean. You know I love you. I just hate it that we can't be together the way that we want to."

Julia shook her head in disgust as her daughter wrapped her arms around his neck, murmuring, "Me too. I love you. Dylan."

They kissed, his hands running all over her back and down her rear. He growled, "Damn woman, I miss this," and with that he squeezed her.

Julia was shocked that her daughter giggled, "Dylan, I miss you too." She reddened to hear that her daughter's conversation was so close to what her own had been just moments before. If she was honest she would admit that she too behaved this way about sex at seventeen. It was simply the fact that Dylan was so controlling and obsessive.

He smacked her bottom and remarked, "Getting a little chubby."

Lily did not protest, but instead said, "I'm trying to lose some weight."

Dylan stepped back and clenched his biceps, "Look at me, I work hard for a living, I don't have a lazy ass job like you. You better keep this bod hot if you want me."

"I'm not fat. I work," Lily protested weakly.

"Let me see," Dylan said with a laugh and from where she stood, Julia could see that he was going to lift her daughter's shirt. She slipped back to the garage door, slammed it as if opening it and called, "Lily, are you out here?"

The two stepped away as she flipped on the interior garage light. She saw Dylan swear under his breath and Lily glared at her, "I was saying goodbye to Dylan, Mom."

"Oh, sorry to interrupt. Have a safe trip home, Dylan." Julia purposely remained leaning against her car. He grudgingly got into his truck; leaned down and gave Lily a short kiss. In a moment he was heading down the drive at too high of a speed. She heard gravel fly as he peeled out of the drive.

Her daughter stomped into the garage, shooting her a look.

"Come on Lily, the guy's a jerk."

"Stop it Mom, you just don't know him."

"He's not even nice to you. He's rude to everyone."

Lily turned to her, a step above her, "People aren't nice to him, and his family is not nice to him. Dylan tries so hard to have people like him."

Julia bit her tongue. Lily moved out of the kitchen and up to her room.

29

On Wednesday, Julia drove the boys to the matinee. They were going to watch the latest Spiderman epic and she would do a bit of shopping at the mall while they did. She was in an excellent mood and thought she might buy herself a new outfit for the lake. This morning she had been in her room, making her bed when she heard Lily's phone ring. From the one-sided conversation she could hear, she learned that Dylan's uncle was taking the work crew of six out of state for a big job. They weren't going to return for an entire week. Lily was whining and complaining. She heard her promise to meet him after work at the park.

Julia was so happy to have him out of state, she decided to not hunt them down and catch them. She wouldn't have to see him for a week and plus she could safely allow Lily to stay with Olivia while she took Cody home to the lake on Friday. She had text Luke first thing, simply stating, "*Will be at lake on Friday*."

He had text back, "*Fantastic*." She had decided that her family could stay at his house, she would of course, not sleep in his room with him. She smiled at the memory of doing just that. It wouldn't happen this time.

**

The family would leave before noon on Friday. With school out there was no reason to wait until later. Angie was working from home now and it would be nice to beat rush hour traffic to see her. Kelsey was bringing Emily with her and the girls were ecstatic to be headed to the lake. The three-hour trip flew by. Emily sat in the front with Julia. The girl's talked non-stop and it was entertaining to hear their light chatter on celebrity gossip, fashion trends, good movies and of course, high school love lives. Julia tried to focus on them and not let her mind wander to when she would see Luke this evening.

After a brief greeting all four kids took off for the beach. Julia noticed that Angie's computer screen was still up with obvious work on it. "Ang, I know you have things to do."

Angie started to protest but Julia held up her hand, "No it's okay, I'd like to surprise Luke at his office."

Angie thought that was a great idea and gave her directions to the architecture firm. Julia took her make-up bag into Angie's room and primped a bit. She put on a shirt not wrinkled by travel and some perfume.

Luke's building was not in the middle of town, it was on an industrial strip across from the small, local airport. She pulled into the parking lot of the brick and largely glass building admiring it. *Designs by Thomas*, very nice.

She nervously opened the glass door; the office was one large open room with long counters in the middle and workspaces along the side. A woman sat at the front reception area, working on a computer, "Good afternoon, may I help you?"

Julia, who had been scanning the people, not seeing Luke, smiled, "I'm here to see Luke Thomas." The woman reached for her phone but before she could push a button, Julia spoke up, "I would like to surprise him if that's possible."

Recognition seemed to cross the woman's face and she smiled. "His office is at the very back of the room, the only space with a wall and a door. It's all glass, so if he looks up he'll see you, but likely he's facing his computer."

Julia grinned, "Thank you so much."

As she moved away the woman picked up her phone and punched in an extension. Julia was passing a desk on the right when another woman moved toward reception. Both women leaned toward the back of Julia, watching her.

Luke was in fact on his computer, his body turned slightly toward the glass wall. Julia glanced at him as she approached the open door. He was wearing black jeans, and white button shirt with thin black stripes, open at the collar. To her surprise, on his nose was perched dark framed glasses. His hair waved over his collar. She silently stepped into his office, facing her was a large desk which he was turned away from, working on the computer at a counter behind the desk. Julia placed her hands on the desk and spoke quietly, "Good afternoon."

Luke whirled around in his chair and caught sight of her. He leaped up and moved around the desk, "Julia, what a great surprise. How was your drive?"

He opened his arms to wrap her in them, hesitated, and then gave her a light hug. She laughed at his movements. "Forget where you were?"

Luke grinned at her, "For a moment. I can't believe you came in here, thank you."

She reached up and touched the edge of his glasses. "I like these, you look sexy."

He pulled them off his face, "Forgot I had them on."

"No, really, I like them."

He hugged her again, "You're here. Do you want to see the place?"

"Of course, I do. It's certainly a beautiful building."

Luke moved toward the door, "I won't show you all the offices, they're just typical. But in the lobby is our photo display of our favorite buildings".

"I'd like to see that." He placed his hand on the small of her back and directed her back to the lobby.

The two women were still at the reception desk, though they had quickly taken a keen interest in some papers on the desk. Luke was oblivious to their interest in him and Julia. "Pat, Debbie." The women looked up as if unaware that they had stepped into the lobby. "Ladies, this is Julia Darby."

Both women gave sincere smiles, “It’s nice to meet you, Julia.”

“This is Pat Fisher a great architect, and this is Debbie Lucas who manages the office and serves as official greeter here.”

Debbie laughed at his description of her job, both women greeted Julia kindly. She smiled back, “It’s very nice to meet you.”

Luke spoke, “I’m showing her our wall of pride.” The two moved to the walls that flanked the glass entrance. The walls were covered with large framed pictures of buildings, anywhere from city structures to luxury houses on lake front property. Julia was amazed at the variety of designs Luke had done. His business was obviously very successful. He briefly explained each one, what it was used for and where it was located. In the top right corner was a gorgeous photo of his own home. He lightly placed his hand on her shoulder, “This is where it all started.”

Julia smiled, “You’ve had an eye for this since you were just a teenager, and it’s absolutely wonderful that you are a very accomplished architect.”

Luke nodded, "I do love my work." They made their way toward his office. This time he closed the door. "How was your trip?"

She laughed, "I had two sixteen-year-old girls with me, and it flew. At Angie's, the girls rushed out to get some sun. The boys were already down at the beach when I left."

He nodded, then reached into his pocket, "Here take my house key, so you can get your stuff in. I have a client coming in at four fifteen or I would leave with you now."

Julia smiled, "I thought I'd cook dinner for you, how's that?" She touched his cheek, "I will see you later."

"Thank you for coming here, it means a lot."

"I really wanted to see it and you at work."

**

In less than an hour, Julia had stopped at the grocery to get the ingredients for dinner, retrieved the kids from Angie's and arrived at Luke's house. She felt a secret thrill using the key to let her into the house and allowed herself a moment's fantasy that this was, in fact, where she lived with her family.

After unloading the vehicle, the girls headed out to the dock with Seth in tow, they soon found swimming floats and a foam water noodle and were gliding along the shore. Julia was happy to have the kitchen to herself. She sliced fresh mushrooms and cloves of garlic, preparing a sun-dried tomato and pasta dish. Luke had a nice collection of cookware and she decided that he must have some culinary skills.

They would eat out on the tall glass topped patio table flanked by six high stooled seats. Clicking on the deck sound system, she headed out with dinnerware. Maroon 5's latest song serenaded her as she stood back and admired the table; it was wonderful to hear the joyful splashes of her kids while she stood on the deck.

Julia was just mixing the vegetables and pasta when she heard the garage door go up. Unaware of her own actions, she straightened her top and pulled her hair from the back of her collar. The door to the garage opened into the kitchen. Luke came in, a bouquet of flowers in his hand. She stepped into his arms and planted a kiss on him. "Welcome home, handsome." After another kiss, he gave her the flowers.

**

Everyone had a hearty appetite; the pasta, fruit and crusty French bread disappeared in record time. Julia insisted on doing the dishes while the ski boat was prepared for tubing. When she returned to the dock, the Castile family had joined the party.

Marcus gave her a brief hug. "I convinced Luke and Seth to join Cody and me for an early morning fishing trip tomorrow."

Julia smiled, "What a fantastic idea."

Kelsey spoke up as she zipped on a life vest, "Don't wake us up!"

It was as Julia sat on the steps that led to the dock, watching Kelsey and Seth riding inner tubes behind the ski boat, that a feeling of extreme sadness overcame her. She rested her chin in her hands on her knees. Next to her, Angie glanced over.

"Oh sweetie, what's wrong?" She pulled Julia against her.

"The kids have grown so much, I'm so sorry that Ken is missing out on their lives. He would have loved seeing them out on the water."

Angie stroked her hair, "It's not fair, is it?"

Julia silently shook her head against Angie's arm. She sat up, "I'm sorry I don't know what got into me. I'm having so much fun; I just looked at my kids and thought about their dad."

"Don't apologize, that's absolutely normal. Of course, you should remember him when you see them. I think he would be proud of how happy you have continued to make them."

**

Luke tried to enter his room silently very early the next morning. He had slept in one of the spare rooms. Marcus was meeting him in half an hour for fishing. Julia was asleep in his room and he didn't want to wake her. Quickly, he grabbed clothes and was nearly to the door when he looked at her. She lay in his bed, the covers wrapped around her feet, wearing a short, sleeveless silky nightgown that was riding at her hips, revealing rather small bikini underwear. Luke groaned out loud, before he realized what he was doing.

Julie opened one eye and caught him, watching her. She gave him a sleepy grin reaching a hand out for him. He lost all will and lay down next to her.

Her hand traveled over his bare chest, "Where's your fishing clothes?"

He caressed her shoulder, "That's what I was coming in here to get. You distracted me."

She grasped his hair, pulling his face to hers, "Close the door," she commanded.

**

In the late afternoon, the teen girls offered to babysit so that the two couples could go out. It was decided that they would eat at The Ocean Odyssey, the best seafood restaurant for miles and then go to Lucky's Tavern, a little dive they used to sneak into when they were teens. Tonight, the bar was featuring a seventies cover band. "Wear jeans," Angie insisted, "We'll look out of place in anything else."

Luke had only enough time to pull a white cotton, short sleeved button shirt from his room before Julia kicked him out to get ready. She decided to wear a blue beaded halter, pairing it with her dark, slim jeans.

The conversation flowed at dinner. The two couples, glowing from the day spent in the sun, laughed and talked as if this was something they did together every weekend. By the time they reached Lucky's, the band was already into its own rendition of "Jetliner" by The Steve Miller Band. The group found a table and ordered drinks. When the band launched into "Sweet Home Alabama" the couples were ready to hit the dance floor.

Later, Angie checked her phone, a text had chimed in. She grinned at her brother across from her, then turned to Julia. "That was Kelsey. The boys are already asleep in Cody's room. She said that Emily is asleep in front of the TV, so we should just drop you two off at Luke's. They'll all stay at our house."

Marcus winked at his brother in law, "If that's okay with you."

"Check, please," Luke deadpanned.

**

The sun was high in the sky when it awoke Julia the next morning. She lifted her head to look over Luke at the nightstand and saw the clock. She sat up, "Oh my gosh, its ten o'clock."

Luke stretched and smiled at her, "Good morning."

"This is awful, it's late, and the kids will be up."

He chuckled, "Jules, it's okay, they know where you are."

She climbed out of bed, "I know but its embarrassing."

30

Julia sat in the boat feeling absolutely mortified as they tied it to Angie's dock. The screen door slammed, and she cringed. Who was she going to have face first? She glanced at the top of the hill and saw Kelsey and Emily with another girl making their way down the steps to the shore. Oblivious of her mother's discomfort, Kelsey's face lit up, "Hi Mom."

"Hi sweetie," Julia responded weakly as she stepped out of the boat. Luke put his hands on her shoulders and gave them a brief squeeze as he moved around her and up the steps.

Julia noticed he gave a big hug to third girl before he headed to the house.

"Mom, last night we went to open gym at Tri Lakes High School."

This took Julia by surprise, "You did? How? Why didn't I know about this?"

"Mackenzie," at this Kelsey motioned with her head toward the third girl, "text Angie, her aunt. Mackenzie's a guard on the Tri Lake team, the best team in the state. We've seen her at the tournaments but didn't know her. She's a senior like Lily. Luke is her uncle." Kelsey was talking in rapid excitement. "You should see Tri Lakes, it's the nicest court I've ever seen. The whole school is new and awesome."

Julia shook her head to let it all register, "You're Nancy's daughter?"

Mackenzie, a tall, pretty girl with long blonde hair nodded her head. Like the other two she was clad only in a bikini, "Yeah."

"Nice to meet you." Julia turned to her daughter, "What about the boys?"

"Oh, they went too, lots of kids were there, and it was a blast," Emily answered.

Kelsey spoke up, "Mackenzie can drive Marcus's boat so we're going out, okay?"

Julia smiled, "Okay, have fun, be careful."

The girls climbed in and Mackenzie started the motor. The screen door slammed again. Seth and Cody raced down the stairs shouting, "Wait for us!"

"No!" chorused the girls.

Julia stopped the boys, "Sorry guys, big girls only." The boys groaned.

"I'm sure Marcus will take you out later." Julia watched the girls speed off and smiled, it reminded her of her own summers here. The boys' complaints were short lived as they grabbed flippers and masks to "scuba dive". Julia had a sudden thought, if Mackenzie was here, were her parents also here? "Cody who's at your house?"

"Everyone," he said strapping a flipper to his foot, "Aunt Nancy, Uncle Randy, Grandma and Grandpa and Uncle Luke."

Julia paled as she thought, "Grandma and Grandpa?" All the people in the house were here when she arrived late in the morning alone with Luke? Her heart flipped over.

**

Luke entered the house while Julia was talking to the girls. He was assailed with the scents of pancakes and coffee. His father sat at the end of the table, the Sunday paper spread before him. At both sides of him were his sons-in-law. The men teased Luke as he came in with words like "Lover boy" and "Stud".

He ducked into the kitchen which was open to the dining area, separated only by an island. Luke kissed his mom on the cheek and reached for a plate.

"It's about time you got here, Lucas," she scolded.

"Sorry Mom, I slept in." His sisters laughed.

Evelyn Thomas held up her hand, "I don't want to hear it. Where's Julia?"

"She's talking to the kids," Luke filled his plate ignoring his sisters' continued ribbing.

"That poor girl has been through a lot. I hope you're taking this seriously," his mother spoke.

Nancy beat him to the response, putting an arm around him, "Ma, don't worry about Lukey, he's been madly in love with Julia since he was sixteen."

This brought a fresh chorus of remarks from the brothers-in-law. Luke closed his eyes and shook his head. When he opened them, he gave his mother an earnest smile, "Don't worry Mom, I'm very serious."

His mother patted him on the cheek, "Good answer."

Angie saw Julia heading to the door and turned to her husband and Randy, "Okay wise guys, be nice."

Julia opened the door with dread. She felt like a teenager caught in the back of a parked car. Luke met her at the door with a mug of coffee, which she gratefully accepted. Before anyone spoke he put his hand on her waist, "Julia, I don't think you've met my brother-in-law, Randy."

Randy stood and shook her hand. Julia set the mug on the table. "Nice to meet you."

Then Luke turned, "You remember my dad." Julia smiled as the elder Thomas stood up.

"Mr. Thomas, so nice to see you."

The tall man with mostly gray hair held out his arms, "Oh no, it's Bob. Julia how nice to see you after all this time." He gave her a kind hug.

Luke steered her toward the kitchen area. Angie was setting a plate on the table. "Morning hon," she hugged Julia close and whispered, "Sorry about the crowd."

Nancy came over, "Julia, great to finally see you again, love your kids."

"They're really impressed with your daughter."

Finally, Evelyn headed to Julia. She immediately pulled the younger woman close. "Julia, so wonderful to see you, you look lovely."

Julia smiled at the woman she had always been fond of, "So do you."

The woman waved the compliment away, and then took both of Julia's hands in hers, "Dear, I am sorry for your loss."

"Thank you."

"My kids tell me you've been a pillar of strength for your children and now that I have met two of them I see you must have."

"Thank you, Evelyn, that means so much."

**

Lily was waiting for them at home when they returned that evening. Julia soon found herself swinging on the porch with her oldest daughter. Lily glanced at her mom and remarked, "You're so tan. Wish I could've gone." Julia felt guilty, determined not to go again without her. She was still feeling so overwhelmed by Luke and all that had occurred with him over the weekend. Love was like a bubble that filled her. Lily grabbed at a heart charm around her neck and slid it back and forth, "I want to take Dylan next time, he'd love it."

With one word, the bubble burst in Julia. She opted not to respond.

Her daughter continued, "I can't wait until he gets back on Wednesday. This has been the longest weekend ever."

"Didn't you have fun with your girlfriends?" her hopes for her daughter's independence from him were dashed,

"Yeah, but you know it's not the same as being with your boyfriend."

Julia knew but was disappointed. "Have you heard from him?"

"Of course, all the time. He's tired of being there."

They were having a conversation, so she asked casual questions, "Where do they stay?"

"At some cheap motel, it's like four guys to a room. Dylan hates that."

"What do they do after work?" Julia saw a frown cross her daughter's face.

Lily shrugged, "I don't know, go out sometimes."

She tried to keep her voice level, "To bars?"

"I guess."

"Does he drink?"

Lily glared at her mother, "Don't start."

"Lily, you're only seventeen, I just don't want you to be influenced to do those things."

Too much, the teen stood up prepared for flight, "Mom, you don't even know. Those guys he's with are into drugs and stuff, he's so much better than the rest of them." With that she slammed into the house.

Julia stared out into the yard. Somehow, she doubted that Dylan was the saint of the group. But, what was she supposed to do?

31

Dylan was over by seven on Wednesday night. Lily had run out to meet him in the truck and Julia thought they were never going to come in. When they did, she did her best to be polite to him. Fortunately, Kelsey was at a friend's house and Seth was busy in his room. She didn't wish to subject her other two children to the reunion. She opted to move to the study and check the progress of her online students.

Julia was unaware of how much time had passed; she'd become involved in reading history essays. She heard raised voices in the other room. Lily's voice was accusing, Dylan's defensive. Julia pushed back her chair, straining to listen. Should she interrupt?

Lily uttered a loud sob, said something in a low voice and soon the front door slammed. The sound of Dylan's truck could be heard screeching into reverse and racing out of the drive. She came out of the study as her daughter headed up the stairs.

"What's wrong?" Julia asked gently.

Lily shook her head, "I don't want to talk about it." Her bedroom door closed behind her.

She did not come out of her room again. Kelsey came home and went to bed. Seth was tucked into bed. Julia closed the house and went to her room. She was about to turn on her television and watch the late show when she heard Lily's voice angry on the phone.

Julia moved toward the door, listening to her daughter's voice. "No Dylan, there is no excuse for that." Just then Julia's own phone buzzed in her jeans pocket. She looked at the screen as she retrieved it. It was Luke.

"Luke," she said in a near whisper, "I'm sorry, but Lily is having an issue. I can't really talk."

"Is everything okay?" Luke sounded concerned.

"Yes, just a fight."

"Jules, you call me when you can. At any hour."

"Oh, Luke, that's not necessary."

"I mean it, if not I'll be calling you by 12:30. Please call me."

"Okay, I promise to call."

From the other room Lily's voice escalated, "Strippers, they were strippers. . . I don't care if they were there for the other guys, you were there. Being too stoned isn't an excuse! Whatever." Julia heard her daughter crying, but instinct told her not to go in.

She heard the song that was Lily's ring tone and tried to will her daughter not to answer. She sighed when she heard her daughter's broken voice, "Yes I love you, and how can you ask that? Because Dylan, you've cheated before! I've never cheated on you, never! Why won't you believe me? I only hung out with girls this weekend, I promised you. You're the one who had strippers at your hotel room, smoking weed and drinking."

Julia's hand was on the door, she wanted so much to charge in, grab the phone and tell Dylan what she thought of him and force Lily to stay away from him. To her relief she heard her daughter say, "I want to break up. I mean it this time, it's over. No, I mean it, leave me alone." The phone clicked off and Julia heard Lily crying, her hand hovered on the door knob.

At that moment she saw Kelsey in the shadow of her own doorway, she looked at her mother and shook her head. "Leave her alone Mom, she won't want you to be in there," she whispered.

Julia sighed and moved back into her room. As she moved to the closet to undress she heard a slight knock and then a quiet, “Lily, it’s me, are you okay?” She felt tears form in her own eyes. Kelsey was such a good girl.

Her phone buzzed on the nightstand and she realized it was 12:35. Her hello was interrupted by Luke’s concerned, “Are you all right?”

“Yes fine, Lily was just fighting on the phone with Dylan, but it seems she broke up with him.”

“Again?” Luke asked skeptically.

“I know, I guess his week away involved pot, booze and strippers.”

“Are you kidding me? Well surely Lily will stay away from him now,” Luke said. They were both quiet for a moment, “Okay maybe not. Man, Julia she is the opposite of you. You were downright unforgiving at her age.”

His outburst stunned Julia, “What?”

“I didn’t mean that.”

“Luke, you can’t believe how sorry I am for the way I ended things back then.”

He sounded contrite, “I’m sorry I should never have said that. It started out as a compliment.”

“An off-handed one at most.” They were silent. “It comes back to you a lot, huh?”

"No, I wasn't thinking of us, just the difference between you and your daughter."

She ignored his answer, "When you know about this stuff going on, do you think that if I had just stayed with you, life would be easier for us right now?"

Luke hesitated a moment too long before saying no.

"I don't regret this life, this family," Julia's voice was defensive.

"Of course you don't, I wouldn't deny you your family." He sighed, "Now I feel guilty as hell for letting that slip out. Please, let's not go there tonight. You've had a rough evening; I've been going crazy here worrying about you, wishing I was there for you."

His last remark helped Julia, "Okay, thanks. Sorry for jumping to conclusions, the last thing I need to do is behave like a paranoid teenager."

"What are you going to do about this situation?"

She let out a breath of air, "I have no idea. It's so exhausting. I know Lily, she'll be back with him before the weekend, and he is such a loser."

"You can only do so much. Now it might be smart to not allow him to be at the house."

"I agree. Do you think I'm overreacting or do you think she's really in trouble with this guy?"

"He's a creep, but a weak one. I think Lily will wise up soon."

"I wish I had your confidence."

"I wish I was with you."

Julia smiled; Luke could hear it in her voice, "Oh boy, that would be great."

"How about this weekend?" Julia was thoughtful. "Busy this weekend?"

"No, I just. . . I don't know, maybe I'm spending too much time on my own romance and not enough time being a dual parent."

"I see," Luke struggled to understand. "How about if I come to help out at the house? We won't go anywhere, work on the house, and hang with the kids?"

"You want to play house?"

Luke got very serious, "No, I don't want to play house, but I'm willing to do that for now."

"You're a good man."

"Would it be easier if I stayed in a hotel instead of the couch?"

"I don't know. The kids don't seem to have an issue with that." Julia ran her fingers through her hair, "I don't know if I'm doing any of this right, but I'm trying. Of course, I want to see you this weekend."

"Okay, but no plans, we'll just be there. Don't mow, or clean or anything."

"Luke, sometimes I think you're too good to be true. Tell me again why you don't want some beautiful young woman with no baggage."

His voice was irresistibly soft as he spoke, "Because you will always be the only woman for me. I love you, Jules."

For the first time in over twenty years, Julia said the words aloud, "I love you too, Luke."

**

The clock glowed 2:43 when Julia heard a truck on the drive. At the end of her bed, Sophie growled and jumped to the floor. Julia's heart pounded, then realization hit her, it had to be Dylan. She grabbed her cell from the nightstand and headed downstairs. Lily's door was closed. Julia didn't see headlights in the drive and moved to the drapes in the living room for a closer look. Sitting on the arm of the couch, she listened. Nothing. If Dylan had been in the drive, he must have left. Julia sank onto the cushion and leaned against the pillow. She hated this so much. The silence lulled her to sleep.

A noise wakened her, and she realized she was still on the couch. Julia clicked the light on her cell phone; it was now 3:05. Once again, she heard the gravel. This time she did glimpse the familiar red truck in the drive. Dylan shut off the engine and in the glow of the open-door light she saw him getting out. What was he up to?

Julia gathered her courage, he was just a punk. She pulled her cell phone out, opened it and dialed 911. She then, opened the front door and stood on the porch, holding back Sophie with her knee. "Dylan, I've got 911 dialed on my phone, if you don't get in your truck this second and pull away, I will call. I mean it, get out of here now." Julia waited. She heard him swear as he climbed back into the truck. Just as he got ready to close the door she added, "Next time you even pull in here, I will call the police." For the second time that night, the truck squealed out of the driveway. She went back in the house, locking the door behind her. It was time to end this.

In the morning, Julia was awakened by Lily standing at the foot of her bed accusing her. "Mother what did you do to Dylan last night? He said you were going to call the cops on him."

Julia struggled to come awake, sitting up, letting her eyes clear. Lily had her hands on her hips, demanding an answer.

"He was here at 2:30 and 3:00, out of his truck, planning to do who knows what."

"So, you were going to call the police?"

Julia was climbing out of bed, "Yes, that is exactly what I was going to do. He was an unwanted trespasser."

Lily shook her head and sneered, "I can't believe you."

"You listen to me, Lily. No one treats one of my children the way he has treated you. No one who does drugs, drinks and sneaks around my house in the middle of the night is welcome here. Dylan has reached his limit. He is no longer allowed to see you here or anywhere else."

"You can't stop me!" Angry tears rolled down Lily's cheeks.

"Well, I'm certainly going to try," Julia began to cry too. "Can't you see that I'm trying to protect you? Protect the whole family? He's not a good person."

"You don't even know him Mom."

"I know plenty, he is bad news, and he's hurting you. No more Lily."

"You can't stop me from loving him."

"Maybe not, but I can certainly try."

"I hate you," Lily ran out of the room, slamming into her own.

Julia watched her go and threw herself back on the bed.

**

Lily didn't have to work that day, so she sulked around the house. Kelsey took Seth to the community pool. Julia resumed her online work. It was just after four when she heard a car in the driveway; she assumed her kids were home from the pool. She heard the back door open, but no voices. Julia was in the middle of an essay and finished it before she got up. As she was headed to the kitchen she glanced out the front window. Dylan's truck was in the drive; Lily was sitting on the ground with Dylan next to it.

"Great," Julia said aloud and headed toward the garage door. She shut the door quietly and made her way silently to the drive. She was coming around the other side of the truck and could hear the couple before she saw them.

"This is how much I fucking love you, Lily."

"Oh Dylan, why did you do this to yourself?"

Dylan's words were not completely clear, "I had to prove myself. You can't break up with me, it's bullshit. I fucking sliced this into my arm, so you would understand."

Julia came around the hood of the truck. Lily was cradling his forearm where he had carved what looked to be an "L" in his arm. It was bleeding and swollen. She gasped out loud, giving her presence away.

"Mom get out of here," Lily hissed.

Dylan looked up at her, his eyes were red, she suspicioned he was high. "Mrs. Darby why can't I see your daughter?"

"Dylan, you're doing things that aren't healthy, that are dangerous, I don't want Lily influenced by you."

"Mom, he's not . . ."

Dylan interrupted Lily, "I love her. I wouldn't hurt her."

"I think you already have." Julia realized that trying to argue with the two of them was pointless. She pointed at her daughter, "Get up and go in the house now."

Lily began to cry, "But Mom."

"Now. Dylan you need to leave."

Lily defiantly kissed him, and then stood up. "You're being such a bitch," she whispered as she stormed in the house. Dylan pulled his usual and peeled out of the drive.

Julia had no desire to return to the house, so she walked along the flower beds, plucking a few dead leaves and petals from the plants. She then pulled out the garden hose and watered the geraniums along the front porch and the hanging baskets. Soon Kelsey pulled into the drive. Seth tumbled out of the passenger's side. The days at the lake and then out today had made both kids deliciously bronze. "Seth, hang your towel on the line before you go in."

"Okay Mom. What's for dinner? I'm starving."

Kelsey walked to her mother. "Mom, can I go out tonight?"

Julia nodded, "Where to?"

"The movies."

Julia tilted her head, "With whom?"

"Derek Kingston, Emily and Matt Schwartz are going too."

She grinned at her daughter, "A double date?"

Kelsey gave a small smile back, "Maybe."

"That would be fine, are they picking you up here?"

"Yes, at seven. I need to get ready."

Julia felt so good to have one daughter headed out on a normal high school date. "Are you going to eat before you go?"

Kelsey was already heading up on the porch, "Do I have time to shower before dinner?"

"Yes, I'll go get everything ready." Julia made a light summer meal of BLT's, leftover potato salad, and melon. No one was surprised that Lily chose not to join them for dinner. She was pleased though, that after dinner she heard Lily in the bathroom helping her little sister with her hair.

**

The teens had left for their date. Seth was hanging out in the kitchen while Julia cleaned up. Lily had moved to the living room; the television was on. "Are Grandma and Grandpa coming for Christmas in July?" asked Seth. Christmas in July was Seneca's claim to fame in the county. The small town decorated its park and city streets with Christmas lights. Vendors set up booths to sell Christmas crafts, and food. There were also carnival games and rides. It culminated in a grand firework display set to Christmas music.

Julia glanced at the calendar on the fridge and was surprised to see the holiday was just over a week away. It had been tradition for the past few years that all of Julia's family had come to stay the weekend. Last year, her parents had come but the weekend had been painful. Julia had refused to go to the park and see other people there. Most were still uncomfortable talking to her. She sighed, at least she had moved beyond that difficulty. It still would not be the same without Ken. He often brought home illegal fireworks he had picked up on trips from out of state and held his own small show the night before. Julia was surprised she had not heard from her parents and Tim but thought they were probably planning on coming. She had better make some calls.

Her parents said that of course it was on their calendar. Her mother politely asked if Luke was going to be there. Her parents had seemed supportive of her relationship with him and she had to laugh to herself. Now that he was a successful architect he had more appeal to them then when he was the long-haired teen aged boy who wanted to keep their daughter trapped at Spring Lake.

Julia marveled at her relationships with her own daughters. Despite all the difficulties with Lily she was at least aware of what was going on. Her mother had never known of Julia going on the pill; she had taken herself to a clinic. Had her mother even known she was sexually active? Even when she went away to college her mother didn't feel compelled to discuss sex with her daughter. Julia couldn't blame her mother on her unplanned pregnancy, she'd been careful with Luke. Still it amazed her that her relationship with her own daughters was more open.

Tim and his family were also coming. In dealing with Lily, she especially appreciated this. Seth was looking forward to all the family being around for the weekend. Julia smiled at her pre-teen son. He had come so far this year. Last summer she had found herself up most nights rocking him through nightmares and tears.

He was scooping ice cream in a cone as he spoke to her, "How about Luke?"

"He's coming tomorrow. Is that okay?"

"Sure, what are we going to do?"

"Nothing big. What do you want to do?"

Seth took a lick of his cone, "Would Luke take me to the batting cages? Or maybe we could throw footballs, practice begins next month. Does Luke know how to play football?"

Julia smiled, "I'm sure he does. I don't know if he's as good as your father, I don't think he played in high school, but I'm sure he could practice tossing the football with you."

Seth nodded as he headed out of the kitchen, "Okay, if he doesn't know, I can teach him."

Julia laughed, looking forward to sharing that statement with Luke later. She looked up and Lily was standing in the door. "*So*, I'm not allowed to see Dylan, but your boyfriend can come shack up for the weekend?"

Julia sighed, "First off we are not shacking up, he will sleep on the couch."

"But I know you stayed at his place without anyone else." Lily accused.

"Yes, but here he will be on the couch, I will be in my room."

"The room you shared with my dad."

"Yes Lily, my husband, the man I loved. The man I miss every day. I never wanted this to happen."

Lily sneered at her, "But hasn't it worked out nicely for you?"

"I know that it seems bad to you, but I never intended for any of it to happen. I am happy to have Luke in my life, but don't you think for a minute that I wouldn't want to have my family back the way it was last year."

"Really mother? Are you saying you aren't glad you got your first love back into your life?" Julia heard her daughter rush up the stairs and slam her bedroom door.

32

Julia felt like the girl that years ago would stand at the end of the dirt road waiting for Luke to come over the hill from his end of the lake and see her after a week apart. He had phoned just twenty minutes earlier saying how close he was. When he stepped out of the car she had the urge to run up and jump on him. Instead, she moved down the walk, as he was making long strides to meet her. They flew into each other's arms and kissed passionately. She tangled her fingers in his hair at the back of his neck.

His eyes were bright as he looked at her, "I'm going crazy. I feel like I did twenty years ago, dying to see you again."

She kissed him, and then spoke, "I know exactly what you mean. My days are unbearable without you."

He ran his hands down her waist, "You look delicious."

One more kiss and she pushed slightly away, "Whoa, we're starting this weekend off completely wrong. The way things are going here, we'll be lucky to get to kiss again."

He groaned, "I know, but seriously Jules, that's okay. I just want to be with you, even if I can't be *with* you."

She laughed, "I actually understand that." They held hands as they approached the porch. The screen door flew open and Seth ran out.

"Hey Luke," to both of their surprise, he embraced Luke in a hug. Luke hugged the boy back, grinning at Julia.

"I heard a rumor."

Seth looked up at the man, "What?"

"Rumor has it that you think maybe you might have to teach me how to toss a football."

Seth looked at his mom accusingly. Luke continued, "Let me tell you now, I will show *you* how to play football."

The boy laughed, taking on the challenge, "I don't know, my dad was first string varsity in high school and he taught me a lot. I'm probably better than you."

Luke ruffled the boy's hair, "I take that as a challenge. And Seth, I brought fishing poles, thought if you wanted, we could check out the fishing action at the quarry."

"Sweet!" said Seth. He headed to the garage and came out on his bike. "Mom, can I go see Kyle before dinner?"

"Yes, watch for traffic and be home in forty-five minutes."

"Okay," the boy called, pedaling down the drive.

As they entered the house, Kelsey flew past them. "Mom, have you seen my lip gloss?" A cloud of perfume followed her. Luke raised an eyebrow at Julia.

"Second date," she whispered, then called to her daughter, "You left it on the coffee table." Kelsey passed them again and headed to the other room.

"Hi Luke," she said as she moved.

"Hello Kelsey, you look lovely."

The girl stopped and brushed at her pink camisole she had matched with white shorts, "Thanks, do I look okay, Mom?"

"Beautiful. Are you two going out alone tonight?"

"I think so, but we might meet everyone at Matt's for a bonfire after dinner."

"Midnight curfew, okay?"

"Okay," Kelsey responded, retrieving the lip gloss and placing it in her purse. A car pulled into the drive.

Soon a tall, thin boy with black hair approached the porch. Julia and Luke were still standing in the foyer. As he held his hand up to knock, Julia opened it. "Hi, Matt."

"Hi, Mrs. Darby."

Kelsey came up behind them and Julia was pleased to see the boy's eyes light up at the sight of her. "Matt this is Luke; he's my mom's boyfriend."

Luke shook the boy's hand, "Nice to meet you, Matt."

"You too." The teens left the house.

Luke glanced up the steps, "Lily home?"

"No, she's at work, I'm driving her everywhere, I have to pick her up at seven."

Luke pulled her close, "Are we alone?"

She smiled at him, returning to the teenager who used to take advantage of every stolen moment. "If Seth watches the time, I'd say we've got about thirty minutes."

"Perfect," Luke replied. He pulled Julia to him, his hand at her cheek, drawing her lips to his. They kissed. Julia reached behind him and locked the front door. She then moved into the kitchen and locked the garage door.

"What're you doing?"

"No one will have their key with them, so this will slow down any surprise visits."

He laughed, "You're good."

"Experienced parent." They both paused awkwardly, realizing this was a reference to her intimate life with Ken. She started to apologize when he reached for her and kissed her. Now was not the time worry about the past. She took his hand and led him to her bedroom. As they undressed each other she smiled, "This is certainly not what I expected to happen this weekend."

He was unbuttoning her jeans, "I tried all the way here to talk myself out of wanting you desperately. The minute you stood up off the porch, I knew I had wasted my time." His hands touched her bare waist, "I wanted this so badly."

A short while later, Julia was fastening her jeans back up. She laughed, "This definitely brings back memories." Luke approached her, pulling his shirt over his head. She took the opportunity for one more caress of his bare chest and stomach. He groaned, "Don't get me started again." Julia turned her back to him and looked at herself in the mirror. She fixed her hair and wiped away stray eyeliner.

"Now let's go get your stuff out of the car."

**

They decided to pick up Lily from work and go out to dinner. They were going to head into New Haven, just ten miles away, and eat at a favorite Mexican restaurant. Julia knew that Lily hated to be seen in her Dairy Bar T shirt, but would be wearing jean shorts, so she grabbed a clean top from her daughter's closet.

When the Range Rover pulled into the parking lot, she took the top to her daughter. Lily, already annoyed at the vehicle and its driver, glared at her mother. "What's this for?"

"We're going out for dinner and I knew you'd want to change your shirt."

"We? The four of us? I don't want to." Lily attempted to hand back the shirt. Her mother refused to take it.

"Sorry Lily, you're going with us."

Her daughter snatched the shirt from her hands and stormed to the bathroom. She climbed into the vehicle a few moments later, flipping out her iPhone. Before she had placed both buds in her ears, Luke turned slightly from the driver's seat, "Hi Lily."

"Hi," she said quietly.

"Missed you at the lake last weekend."

"Had to work," she said and turned her music on.

Dinner began awkwardly, but Lily seemed to warm up as she ate. She was soon describing a mother who came in with six kids and ordered double cones for all of them. It was a funny story about spilled ice cream and a toddler eating it off the ground. The foursome laughed easily, and the atmosphere was more comfortable.

Luke asked Lily if she had any plans for college the next fall. She told him she was interested in living on campus at a big university. Julia suggested that the two of them take a college trip during the next week, to tour campuses.

Luke had just given the waitress his card to pay the bill; when suddenly Dylan was standing at their booth. Julia looked at the young man. He was wearing loose cargo shorts down nearly to his ankles, unlaced sneakers, and a white tank. His unruly hair was covered mostly by a cap. On his lower arm the "L" now puffed, bruised and painful. It would be permanent. His eyes were once again red.

He looked directly at Lily, ignoring the rest at the table, "Lily, I need to talk to you."

Lily flushed, “Dylan.” Julia looked at her daughter accusingly. Her daughter’s expression was complete surprise, “How did you find me?”

“Andrea at the shop heard your mom say you were coming here, we need to talk!”

Lily made a move to rise and Luke stood up. “Dylan,” he said quietly but firmly, “Lily can’t talk now, let me walk you out.”

Dylan slapped his hand on the table, a few people nearby turned. “I need to talk to you.” He turned glaring eyes on Julia, “Let me talk to her.”

Luke firmly placed a hand on Dylan’s shoulder, a few inches lower than his own, “Dylan, let’s go. No need to cause a scene.”

Dylan shrugged the hand off but turned with Luke and followed him out the door. Julia looked at her daughter who had tears welling up in her eyes. Julia had to admit, it truly looked as if Lily did not welcome the sight of him. When the waitress returned for Luke’s signature, Julia signed it not certain if he would be back in. She took the card and receipt, keeping her eye on the door. Soon Luke stepped in, motioning them to join him. Seth remained quiet throughout all of this.

There was no sign of the truck in the parking lot. The four climbed quietly into the car. Julia decided to wait and question Luke once they were alone. Lily however, spoke up. “What happened?”

“Nothing really. I just told him this wasn’t the time to try to see you.” From the flush of Luke’s face, Julia was not convinced it had been that simple.

Lily was silent for a moment, and then said in a near whisper, “I’m sorry.”

No one spoke as they headed back to Seneca. Seth went to his room when they got home. Lily slumped in front of the television. Julia and Luke settled onto stools at the kitchen island. She made them coffee.

“Thank you for handling that.”

He lightly touched her hand as she sat out mugs, “It’s what I want to do for you.”

She came around the counter and placed both hands on his temples, “I like the sound of that.”

Luke pulled her onto his lap and kissed her. “I know none of this is easy, we’re hundreds of miles apart. I have a business at Spring Lake and you have teenagers in school here in Seneca, but somehow I want us to make this real.”

She rested her forehead against his, “Me too, Luke.”

They heard the front door open and she moved back to her side of the counter. Kelsey must have returned from her date. Julia looked at the clock, 11:15. Early? She was surprised. They waited for Kelsey to walk in. She didn't.

Julia moved to the doorway looking for her daughter, instead Julia heard her voice and it was angry. "How could you? Lily, I've never been so embarrassed in all my life!"

Julia couldn't hear Lily's words, but she responded in a question. Kelsey's voice was accompanied with angry tears; Julia could hear them as she spoke. "I went to Matt's for a bonfire tonight. All the guys were laughing because today some of them went to the quarry to swim."

This time Julia heard Lily moan in response. Kelsey's voice rose even more, "That's right; they saw you doing 'it' in Dylan's truck. Right there in the middle of the afternoon for all to see. My own sister the town whore." With that Kelsey ran up to her room.

Luke had come and stood beside Julia, but she hadn't noticed. Soon Lily flew past, headed to her own room. Julia wasn't aware that she was shaking until

Luke wrapped his arms around her waist, from behind her. "Oh baby, I'm so sorry," he whispered in her ear.

Julia was out of words. She hugged Luke and whispered, "I think I'm going to go to bed."

He kissed her forehead, "I think that's a good idea. You go, I know where everything is, and I'll settle myself in and lock up."

"Thank you. For everything." She gave him a soft kiss and moved up to the steps.

Julia washed her face, and brushed her teeth, put on a tank top and boxer shorts and climbed into bed. The kids' rooms were all quiet. She had peeked into Seth's room, he was asleep. Though she had stood silently at both girls' rooms, she didn't open their doors.

Now she lay, staring out the window at the moon. Her eyes burned with unshed tears, her heart was heavy. Suddenly she heard someone come in. She turned to see Luke in her room. "What are you doing?" she asked.

He lightly closed the door and moved towards the bed, "Breaking the rules," he replied climbing in next to her. He pulled her close; she lay on his chest, breathing in the warmth of him. Now against his skin, the tears flowed.

33

Julia opened her eyes, amazed that she had slept without waking once. The sun was just peeking in the window. Next to her the bed was empty. When had Luke left? She put on her robe and headed out into the hall. One glance showed her that Seth's room was empty. She went down to the kitchen; on the counter was a note, "Gone Fishing!"

Julia grinned and headed back up for a shower. In the shower, the reality of her daughters came back to her. How was she supposed to handle this one? Kelsey needed a lot of consoling. What about Lily? Obviously, she had left work and went with him. Wasn't he working?

Julia felt a pang for Lily, as horrible as Dylan was and that she was not supposed to be with him, she was sorry for her too. Teens were so stupid about sex. It was just typical of a young couple to not be discreet about where they had sex. Though she herself had never been foolish enough to be where others could see her; in a vehicle in the daylight, she could certainly remember some inappropriate places she and Luke had chosen. If this was a normal teen relationship she could act as the disapproving yet sympathetic mother. Unfortunately, this was in total defiance of her rules about Dylan. So now what? Did she need to send Lily off to a convent? Julia laughed aloud at this notion.

She was in the kitchen making herself some toast when Kelsey came in. She looked at her mother still angry, "What are you going to do about your daughter?"

Julia was surprised, "What do you mean?"

"Mom she's out of control. Dylan is the biggest stoner loser. He sleeps around; did you know he dropped out of school?"

Julia tried to process this new information. Kelsey continued, "You have to force Lily to stay away from him. You've been way too easy on her."

"I don't think I've been easy on her," Julia found she was defending herself against her own daughter, "I've tried desperately to keep them apart. Look I'm so sorry for your embarrassment last night. I'm sure it was awful, but kids aren't going to hold this against you."

Kelsey suddenly resembled her sister as she shot back, “Oh please, Mom you have no idea how mean kids are. I’ll hear about this for the rest of the year.”

Lily chose that moment to enter the kitchen. Kelsey turned her back on her sister and fixed a bowl of cereal. Lily spoke to her sister’s back, “Kels, I’m so sorry about last night. What I did was totally stupid and I’m sorry that you found out and people embarrassed you about it.”

“People didn’t embarrass me, you did.”

Lily tried to placate her, “Look I know you don’t understand how it is.”

“You mean understand what it’s like to be slut?”

Julia jumped in, ‘That’s enough.” She grabbed her coffee off the counter, “Can I talk to you outside, Lily?”

Lily followed her mother out to the swing. She glanced at the drive, “Where’s Luke?”

“He took Seth fishing.”

Lily looked surprised but said nothing.

“Lily, you have to quit seeing Dylan.” Lily opened her mouth to protest. Julia held up her hand, “This isn’t about the park; this is about the kind of person Dylan is. You probably know way more than I do, of the trouble he’s been in, is still getting in. He’s leading you right down that path. Come on Lily; picture the life you want in the future, think about that right now. Think about the future you want." Julia was silent for a moment; she could tell that Lily was thinking about it. After a moment she spoke, "Dylan doesn't fit into that future, does he?"

Lily slowly shook her head. Julia nodded, "I thought not. Lily, you have to end this before it ruins the person you are."

Her daughter mulled over it then spoke, "Mom, I know what you're saying. I know Dylan is doing bad things, but Mom he needs me so much. He has no one. I'm the only one who can talk him out of doing dangerous things. If I'm not there, something really bad could happen to him."

Julia's heart hurt for her daughter. This was the Lily she knew and loved. She had been fooled by this boy. He'd really convinced her that she was his reason for survival. Julia struggled with how to respond. "Have you been able to stop him from anything permanently?"

"Yes, a couple of weeks ago he wanted to kill himself, I talked him out of it." Julia doubted this. "He tried coke and I warned him that if he did it again I would be gone."

"But Lily, is he ever going to change enough to be the boyfriend you should have, that you deserve?"

"Mom, I can't explain it to you, I love him so much. He makes me feel so special."

Julia was about to respond when the Range Rover pulled in, bad timing. Luke seemed to sense it; he glanced up then spoke to Seth. They climbed out of the vehicle and headed straight for the garage. When Julia turned back to her daughter, Lily was watching her. "Mom you obviously are madly in love with him. That's how I feel too."

"But Luke is a good, honest person."

"Did Grandma think he was right for you?"

Julia hesitated. "Not always. I wanted to stay at the lake and go to college there to be with him, she didn't want me to settle there and not experience life."

"And you thought she was wrong, you still do, right?"

"It isn't the same, Lily. Luke wasn't like Dylan."

"Come on Mom, he got drunk and cheated on you."

"Yeah and I dumped him."

"Yeah, but you regretted it didn't you?"

Julia put her hand on her daughter's leg. "Honey, I know this all sounds very similar, but it's not. Look at Luke." At this point he was at shooting basketballs in the driveway with Seth. “Can you honestly picture Dylan as him in twenty years?”

“Maybe with my help,” she responded weakly.

“That’s the point; Luke didn’t need my help to become the person he is. You deserve the chance to grow as your own person, discover what you love to do. Learn all you can. You are way too young to be responsible for the survival of another human being. Dylan will demand that you do all of that for him. That’s not fair to you. You deserve to be loved because of what and who you are, not because you’re there when someone needs you and can take care of them.”

Lily was quiet for quite a bit. Finally, she said softly, “But I don’t know what to do about Dylan.”

“You don’t think staying away from him will work? I know you haven’t done that yet.”

“I don’t know if it will or not.”

“Lily, please try.” Her daughter nodded and for the first time in a long time, Julia felt some hope in this situation.

**

Later in the afternoon, Luke was on the riding mower, Seth was using the blower to keep grass off the walk and Julia was trimming the weeds when Matt pulled up. Julia greeted him and then told him to just ring the bell, Kelsey was home.

Julia continued to work as she watched Kelsey come out and sit on the swing with Matt. It was obvious that he was making her feel better. When he shyly took her hand, Julia smiled and turned back to the trim.

Later that night, Kelsey had gone over to Matt's house for dinner. Lily had invited Olivia over; this was a positive turn of events. They were eating dinner on the patio when Seth brought up next weekend. "Luke are you coming for the Christmas in July festival? Uncle Tim, Aunt Beth, Scott, Alex, Grandma and Grandpa are coming, they always do."

Luke turned to Seth, "What's the Christmas in July festival?" Seth rambled on about the many events of the weekend. Julia blanched. She had not invited him, she was not sure if she wanted to subject him to her extended family as well as all the drama he had been witness to this weekend. As was typical, Luke picked up on her hesitation, "No Seth, I think I will be at the lake with my family," he said coolly.

To her surprise, Julia saw Lily give her mother a glare as if to say, "Way to go, Mom." Lily turned to Luke and said, "It's pretty lame."

Olivia agreed, "Just kiddy rides and fireworks with lame Christmas music."

Seth disagreed, "No it's cool, Luke you should come."

Luke aimed his look at Julia, "No, I don't think I'll be able to make it. Sorry Seth."

Lily elbowed her friend. "Come on Seth, help Olivia and I get the strawberries and shortcake." She raised her eyebrows meaningfully at her mother and herded the other two into the house.

Julia looked across the table at Luke who was obviously angry. "I'm so bad at this. You must be really sick of me."

He looked at her, his eyes dark, "Do you just lie to me when you agree about wanting this to last? About this being serious?"

Julia had her elbows on the table; she put her head in her hands for a moment. "No Luke, I'm not lying to you, I'm totally serious. I just keep thinking that, I don't know. That this is moving too fast, that it can't really work out."

Luke was not appeased, "Julia, back when this first started, I told you it wasn't normal. We weren't strangers meeting and getting to know each other. We may have spent what seems like a lifetime apart, but when you showed up at the lake again, it felt like we were just picking up where we left off." He looked out at the yard, "I thought that was how you felt too."

"I do Luke, I do. I just still feel . . . guilty. I feel guilty for how you didn't get to have kids, I feel guilty for when I saw you last summer and what we did, I feel guilty that Ken died and now I have you and it's like I got what I wanted," her voice was a whisper, the kids were just inside.

Luke shook his head in disgust, "You didn't wish him dead. Looking at what you go through daily, I know your life would be a lot easier if he were sitting here and not me." She started to protest, he waved it away, "Can't you just look at this as a good thing? Your life was destroyed last year, and then this year something good happened. You have someone who loves you, who wants to be a part of your life. All your life. Why can't you believe that? It's like you can't allow yourself to be happy. Right now, you're so miserable, struggling through the tough times your teenagers are having. Being a teenager sucks, don't you remember? But it won't be long before they're off having their own lives. Remember when your parents became distant relatives? When suddenly you were calling your own shots? Your kids are close to that and what will you have when they're gone?"

Julia looked across the table at the man whom she had loved since she was fifteen years old. Luke had said things that she had desperately needed to hear. "I want to have you, Luke." They both stood up and held onto each other. She kissed him and then said, "Can you forgive me for being so stupid?"

He shook his head, "See always the guilty one. Don't apologize, just kiss me again."

"Gross," they turned as Seth spoke the words from the other end of the table.

Luke laughed, "Sorry buddy, your day's coming."

"No, I don't want to kiss girls."

Lily and Olivia were behind him, "Oh you will, Seth."

**

It was after midnight; the moon was nearly full. Luke and Julia sat on a blanket in the yard watching the bats fly past the barn light. They had returned out here after the kids had gone to bed.

A bottle of wine sat beside them, mostly empty. Luke picked up his glass for a final swig. "How much fun would our late nights have been with this?"

Julia laughed, "What are you talking about; I think we had our share of cheap beer or wine."

"Maybe. Remember when you snuck out of the cabin and met me in the woods?"

"You and John were camping."

He nodded his head, "We kicked him out of the tent pretty quickly, didn't we."

Julia shook her head, "We weren't any better than Lily and Dylan." Luke put his arms around her waist, "We were shameless."

He put his hands just under the hem of her top, "Hey don't blame me, you were the one who spent all day wearing two tiny pieces of material."

"Yeah, well I seem to remember that you never had a shirt on yourself."

He kissed her neck, "No wonder we couldn't control ourselves."

She looked up and laughed as he nibbled her neck, "What's your excuse now?"

"Too much time apart."

"I'll give you that. It's my house, and I'm considering the only way to do what I want is to sneak into the garage."

Luke was still holding her close, "Garage? I'm game."

"Really? I couldn't tell." She pushed his hips from hers. "Okay let's talk about something else, before we do something I'd be ashamed of my daughters doing."

Luke laughed and moved away from her. He laid back down. Looking up at the stars, he folded his arms under his head. "Let's talk about marriage."

Julia, sitting on the edge of the blanket, nearly fell over. "What did you say?"

He sat up, "I'm serious. This certainly doesn't come as a surprise, does it?"

She smiled at him, "No, it doesn't."

Luke smiled back, "Good, because I do want to marry you."

Julia took a deep breath, "I want to marry you too. Wow, we actually said it out loud."

He took her hands, rubbing his fingers over the tops of hers. "Did we have to do that for you to think it was real?"

"I keep telling you that you're too good to be true and you don't believe me."

"No, I'm not."

"Really, Luke? Let's see, you've forgiven me for sending you away over two decades ago. Over a year ago, I chased you off again."

"Well, you were married."

"Then this summer I show up at the lake with my three kids and crazy life. You treat me as if I just was gone for a weekend and let me back into your life."

"Let you back into my life? Julia, it's what I've been wanting forever. This year I did get the same feeling from you, I'm not crazy. You come back into my life; you act like you're interested. I'm not going to take it easy. Jules, when you came to the lake alone, that was it, I was a goner."

He grabbed her chin and pulled her toward him and kissed her. "Okay, now that we've established that we love each other and that we're lucky to have each other, can we get back to the subject of marriage? Some of us have already turned forty this year."

"You're almost too old to marry," she teased

"Can we get married?" he refused to get off track.

Julia looked at Luke, he was no longer joking. She gave him a sad smile, "I don't know when. I have an obligation to my kids to stay here. They've lost so much, and their ages are the worst for starting somewhere else."

Luke ran his hands through his hair and sighed. “I know that’s true and you’re right. I’ve investigated the area and there isn’t much work for me here.”

“Work for you here? Luke, no way. You have a fabulously successful business there and you can’t leave the lake or your house.”

“But I would. Those things aren’t as important.”

“Thank you. But your business, no you cannot leave it.”

“What if we had a commuter marriage?”

Julia mulled it over. “You mean we see each other on weekends and holidays?”

“And you don’t have to work over the summer, so you and the kids could spend the summers at the lake.”

Julia took some time to think. “When Kelsey graduates, it will just be the beginning of Seth’s freshman year; it would be a good time to transfer.”

Luke nodded, “Then that’s only three years.”

“Less by the time we get married.”

“How long do we have to wait?”

Julia balked, “Luke we’ve only been seeing each other for a month.”

“A month and four years.”

“Yes, that counts for something.”

"Okay so a fourth of July wedding is out?"

She nodded, "Yes, it is."

"How soon can we get engaged?"

She looked at him, "Are you in a hurry because you think it won't work out?"

"No, I just want to be married to you. A lifelong fantasy."

"I have to talk this over with the kids."

"Okay." Luke stood up and pulled her up to face him. "You tell me when the time is right, and I'll take care of the rest."

**

The next afternoon, she prepared a large meal, convincing the girls to take part, while the boys returned to football practice. Kelsey peeled potatoes, Lily made biscuits. They seemed to have recovered from the Saturday night disaster. They were talking to each other in normal tones. Her relationship with Luke suddenly became the topic of discussion. Lily was telling Kelsey how "Mom almost blew it" over the holiday weekend.

Kelsey was in complete agreement that her mom wasn't good at this dating thing and last week she'd practically had to force them to go on a date.

Julia protested, "But I'm just out of practice."

"Well Mom, you better get in practice if you want to keep him."

Julia smiled a secret smile, "I don't think I'm going to lose him."

She was unaware that the girls were watching her. Lily swooped down first, "Are you guys going to move in together?"

Kelsey answered, "That's dumb, where?"

"No, we're not moving in together."

Kelsey tried to guess next, "Did he pop the question?"

Lily's turn to respond, "Already? It's only been a month."

"This time," Kelsey said.

"True."

Julia turned back to the oven, "You two don't even need me, you've got this all figured out."

"No Mom," they both chorused. "What's going on?"

Julia turned to her girls, "We were just discussing the future last night."

"And?"

"And I want you both to know that I know how important high school is and I would never think of moving while you're in high school."

"I would hope not," said Lily, "this is my senior year."

Kelsey shrugged, "Whatever, Tri State would be an awesome place to play basketball."

Both Julia and Lily turned to her in amazement. "I'm just saying I might consider it."

"Well that's two less years," replied Lily. "Are you guys seriously talking marriage?"

"I won't do anything that we all don't agree on."

Kelsey put her hands on her mother's shoulders, "Mom, we all like Luke, he's great."

Lily nodded, "She's right Mom, you guys act happier together than any of my friends' parents."

"Look girls, I loved your dad so . . ."

Lily cut her off, "Mom this isn't about dad. I'm sorry for the stupid things I said before about Luke. I think it's great that you guys found each other again."

Kelsey smiled, "The way Angie moved into town and then Luke showed up at the lake, so romantic."

Both Julia and Lily stared at Kelsey. Lily grinned, "Oh no, guess who else is in love."

Kelsey blushed, "I am not."

Lily cackled, "You have never used the word *romantic* in your life, you've got it bad." Julia laughed too.

Kelsey struggled to get the attention off her, "So did he propose, Mom?"

"No, he told me to tell him when I'm ready."

Lily spoke again, "So are we still talking years away?"

"Well, that's just it. Luke thinks we could have a commuter marriage."

"What's that?"

"We would be apart during the work week. We would be together during the weekends, holidays, and if I didn't teach, we could live at the lake in the summer."

Lily nodded, "That could work. So how soon does he want to get married?"

Julia laughed, "Like I said it's pretty much up to me."

34

The next four days gave Julia way too much confidence. Lily did stay away from Dylan. She didn't complain when Julia continued to take her to and from work. She was even willing to spend the rest of her time at home. Julia was elated, feeling this was over.

By the time Thursday rolled around, the house was ready for company. She had put all three kids to work. Not a corner had been left untouched. Every bed had clean linens. Towels were laid out for each guest. The fridge was full. Dishes had been prepared. The neat yard had been maintained. Not a single sock remained in the laundry room.

She imagined her parents would arrive first in the late afternoon, followed by Tim and his family from the Indianapolis area and Luke from the lake in the evening. Julia and the kids finished lunch and cleaned up the kitchen. She discovered that she had forgotten her mother's favorite tea and decided to go to the grocery herself to get it. Still in her most faded, torn jeans and an old basketball T-shirt of Kelsey's that was a bit tight, she grabbed her purse and headed out. Julia was certain to be home before company arrived.

At the grocery, she climbed out of her car and headed toward the store. She heard a male voice some distance behind her call, "Lily?" She turned around, it was Luke. He laughed and sprinted to her, slamming the door of his Range Rover. He caught up with her and grabbed her around the waist. "What the hell are you doing dressed like that?" He kissed her.

She looked at her outfit, "I look hideous, don't I?"

"No far from it, I was almost to your house when I saw your car pull out, I followed, but when I saw the person get out of the car with those tight jeans and teeny shirt, I thought you were Lily."

She smacked at his shoulder, "Liar."

"I'm not kidding; the bag boy would've been drooling over you." He grabbed her close again.

"Okay hot stuff, behave yourself, this is a small town. What are you doing here so early?"

"I felt like it. I couldn't wait any longer."

"You may change your mind, when my folks get here."

"Another good reason to get here first, gives me some time to do this." He kissed her again.

She pushed him away, laughing. "I may have to move sooner than planned."

He caught up with her, grabbing her hand, "Whatever it takes."

**

The weekend went very well. Luke was well received by everyone. Julia's dad was fascinated by his business, and they had lengthy discussions on the world of architecture.

Kelsey was still dating Matt and attended the fireworks with him. Julia saw them with a group of young couples. Lily met up with some of her girlfriends. Later in the night, Julia also spotted Dylan. He was with a group of rowdy young adults, surrounded by beer bottles and smoke. He had his hand in the back pocket of a girl's jeans.

That night, Lily slept on the air mattress on Julia's floor, and late she heard her daughter crying quietly. She decided to leave her to her sorrow. It was all part of the process.

Her family all planned to leave on Sunday. The entire household went into New Haven for brunch, and the relatives headed to the highway from there. Luke was not ready to leave.

Early afternoon found the couple on the porch swing. He was stretched out with his head in her lap. Julia ran her fingers through his hair that she loved so much. Occasionally she would point out the discovery of a strand of gray. Luke insisted she was imagining things.

"I haven't got to talk to you alone. I was hoping I could stay a few days longer."

"I must teach tomorrow morning. Can you entertain yourself? Break from work?"

"I have to be gone for a week, beginning on Thursday. I'm flying to California for work."

"Sounds fantastic," Julia imagined a trip away with Luke.

"I would love to take you with me, but I know now isn't the time. I had another idea. Are you taking a vacation this year?"

"We haven't planned one."

He sat up, "When I get back why don't you all come spend a week at my house?"

Julia nodded, "That is a great idea. The kids would have a great time"

"I think I could keep busy with the kids. I'd love to see you teach, though."

"No way, this will be an absolutely boring lecture in Intro to Psychology."

The front door opened, and Lily stepped out. Luke sat up to give her space on the swing. She shook her head and sat on the porch steps.

"Luke, where did you go to college?" she asked.

Julia almost answered that he attended the local college at the lake, but he surprised her when he answered, "I got my master's degree at Ohio State."

"Really, that's one of my top choices," responded Lily.

"I'd love to take you on a tour; it's been years since I've been there. Could we go this week?" he was instantly excited.

"You're going to be here?"

"For a few days more."

"Cool, I'd love that. I'll get online and see when they have tours." She pulled out her phone to look.

Julia's head bounced back and forth as they conversed, she spoke up, "Hey, do I get to go too?"

"Of course," Luke said.

"Yeah Mom, you'll be paying for it someday."

Lily discovered that they could have a tour on Tuesday and emailed their registration to attend. Kelsey agreed to clear her calendar and stay home with her brother.

35

Julia felt like it had been weeks since Luke had been there though he'd only left for California a day ago. She found herself in a slew of single parent issues. On Thursday, Kelsey who'd just gotten her license a month ago, had been in a fender bender, not her fault but now Julia had to deal with insurance companies, getting estimates, and car repairs. She had given Kelsey Lily's car to use and Lily had felt that was decidedly unfair. She became bitter about her captivity and Julia suspected that she may have been in contact with Dylan.

Tonight, she was to attend a cookout/meeting about varsity basketball camp at the coach's house and she also needed to meet at the football field with Seth. Julia had finally informed Eric that she would be late to the girl's meeting and would try to leave as early as she could from the football meeting. After the basketball meeting, Kelsey was headed to Matt's. Julia and Seth headed home. Her cell phone chirped in her purse, and she answered it.

"Hello darling." It was Luke. Julia glanced at the clock. It was 8:45 her time, it must be 5:45 in California.

"Hi. Are you done working for the day?"

"Yes finally, what are you doing?"

"Just left a basketball meeting and a football meeting," She pulled into the garage, exhausted.

"Both at once?"

"I jumped from one to the other."

"Oh babe, I'm sorry you have to do that stuff yourself. Make any progress on the car?"

She laughed, "Are you sure we're not already married? This conversation sounds awfully familiar."

"I know, I just hate you having to take care of things yourself."

For reasons she couldn't explain, Julia felt a bit of irritation, "It's been over a year Luke, I've gotten used to it for the most part." He was silent for a moment. "I'm sorry; did that come out the wrong way? I just feel like talking about things other than my day to day tasks."

He seemed to recover, "Okay. How about I miss you? I can see the ocean from my window, and I would love to walk along the shore with you."

"Ahh, barefoot in the sand with you. Would you be shirtless?" the expanse of green lawn out the kitchen window did not seem as appealing.

"Would you wear a bikini?"

"Okay, fantasy over, we will stick with barefoot. Are you getting to do anything fun while you're there?"

"Yes, a couple of dinners out, a tour of the city. The company is treating me well because they want me to design a beautiful building for them. Have you figured out when you're going to spend a week with me?"

"Well I looked at the calendar and maybe a week from Monday would be good, my summer class will be over, and the camps haven't started yet."

"Monday, can't you come on Friday?"

Julia laughed, "If Lily can get the weekend off too, then we will try. That's one week from today."

"What do you want me to bring you?"

"Bring me? Ken quit bringing me gifts from business trips, years ago."

"I'm not Ken," Luke responded quietly. Then in a lighter tone, "I already bought all of the kids something.

"This is going to be bad. They're going to have you under their thumb in no time."

"How about you? Any requests?"

"Just you."

He sighed, "I'll be flying home on Tuesday. I should be done then."

"Have a good night, Luke. I will be thinking of you."

"I'll be thinking of you too. I love you."

"I love you too,"

**

Julia was completely exhausted that night as she locked up the house and headed to her room. As was her habit as a single woman, she got ready for bed, then watched something on her laptop. The glow of her screen was not visible from the hall and it must have looked like she was asleep at 12:30 when Lily snuck outside. She might have gotten away with it, except that the beer bottle that Dylan had been drinking when he got out of the truck clanged against the chain of the swing, as the couple sat down. The slight noise was heard by Julia. Sophie had apparently joined Lily downstairs.

It was beginning to be a familiar routine of pulling clothes over her nightwear. This time she went to the living room window and peered out. Sure enough, there was Lily and Dylan on the swing wrapped around each other. Julia swore under her breath and sat down on the couch. What should she do that would be most effective? She was out of ideas. She peeked out the window again, it looked as if they were having an argument.

Lily was pointing at the beer bottle on the porch and pulling something out of his pocket; it looked like a bag of something. Weed? Probably. He grabbed it from her and shoved it back into his pocket. Now he was yelling something.

She was shouting back, though Julia could not make out words, the volume of their voices carried in through the window. Lily was getting ready to head back into the house, as Dylan stumbled back to the truck. She saw him reach in the bed of the truck for something. It was a beer. He twisted the cap as he climbed in. Lily slammed into the foyer but stayed by the door. Julia could hear her sobs but remained at the window. He was at least drunk and a danger to be out on the road. She would call the sheriff and report him.

He squealed his tires loudly, sending gravel flying as he took off down the drive. Julia was about to reach for her phone when a light caught her eye. Dylan had pulled out of the driveway and having gone no more than twenty yards was stopped by a patrol car. Julia realized they had been by her house more frequently since the night she had previously called them. In a small town like this, most likely her status as single parent was well known.

"Good," she said out loud. Lily walked to the doorway of the room.

"Mom, I can explain."

Julia continued to watch out the window, "Don't bother, come here and see Dylan."

From the window they could only see the headlights of Dylan's truck and behind it the flashing lights of the patrol car. Lily put her hands over her mouth, "Oh no." She made a move to go out, Julia caught her arm.

"Don't even think about, Dylan is getting exactly what he deserves."

36

"Go to the lake." This was Luke's idea when Julia talked to him Sunday. She explained that Lily had talked to Dylan's father and discovered that he was in jail for three days. There would be a court hearing for any further sentencing in the future.

"When?"

"Now, tomorrow, sometime before he gets out of jail. Get her out of Seneca."

Julia could see this as a good suggestion, "Great idea. Take her before he even knows where we are."

"Don't tell her where you're going. Pack when she's not around, if you can."

"When will you be home?"

"I'll catch the first plane out tomorrow."

"But Luke, you said you needed to be there until Tuesday. "

He was insistent, "I can finish up what I need today. I will call you with my flight plans, if I can't be there before you, Angie has a key."

**

Julia pretended to be sympathetic and sent the two girls to the mall with her credit card. She told them to each buy a new summer outfit to help cheer Lily up and stop for a pedicure while they were at it. Next was a call to the neighbors, Kyle's parents, to tell them she was taking the kids on a surprise trip. Could they get her mail and papers, and could Seth come play for a couple of hours while she packed?

She had covered the contents in the back of the vehicle with a blanket. When the girls returned, she ordered Kelsey to put her car in the garage. Julia had the house ready for time away. She told the girls to hop into her vehicle, they needed to pick up Seth at the neighbors and then she had a surprise for them. Lily set her purse on the floor of the front seat, then realizing her sunglasses were in Kelsey's car, ran to the garage to retrieve them. This was the perfect opportunity to snatch her phone from the outside pocket of her purse.

Seth was extremely excited about an unexpected trip and was the first one to ask if it was overnight. Julia gave no hints, but when she turned on to the interstate, the girls looked in back and discovered their luggage. She gave in to their questions about ten miles away from the city. "We're going to vacation at the lake for a while."

Seth was whooping it up, Lily in the passenger's seat asked, "Spring Lake?"

"Yes."

"I thought Luke was in California."

Julia nodded, "He is, he won't be back until probably tomorrow. But, Angie has a key and we're welcome to his house."

Kelsey was puzzled, "Why are we going if he's not even there?"

"It just seemed like a good time before you and Seth go to camp."

Lily looked at her, "What about my job?"

"I called them."

Kelsey persisted, "When did you decide all of this?"

Lily gasped, "This is about Dylan." Julia stared at the road not answering. "I'm right, aren't I? You want to leave while he's in jail so that he won't be able to find me, when he gets out."

Julia looked at her daughter without words, confirming her guess just the same.

"Mom, he'll be devastated when he can't find me." She reached into her purse for her phone and let out a shriek. "Where is it? Let me have my phone. Let me at least text him so he'll know where I am."

Julia shook her head, "And let him show up there? No. Dylan is being charged with driving under the influence, open container and drug possession. You're not going to have any contact with him."

"What are you going to do, hold me prisoner at your boyfriend's house?" Lily's voice was rising. Her eyes were scanning her mother's body and car seat, hoping to glimpse her phone.

Julia had it safely tucked into her front shorts pocket, powered down. "If that's how you think of it."

Lily slumped down in her seat crying. Julia glanced in the rear-view mirror. Seth, frowning was pulling up a game on his phone to shut out the fight. Kelsey looked up, catching her mother's eye in the mirror. She gave her an approving nod.

**

Angie had phoned her an hour ago; a call from Luke had her informed of the plan. She told Julia to go straight to Luke's house; she would be there to meet them. Julia felt her friend's presence was a bonus. She was right, Angie's open arms were just what she wanted when she climbed out of the car, three and a half hours later.

Lily climbed out of her seat and walked right toward the water. Julia watched her daughter trudge out to the dock and sit cross legged on the end. She felt a pang; this was exactly what she had done as a girl when she needed to think. Maybe time on the water would help Lily.

**

Lily stared unseeingly at the lake. The beauty of the beach and the serenity of the waves making their way slightly up to shore and rolling out again held no interest to her. She was outraged that her mother had forced her on this trip. Last night had been so horrible. Why did Dylan keep doing this stuff? Coming to her house, wasted, was ridiculous. Her mom had called the police before, what was he thinking? Lily knew in her heart that was the problem, he was never thinking. Dylan reacted by emotions only.

He felt that Lily was his and when he wanted to see her, she should be there. It didn't matter to him that he had cheated on her, he was weak. Somehow, he always made it her fault. Tears burned as she told herself that maybe it was finally time to end it. The thought of being without him was scary, but she knew it was wrong. Her reputation in Seneca was shot. No boy would ever date her there. She was lucky to still have Olivia as her best friend. She would ask for a new number, she would block him from social media. The time to change things was now. If only she could do it. She felt like a traitor for these thoughts when he was sitting in the county jail. Poor Dylan.

**

Angie took the boys to her home a couple of hours later. Lily had not come back into the house, Kelsey joined her at the water. Julia wandered aimlessly about Luke's house. She was still too tense from the whirlwind plans and drive to relax.

She stepped into his home office and looked around. He had his laptop with him, a bare spot sat on the desk for it. She glanced at the frames on the wall. She saw a picture from an Ohio State football game and was surprised. How had she never known that he had lived in Columbus while getting a master's degree? Why should she know? She looked at the year listed. She was pregnant again, with Kelsey, that year. She and Ken were buying their first little house. Ken had just been promoted to Assistant Manager in his department. Julia had worked part time at a bridal shop, to help make ends meet.

Luke had been living in a campus apartment, enjoying the college life. She moved to the next photo of the ribbon cutting at his company. She glanced at the various men and women surrounding him, especially the women. A couple of the women were attractive, dressed in business suits. Was he dating one of them at the time? Julia felt ashamed of herself as she climbed the steps to his room, but she couldn't resist looking into Luke's life. In his closet, she ran her hand across the many shirts. They ranged from crisp cotton dress shirts to soft casual wear. Many she had seen him in. She stroked the sleeve of the black and white one that he had on the day she surprised him in his office.

Next were pants hung up, and then a few suits. Julia hadn't seen him in a suit since her senior prom. She chuckled, picturing him in a black tuxedo with a pink cummerbund and tie. These were expensive looking suits; charcoal, and black pinstripe, navy. What women had he taken out wearing these?

Julia shook her head, disgusted at the jealousy she was feeling. Still, like a glutton for punishment she moved to his dresser. He had a small jewelry box which she opened. In it was a sport watch he probably wore on the lake. Some cuff links, a few tie clips. There was also a silver chain, was this a gift from a woman? The silver band, obviously from his brief marriage to Gina, lay there. That relationship didn't seem to bother him, why should any others?

"You're being ridiculous," she said aloud to herself, but instead of stopping she moved into his bathroom. She had heard somewhere that the medicine cabinet revealed many secrets. Julia opened his and closed it quickly. She immediately regretted looking in there. Of course, she opened it again. Inside among bottles of aftershave and shaving cream was a bottle of peach scented body lotion. Julia picked it up, it was partially used. Had a woman lived here and this was hers? It had to be a woman's, Luke was obviously not wearing peach lotion. She looked at his toothbrush holder, only one. Julia opened the drawers of the vanity. The first held the usual combs and nail clippers. She pulled out the second one, and gasped. In this drawer was an open box of condoms. Her heart sank. They weren't for her.

"What'd you expect?" she berated herself. They hadn't been together that long, and Luke was a typical man, he wouldn't even think to get rid of the evidence of another woman. Julia forced herself to leave his bedroom and quit snooping. It was her own fault she was feeling so miserable.

She went to the kitchen, deciding to make some dinner for the girls. Opening the pantry, she found the makings for spaghetti and set about cooking. Opening a cupboard looking for spices, she found a selection of alcohol. There was a bottle of Peach Schnapps. Wasn't that an obvious woman's alcohol? "Stop it!" Perhaps coming here without him was a bad idea.

While the pasta was boiling, she headed out to the deck. Lily was dangling her feet in the water; she was down to a tank top and shorts. Kelsey had taken off the boat cover and was stretched out on the front seat. Lily looked up, when she felt Julia's weight on the other end of the dock.

"I'm cooking dinner if you girls are getting hungry." She glanced around the lake. "Think we can get this thing gassed up and out on the water later? It would be fun to take a spin around the lake."

Lily shrugged noncommittally, but Kelsey voiced her agreement.

37

Julia reclined on Luke's big king-sized bed, the soft cotton navy sheets lightly covering her. She turned on her side, hugging the extra pillow wishing it was him.

The house was quiet; the open bedroom window let in the sound of the waves against the shore and the locusts buzzing. Both were familiar sounds which brought her peace.

She was anxious to see Luke tomorrow, and push away the insecurities that had filled her evening. Why was she suddenly so unsure of what was going on between them? It was just this morning that she'd called him to tell him of Dylan's arrest. Luke, as she should have expected, jumped right in with a kind offer that was also a great suggestion. Now, here she lay at midnight in his bed, acting like a jealous wife because she had found proof that in the last twenty years he had other lovers. Who did he love now?

**

When Julia went downstairs in the morning, she found Lily in the office looking through the desk drawers. "You're not going to find any devices," she said quietly.

Lily jumped and slammed the drawer shut. "Come on Mom, just one text. It's very important."

"I'm not giving you the chance. Lily you have to give this relationship up."

"You don't understand."

"No, I don't, on top of everything else that Dylan has done in the year you have known him, now he's in jail because of drinking and drugs. You were fighting with him that night."

Lily closed her eyes, her heart and head were at war, "I know, but when I think about him in jail..." a tear rolled down her cheek. Instinctively Julia moved to hold her.

"Don't," Lily said, pushing her mother's arms away and walking out of the house.

**

When a car pulled into the driveway later, Julia's heart leaped, could Luke be home already? Soon there was a knock on the door, and she knew it must not be him.

It was his niece, Mackenzie. "Hi, Aunt Angie said Kelsey was here for the week. I thought I'd come over and see if she wants to do something."

Julia smiled, "That's great. Her sister Lily is here too, she's a senior like you. They're out on the dock already. Want me to take you out?"

"That's okay, I know my way around." The teen girl headed through the kitchen. Julia sometimes forgot that these people were Luke's family and they had spent years at this house.

She went to the glass door and watched Mackenzie approach her girls. She was wearing shorts and a tank top, her bikini strap peeking out the sleeves. Kelsey, already lying in the sun, jumped up and hugged the other girl. Lily, sitting in the boat, not in a swimsuit, looked up. She did seem to nod politely as the other girl sat on Kelsey's towel with her.

Julia made coffee and munched on toast. She was having difficulty shaking the feelings of depression. All of this with Lily was wearing her out. To compound things, she had been completely stupid, nosing through Luke's things. Now she was in a decidedly bad mood.

Maybe a swim would help. She headed up to Luke's bathroom to put on her suit. Upstairs, she pulled her cell phone out of Luke's closet and checked it. No missed calls or messages.

Julia was down to her bra and panties when she heard a noise behind her. Before she could turn around she felt hands unfastening her bra. She made a small sound like a scream, when a voice at her ear spoke, "Perfect timing." It was Luke. His hands removed the garment.

She turned around in his arms. "How are you here, already?"

"All night flight," he said between kisses, his hands roaming over her curves. "Definitely worth it."

Her insecurities were gone, as she grabbed his face and kissed him back. Without letting go of her, he managed to get them onto the bed. She made fast work of unbuttoning his shirt, her hands delighting in the feel of his bare chest. His jeans were on the floor in moments. Julia's tension rolled into passion and she reached for his hips. Luke responded eagerly. It wasn't long before he collapsed next to her on top of the comforter. "I don't think I can move."

She gave him a lazy grin, pushing back the hair from his face, "You don't need to. I'm so glad you're here."

He lay with his eyes closed, but answered, "I couldn't stay another minute. It was killing me, trying to sleep in my cramped plane seat knowing you were sleeping in my bed."

She continued to play with his hair, "You managed to get me back into this bed in record time." His eyes closed again, "Get some sleep. I better get outside before the gang realizes we're both up here." Julia reluctantly kissed him and stood up. He lay sprawled out naked, on the bed. "You might want to get under the covers."

Luke yawned, stretched and stood up. He walked over to his dresser and pulled out his swim trunks. "I can sleep in the sun," he reasoned.

When Julia and Luke joined the girls out on the dock, Lily was still not wearing a bathing suit or sitting with the other girls. All three looked up in surprise when Luke said hello then walked to the end of the dock and dove off. Julia shook her head; could he resemble a man of his age at all? Laying out another towel and sitting on it near the teenagers, she felt frumpy and old.

Luke came up out of the water, pushing his hair off his face. "Where's Seth?"

"I think we've lost him for the week, he's moved into your sister's house."

Paddling over to the end of the dock nearest Julia, he leaned against it, still in the water, "I should have known." Julia was lying on her stomach, facing him and he toyed with the idea of kissing her. He glanced at the others, they were all watching.

Mackenzie spoke up, "Hey Uncle Luke, Uncle Marcus lets me take out his boat. How about it?"

"I don't know Mackenzie; I've seen you driving like a maniac down this road."

"Whatever, I'm a better driver than you." Luke's response was to slide his hand along the surface of the water, sending a spray of it at the girls. They all screamed as Kelsey and Mackenzie jumped into the boat with Lily.

He laughed, and then spoke, "Okay you can take it out, but be careful, Mackenzie."

She leaped out of the boat and headed to the house to retrieve the keys. Luke was about to call her back, but Julia guessed his thoughts. "The gas is already in it, we went out in it last night."

He looked at her in surprise, "You did, huh? You remember how to do that?"

"It's not rocket science, Lucas. Your toys might get faster and more expensive, but boats are boats."

Julia was pleased to see that Lily remained in the boat as Mackenzie sped off. Maybe she would warm up to this yet. Luke had taken Kelsey's towel and spread it out next to Julia's. He was flat on his back, his eyes closed. She knew he was close to sleeping. She watched him next to her, so beautiful. Unable to stop herself, she casually said, "Do you like peaches?"

Without opening his eyes, he answered, "I guess, why?"

"Just wondering," she lay down next to him feeling foolish.

"That's a weird question," he mumbled.

She didn't know how much time had passed, she heard the boat approaching the dock. Hearing Lily's voice mixed into the conversation, she decided to keep her eyes closed as they arrived. Julia realized that her fingers were entwined with sleeping Luke's, but to move them would be proof that she was awake behind her sunglasses. If Lily had loosened up, she didn't want to ruin it.

The girls were climbing out of the boat. She recognized Mackenzie's voice, "Oh, look how cute they are."

"They must have worn each other out," Lily answered rudely.

Mackenzie answered, "We weren't out there that long."

"Not here, wasn't it obvious when they came out in their suits?"

Kelsey's voice was disgusted, "Lily, shut up, that's gross we don't want to think about that."

"Why do you think we're here?" Lily said bitterly.

Her sister replied, "You know why we're here, and it's not about Mom."

Lily snorted, "Whatever, that was just an excuse to get her back here to him. He's her priority now."

Julia was ready to respond. She nearly rose when she felt Luke's grip tighten on her hand. Apparently, he was feigning sleep also. She forced herself to relax and remain quiet.

"I can't believe you, Mom's not the one screwing up your life, you are," Kelsey retorted. At that, Julia could hear rushed footsteps head to the house.

It was silent on the dock for a moment. Kelsey finally spoke, “Sorry to do that in front of you.”

“Is this about that guy she was dating?”

“Yeah, this weekend he was busted for drunk driving and thrown in jail. That’s why we showed up here yesterday. Mom’s trying to keep her away from him and your uncle thought we should come here.”

“Good idea. Look, maybe tonight we can go into town with her and get her mind off him.”

**

Later that night, Luke caught Lily in his study trying to get on his laptop. He stood at the door watching her. He was beginning to understand the complete frustration that Julia was feeling. This girl was obsessed. How were they going to get her over him? Quietly he spoke from the doorway, “Its password protected.”

For the second time that day, Lily jumped at being caught. She flushed but attempted to lie her way out. “I just wanted to do some work for a class I’m taking at Mom’s college.”

His voice remained steady, “Class ended last week, that’s how your mom was able to come here. Lily, you can’t contact him.”

"That's none of your business," she hissed.

Exasperated, he raked his hands through his hair. "Lily, I care about you, that's why I'm involved."

"You're not my father."

"Is Dylan going to go to Ohio State with you next fall?" Luke tried another tactic.

As Lily looked away, her eyes spotted his college pictures. "No," she said softly.

"Is he going to stay in Seneca and patiently wait for you for four years?" She didn't respond. "Will he be happy that you're off to college?"

She turned this on him, "Were you happy for Mom when she went to Ashland?"

Luke nodded as if to say touché, but responded, "No I wasn't, and because I was insanely jealous, I lost her." This quieted Lily down. "I can respect your desire to work hard to keep a relationship working. Your mom and I didn't work hard enough. But the difference is we treated each other right. Your mom is fighting so hard, because she can't stand to see Dylan hurting you.

"He can't live without me."

"He can't live with himself."

"If he doesn't have me, he'll hurt himself."

"But if he has you, he hurts you instead."

This caused Lily to pause. She moved away from the desk. “I don’t want to talk about this anymore; I don’t want to think about this tonight. I guess I’ll go to town with Mackenzie and Kelsey.” As she moved past Luke, he lightly patted her shoulder.

38

They were walking. Luke had convinced Julia to put on her jeans and tennis shoes and join him in a walk. To add to the appeal, they had driven over to the other side of the lake, the side where they had both lived. The dirt road and paths in the woods were very familiar to them.

Now as dusk was approaching, they trudged along, hand in hand. She enjoyed seeing each cabin. As they passed the back of his boyhood home, his dad was climbing out of his car. It was as if they were back in time. He waved at them briefly, calling "Hi kids" before heading into the house. Julia laughed.

Luke pointed to his first boat, a metal rowboat sitting on cement bricks with a blue tarp over it. He pulled her in that direction, "Want to go climb into our first love nest and make out?"

She steered him back to the road, "You never change, do you?"

He tried to look innocent, "I don't know what you're talking about."

They walked on. "So, who was your next girlfriend after we broke up? Not your next date, but your next girlfriend?"

Luke turned to her surprised, "What? Why are you asking me that?"

"I'm just curious. I don't know much about your life for the last twenty years. We've talked briefly about your marriage to Gina, but nothing after that."

"But why would you want to know about that?"

She could feel his eyes on her, but stared at the road instead, "It's just a part of your life I know nothing about."

"But why would you want to?" He walked along in silence. "It's like me asking; how long after you dumped me did you go out with Ken? How long before you were sleeping with him? How many chances did you take with him before he knocked you up?" His voice was quietly angry.

She let go of his hand and stopped, "Luke, why are you saying that stuff?"

"That's what you were doing to me, weren't you?"

Julia turned on him, “Maybe I was just wondering who wears peach lotion, or drinks Peach Schnapps, who bought you nice jewelry, who do you go out with when you wear nice suits? Who were all the condoms for?” She immediately closed her eyes, regretting each word that had leaped out of her mouth.

Luke stopped and muttered, “Shit.”

“I didn’t mean to look, but once I did I went crazy,” she explained.

“Julia, I’ve just never got around to getting rid of those. None of it means a thing to me, so I never thought about it.”

“I know, I was just jealous.”

Luke walked on, she caught up with him. “You have no right to be jealous,” he said after a while.

She was surprised at his tone. “What?”

Now he stopped and looked at her, his eyes near disgust, “You have no right to be jealous. You don’t know what jealous is. You found things in my house that proved I was involved with other women? How do you think it is for me? Every time I look at Seth, I see a boy who is already growing so big that I know someday he’ll tower over me and be twice as bulky, like his father. I see the dark brown hair and facial features of Kelsey’s that are the spitting image of her father. And then Lily, she looks so much like you and then I look at those brown eyes and know they're her father's. Those kids are a combined re-creation of the man you were married to for nearly twenty years. You had a whole life with him. He got to see you pregnant and watch you give birth. He celebrated all your children's birthdays and was up at night with you when the kids were sick. Their first days of school, or first teeth, or first ball games were things the two of you shared together." He paced as he spoke, "For decades he shared a bed with you. You sat next to him on the couch and watched countless movies. You exchanged dozens of birthday presents, and Christmas presents. No matter what you now have with me, you will always go to the cemetery and shed a tear for the man you lost earlier than you should have. That's all okay, I know. But dammit Julia, how dare you try to act jealous about anything in my life when I have to live with that every day." With his final words, Luke took off at a run, leaving her at the edge of the woods watching him disappear in the trees.

Julia stood at the on the road, tears streaming down her cheeks. She was so ashamed of herself. All her energy was zapped, so she leaned against a stump, waiting for him to return. Soon, she realized that he wasn't coming back. Her old cottage was just up ahead. It was closed tight; the owners were obviously gone.

She moved around to the front yard and headed down the steep stairs to the water. Julia stepped out to the dock, the sun nearly gone now, and sat down cross legged. Why she was once again determined to ruin her relationship with him? Did she have some twisted wish to punish herself and not allow herself to have him? Was all of this because of what happened when Ken was still alive? Julia reasoned that it probably was. She didn't deserve this happiness. But she had it anyways. Sometimes she thought she just couldn't grasp that he was back in her life, wanting her back, wanting what they had always wanted. It still seemed miraculous that he was hers again.

Her life hadn't exactly been golden. She broke up with her first love, got pregnant by a boy she really didn't love. Things seemed good for a long time after that. She had three children, her marriage, though not perfect, was good. Then there were those horrible moments last year; she was disloyal to her husband and in the same summer he died. Lily became involved with Dylan. Julia became a single parent and provider to three. She had to admit that most of the fall and winter were a blur. She wasn't even certain how she'd survived.

Then in May, they'd come up here. She had returned, and Luke was here waiting. It was amazing. In no time, they both realized that the love they shared was still as strong as ever. Just last week her kids said they'd be fine with her and Luke getting married. Marriage to Luke was a young girl's fantasy. Her fantasy. And Luke, he was trying to be there for her and help her with the rest of her life.

When things had taken a nasty turn, he had once again come to her rescue and she was here with her family. So now, she sat alone in the dark because she decided to be jealous of his past. And what had she discovered? She was the one to cause jealousy. How could she have been so blind? Body lotion freaked her out. What did she think three kids by another man could do? Julia put her knees up and rested her head against them. How was she going to make this right? She looked around; she had no idea where to find him. After a while, she smiled, he'd know where to find her.

The sky was almost completely dark. The small sliver of moon gave little light. Julia heard his steps on the stairs, heard the creak of the dock as he stepped on it.

Luke got to the end of it. "Julia?" he said. He knelt and felt objects in front of him, it was clothing. "Julia?" he said again.

She pushed slightly away from the dock, her movement causing the sound of water ripples, "I'm right here, Luke," her voice was seductive.

He strained to see her, caught the pale reflection of her skin as she moved below him. "What're you doing?"

"Swimming, "she said simply.

"What are you wearing?"

She laughed, "Oh come now, Lucas, I think you know what I wear when we swim in the moonlight."

She saw the flash of his teeth as he grinned. "I do recall a few late-night swims off this dock." As he spoke he pulled his T shirt over his head. She heard the zipper of his jeans. Soon he was close enough for her to see as he lowered himself into the water. "It's cold," he complained.

Julia moved toward him, "It won't be."

He reached for her. She wrapped her arms around his neck and her legs at his waist. "Luke, I'm sorry."

He pulled her close for a kiss, "It's okay."

She pushed back, and stroked his cheek, "No it's not. I don't know why I keep trying to ruin this relationship."

He looked at her seriously, "Maybe you don't want it."

"No, no that's not it at all. I think that something inside of me thinks I don't deserve it or that I could never be lucky enough to have you back."

"But babe, I'm right here, back with you. Back to stay."

She felt tears welling up and for a change they were happy tears. "Lucas Scott Thomas, will you marry me someday?"

He stepped back, losing his balance and dropping her. She went briefly underwater. Luke grabbed her hand and pulled her back

She pushed water from her eyes, "No would have worked just as well."

He grabbed her again, "Did you just propose to me?"

Julia smiled, "Yes I did. This is my way of showing you that I want this to work. I want us to last forever this time."

Luke pulled her up to him, "Julia, I will definitely marry you. I'm definitely going to marry you."

They laughed and kissed at the same time.

**

Julia and Luke were freezing by the time they arrived back at the house. Putting on jeans, shirts and shoes over soaking wet bodies was not pleasant. Even their hair was dripping as they headed back to the car. The night was humid, so they put the air conditioner on as soon as they got in the Range Rover. By the time they arrived at the house, they both felt disgusting.

Luke grabbed clean clothes and headed to the guest bathroom. Julia took a shower in his room. She was still upstairs when Mackenzie dropped the girls off. Luke was watching television as they made their way into the house. They both seemed to be in good spirits. He was glad to see Lily smiling and chatting. He felt sorry for the girl, she was being psychologically controlled by someone she was certain that she loved. If she could have fun without him here, maybe she could remember how good life could be. An idea struck, "Lily have you ever driven a jet ski?"

Before she could respond, Kelsey jumped in, "I want to drive it!"

"He asked me," her sister put her hand up toward her.

"One at a time, maybe Lily can teach you, Kelsey." The responsibility seemed to please the elder sibling.

The girls were deep in making plans with Luke, when Julia headed down the steps. She saw the three of them head to head, he was a wonder. Tonight's proposal had been the right thing. Because her presence seemed to lately annoy Lily, she moved silently into the kitchen.

39

By the next afternoon the three teen girls were racing around the lake, alone or in pairs. Cody and Seth had returned to the house and were engaged in some sort of competitive diving contest. Luke and Julia had the deck to themselves, eating lunch. He had taken the day off, and even though there were kids everywhere, at this moment it was as if they were alone. Her eyes followed the expanse of the lake, how many times had she watched this body of water over the years? It was the place she dreamed about, the way the sun formed a pool of pink as it went down over it each night. The family of swan that appeared early in the spring. She and her mom would delight in seeing how many cygnets would hatch. Then looking out for the parade of white as the family glided across the lake as if it was their very own. Her afternoons were always spent with Luke. After a catch-up on their hours apart, as they sat at the end of the dock, he in the boat, she is holding on to it. He would either park and stay at her place for a swim, or often, she would climb in and they would head out to some friends to ski.

Now, her own children were delighting in a Spring Lake summer. Thoughts of Ken and his right to be here threatened to take over. She sipped her ice tea, forcing herself to not let that particular sadness ruin this happy moment. Instead, she looked at the man across the table from her. If last night really happened, he was her future husband. When would they sit down with the kids and plan for this change? Not this week, she could not risk losing the smile on her eldest face that she was now seeing as Mackenzie and Lily climbed off the jet ski. It could wait. The next several days were all about fun and Lily's freedom.

**

The next day was not to be a day of fun. It was early in the morning when the phone rang. Glancing at the screen, she recognized the numbers as her neighbors at home. The words from her neighbor, stunned her. She sat on the bed, elbows on her knees, and face in her hands. Luke walked in from the bathroom and found her this way.

He ran to her and knelt beside her. "Jules, what's wrong?"

She looked at him, "The neighbor drove by the house this morning. From the road, he thought something looked funny, so he drove up the drive. The front door was broken into, someone has trashed my house."

"Dylan," Luke said in a whisper.

Julia used her phone to find a number and began to dial. When she was connected with the right person she asked, "Can you tell me if Dylan Specter has been released from jail?" She listened. "Okay I understand that may be confidential information, but my house was broken into last night. Yes, 3143 County Road 72. That's right, I'm out of town. What I'm asking you to do is check on Dylan Specter, I have no doubt that he did it." More response, "I will be in town later this afternoon. Thank you." After she ended the call, she looked up at Luke, "That bastard broke into my house and ransacked it. I know he was looking for Lily or a clue of where she is."

Sitting on the bed beside her, he thought for a moment, "Okay, let's call Angie and Nancy. Nancy will keep the girls, Seth will stay with Angie. We need to get back to Seneca."

They went down to the kitchen. The girls were having breakfast. Julia didn't waste time; she told them exactly what had happened. Before she could say anymore Lily groaned. She looked at her mom, "It was Dylan wasn't it?"

Julia looked at her steadily, "Do you think he would do that?"

Lily nodded gravely, "He was looking for me. I'm sorry, Mom. I know you probably won't believe me, but I'd decided last night that it was time to break it off for good with Dylan."

**

The mess in the house was unbelievable. Glass was shattered on the outside door, and the screen was ripped away from the inner door. She stepped into the house; kitchen drawers were tossed on the floor, the contents all over. In the study, every desk drawer emptied, the laptop smashed on the floor. The only bedroom vandalized was Lily's. Nothing had been untouched in her room. He had even written profane names on the walls with the markers she kept on her desk.

Julia cried into Luke's shoulder. An officer returned to the house, to go room to room with them. Dylan had already been brought in for questioning. His hand had been sliced when he had punched through the glass front door. The police were certain he was the culprit.

Luke was repairing the door later that night, as Julia worked on cleaning up the kitchen. All the silverware and utensils were being run through the dishwasher. At present, she was picking up the variety of items that had made up the junk drawer. She put batteries back in, matches, a chip clip. Locating a stray golf tee under a bar stool, she said aloud, "Ken, you lucky bastard, you missed out on all of this." Julia rolled it around in the palm of her hand, letting the point stab her skin. "What would you do if you were still here, how would you handle this?" She picked up a golf ball, "Why aren't you here, she's your daughter too, why did you leave me with all of this?" At those words she flung the golf ball out of her hand, it bounced on the counter, shattering a coffee mug. Luke came running into the kitchen. He found her on the floor, crying. He sat down and pulled her against him, she looked up, her tears spiking her lashes, "Aren't you sick of all of this? Me crying all of the time, all of this crap?"

With a kiss to the top of her head, he nodded his agreement, "Yes, I am."

She was surprised by his response. "You don't have to do this."

He sighed, "Yes I do. That's the point. If we make it past all this early in our relationship, we'll be on a constant honeymoon for the next twenty years."

The words lightened the mood, "Sounds great to me."

He pulled her up, "Let's order Chinese food. Got anything to drink around here? I think we could both use it."

She gave him a weak grin, "Sorry I'm fresh out of Peach Schnapps,"

**

Luke poured her another glass of wine. They'd just finished the last of the fried rice. She lifted it and gave him a lopsided grin, "Another glass of this and I might be officially drunk."

He held up his hands, "If you are, I'm not responsible for what happens here."

Her eyes widened, "We're alone aren't we?"

Luke laughed, "You just figured that out?"

She grabbed her glass and stood up from the table, "Let's move this party to another room."

40

They had returned to the lake a day later, that was when she received an update. Dylan had pleaded guilty and was now housebound with an ankle bracelet for 30 days awaiting trial. Julia and Luke discussed what they would do next. She'd looked at the calendar and realized that next Monday was the week that Kelsey would be heading for basketball camp and Seth was going to football camp. She couldn't imagine bringing Lily back to town and risk Dylan contacting her. Julia opened her phone to make a call. She asked Tim if he was interested in keeping Lily with him for a week or two. When she explained all that had happened, Tim agreed and promised to set up some counseling sessions for Lily with his friend, the school guidance counselor.

The plan was to get Lily from the lake, directly to Indianapolis without ever taking her back to Seneca. Lily had initially fought her mother on this. She couldn't imagine not seeing her friends until it was time for school to start. It all changed, however, when Kelsey came home from Mackenzie's house. She had been on Mackenzie's phone checking her Instagram. Dylan's crime was all over everyone's posts and they were all gossiping about Lily's crazy boyfriend. Lily was embarrassed; so much had already been spread about the two of them.

With heavy heart, she reluctantly agreed that visiting her uncle would be best, even if it was boring. On Saturday, Julia and Lily would head off on a two-hour drive to meet Tim at a halfway point.

**

Lily was furious with Dylan for ruining the remainder of her summer. At the same time, she was afraid for him. What might he do if he was trapped in his house, and she was far away? Maybe she should have given in to his pleading the other night. They had gone to Mackenzie's, she had convinced her new friend to let her use her phone when Kelsey went to the bathroom. Though reluctant, Mackenzie had allowed her to take the device up to her parents' master bathroom and agreed to cover for her when Kelsey returned. Her first text from the strange number went unanswered. Finally, her, *Dylan, this is me Lily* prompted a call. He was desperate. That was the only justification for his mood to be swinging between fury and sorrow.

"Hell, Lily why did you leave me? Jail was the worst experience of my life. This is all your fault, you and that bitch mom of yours."

She felt strength being a state away, "Dylan, stop calling her that. She didn't call the police on you." He shouted his disbelief, laced with an unbelievable collection of profanity.

Her angry silence warned him to use a different tactic, "Please baby, I've seen things in jail that I'll never forget. My old man punched me for costing him bail money. My uncle fired me. Let me come to see you, you're the only person who loves me."

Voices below alerted her that the other girls were getting prepared to head out. She needed to cut this short, the excuse of a bathroom break was wearing thin. "Dyl, I can't. If you showed up here, my mom would kill me."

"She won't have to see me, you can come up with an excuse to get away. Just tell me the name of the city and I'll find a way to see you." Once again, her hesitation was apparent, his anger returned, "I'm not fucking around, Lily. Tell me where the hell you are. You owe me this.

My life has been dragged through hell because everything I've done is for you. Where the hell is this damn lake? You selfish bitch, you owe me this. Where are you?" his voice was near yelling. There were footsteps in the hall.

"Dylan, I have to go. I'll call when I can. Please don't call me back. Let me call you. I love you, honey," she clicked off the phone and stuck it in a vanity drawer. The girls were outside the bathroom as she opened the door. "Sorry guys, I was trying to do something with this mess." She gathered the ends of her hair. "Mackenzie, do you have a hair tie in one of those drawers." Message was received.

Mackenzie nodded, "I'll grab one, let me use the bathroom really quick." The sisters agreed to meet her at the car and headed downstairs. Later that evening, Mackenzie had whispered that she was going to have to block Dylan's number, he was blowing up her phone. "He's been sending a million texts, demanding to know what city we're in. Will he show up here?" Lily's instinct was to defend him but realized that the last thing she wanted was him here.

**

When she climbed in her uncle's car, Lily cried, as was to be expected. Julia was saddened to leave her, but knew it was the right thing. She had a very difficult time watching her brother's car pull away with Lily in it.

That evening, she and Luke sat on the deck after the kids had gone to bed and argued about the following week. "I don't want you there alone."

"Luke, he's a kid. He's not going to hurt me; besides he's under house arrest."

"How many times do the police have to come to your house, for you to know he's not stable?" He took a swig of his drink.

Julia swallowed some of her own, hoping that she would sound more confident than she felt, "If he steps a foot out the door, the police pick him up."

Luke shook his head, "I'm not comfortable with this, at least come back up to the lake when the kids are gone. Your classes haven't started." He reached across their seats and squeezed her hand, "We could be alone here."

"You give a very convincing argument. I suppose I could head back up here on Tuesday."

Luke got up and nudged her to move over, he squeezed into the chaise lounge with her. “We have a wedding to plan.”

“Luke, do you want a big wedding?”

“I want whatever you want. For all I care we can run to Vegas or have a big church wedding. The courthouse in town is fine too. I’m the guy, this is your call.”

“I think maybe alone would be nice.”

41

Leaving the lake after eight days felt like it used to when the summer was over during her teen years. Julia was amazed at how accustomed she'd become to being with Luke. She forced herself to seem enthusiastic for the kids on the trip home. After all, they were headed to camps, both were excited for the adventure. She had spent a hectic night doing laundry and running to Walmart. Somehow, she had misread the paperwork and didn't realize that Seth's camp bus left at 9:30.

Now Julia held a coffee in one hand and put boxes of cheese crackers and granola bars in large Ziplocs with the other. The phone rang, and Kelsey got it before she did, "Mom, that was the auto body shop, they can take my car this afternoon."

"Perfect, it will be ready when you get home. Okay you have to be at school at 1:45, I'll just follow you in my car to the shop and then we'll go to school together."

Kelsey protested, "I already packed my stuff in Lily's car because I was just going to leave it at the school until Friday."

"That's okay; I'll just drive it and follow you." They agreed on the plan, and Julia headed out to take her son to his drop off. Seth's enthusiasm for camp was matched by all the middle schoolers climbing into the school bus. He barely had time to give his mother a hug before he launched himself into the back seat with their neighbor, Kyle.

The yard was a mess, so in between errands, she threw on a pair of shorts and another cast off tee from the girls. She managed to get the front and back complete before Kelsey waved her in. "I made you a sandwich, Mom. We have to take the car in before we go to school, remember?" Kelsey appeared to be the parent. Julia thanked her and ate. "Are you staying here alone this week?"

Julia swallowed the bite she had taken, "No, I think I might go back to the lake tomorrow."

Kelsey smiled, "I thought so. Anyway, with Dylan around it's kind of creepy here."

"You sound like Luke, Dylan is on house arrest, if he leaves the house he's back in jail."

In just a few minutes, Kelsey was handing her the keys and herding her to the driveway. Julia looked down at her outfit and rolled her eyes. "Hey, I'm not getting out of the car at school." She followed Kelsey, driving the damaged Honda. The body shop was not in one of the better blocks in town, lots of decaying houses, broken down cars out front, couches on the porch.

She stopped at the curb, allowing Kelsey to pull ahead of her. As she was stopped she looked ahead, two doors down was a vehicle she recognized, Dylan's red truck. Was this his neighborhood? Though she'd never admit it to Luke, the thought made her shiver a bit. How crazy was she? Julia pulled in behind her daughter and got out of the car to speak to the mechanic. Soon the two women were both in the Lily's car, headed to school.

At last she had both kids off to camp. Julia was tempted to take a nap, but instead chose to finish the yard. She was still in her old clothes. This way she could head to the lake as soon as she wanted tomorrow. As she was putting the lawn equipment in the barn, she looked around. Was she really planning on moving from here in the future? This had been a great place to raise her family, so many happy memories filled the place; holidays, birthdays, bonfires out back, picnics on the front lawn, the five of them crowded on the couch to watch a movie. It had been great, but that was when two parents lived here.

42

The laundry was done, and she was putting things she wanted to take with her directly into the suitcase. Julia couldn't remember a summer when they'd been gone so often. Night was falling fast, and she was exhausted. Grabbing a bag of white cheddar popcorn and a diet soda, she settled onto the sofa, channel surfing while she ate. It wasn't long before she dozed off.

A noise woke her; she sat up, her back stiff. Julia reached for her cell phone on the coffee table, it was almost 1 a.m. She glanced at the television again as she heard another noise outside. Julia grabbed the remote and shut it off. Was that a car? Sophie was outside, she could hear the dog's incessant barking. The curtains were open, and she felt vulnerable. Sliding off the couch, she decided she would peek out the front door. Julia had just made it to the doorway of the living room when she heard a loud thud against the picture window.

A voice swore and then to her dismay she clearly heard the voice shout, “Lily.” It couldn’t be! The window was crashed against again and she distinctly heard Dylan’s voice, “Lily, I know you’re in there. Lily!”

Julia saw that she’d left her cell phone on the coffee table. Maybe if she crawled in he wouldn’t see her. She got on her knees and made her way in. Just as she placed a hand on the phone she saw movement. Dylan’s body leaped at the window, it shook but didn’t break. She could see blood on his face. He continued to scream her daughter’s name.

“She’s not here!” Julia yelled without thinking. “Go away, Dylan.”

“Lily let me in, I have to see you one more time.”

Julia stood up and was heading out of the room, when she heard him smack the window.

“I see you! Lily, you bitch, let me in.”

Julia hid in the hall but called back, “It’s me Dylan, her mom. Lily’s gone away. You need to go; the police are going to find you here in a minute. She’s not here. Go away!” She dialed 911 as she moved.

“I see you!” He screamed at the darkened room. Julia looked down at herself and realized that she was wearing her daughter’s clothes.

"I saw you today, I know you're here. Let me see you!"

The 911 operator came on asking her emergency. Quietly, she filled her in on the situation. Julia heard him moving away from the window. Was the house locked up? She thought the front door was but wasn't certain about the garage door. Julia scrambled to the kitchen. As she reached for the door, the knob turned, and Dylan pushed in. He shut the door on Sophie. She continued to bark and scratch, attempting to get in.

Julia turned to get away from him.

"Lily!" he roared and grabbed at her hair, pulling her back to him.

She moaned, but tried to turn her face to him, "Dylan, Dylan look at me, I'm not Lily. She's not here. I told you. It's just me." Just then they both heard approaching sirens.

"I wanted her to see me."

"She's not here," Julia tried to get out of his grasp; he'd taken hold of her arm instead of her hair. He was definitely on something.

"I'm going to kill myself," he pulled a hunting knife out of baggy jeans. "I want her to see me do it, so she'll know it's her fault."

"Dylan," she sighed, though the knife was causing her to tremble, "She's really not here, she went away. Go now, the police are coming, you'll be in more trouble if you're caught in my house."

They both heard the crunch of gravel. His eyes, red and unfocused, scanned the house, "Too late." He pulled her by the arm. "Come on."

She tried to fight him, "No Dylan, let me go."

He grabbed the knife and waved it at her, "Come on, bitch."

Dylan led her into the small half bath on the main floor. He sat down against the vanity, forcing her to sit across from him. He moved her, so her back was against the door. "They're not going to shoot if you're there."

Her cell phone clattered to the floor between them. Dylan looked at it.

"I wanted her to be here," he looked at Julia accusingly.

"She needed to get away, you two can't be together."

"I want to cut my throat."

Though at this moment she didn't care if this boy was alive or dead, Julia decided that keeping him talking was best. She could hear footsteps around the house and hoped it was only a matter of time before the police found them. "Dylan, you don't want to die. You're young, you'll find someone else."

He gripped her arm, the knife close to her wrist, "She's the only one, the only one."

"No, you can love more than one."

He looked at her as if realizing for the first time who she was, "Yeah like your old man died, now you have that new guy. What's his name?"

At least he was talking, she thought, "Luke, his name is Luke."

Dylan nodded, "Right, Luke, Luke. Luke and Lily. Luke and Lily." He smiled and pushed up the sleeve of his sweatshirt. "See how sweet this is." He pointed to the ugly red "L" he had sliced into his arm. "That's what you need," he grabbed her arm. She struggled. Dylan took the knife and sliced a deep "L" into her forearm. Blood spurted, and she screamed. He clamped a hand over her mouth. "Quiet, bitch," he hissed.

She nodded to him, her eyes promising to obey, tears poured down her cheeks. He lowered his hand cautiously. Julia looked at her arm. She glanced up at the hand towel by the sink, and motioned with her head, then grabbed the towel and wrapped it around her arm.

The police were calling for her and shouting Dylan's name. Dylan rocked back and forth. "Shit, shit. I just wanted to die for Lily. I just wanted to show her how much I loved her. How much she fucked up my life."

"Dylan, go with the police. They can get you help. You can get through this. You're young; you have a life ahead of you. Don't make a mistake tonight."

Footsteps were heard outside of the door. Dylan called out, "She's against the door, and if you do anything I'll hurt her."

"This is the Seneca County Sheriff's Department, are there others in the house?"

"No, just. . ." Dylan smacked her face to quiet her. "Shut the hell up." Julia put a hand to her stinging cheek and fought back tears of pain and frustration.

The deputy's voice came again, calm and sure, "Let her go, Dylan. We don't want to hurt you."

"Dylan please, let's just walk out of here together," Julia whispered to him.

He seemed to be losing his stability quickly. Once again, he was rocking back and forth. "When Lily gets here, I'll show her, I'll show her."

"Come on, let's go out now," Julia moved as if to stand.

He grabbed her tight. “No, we wait for Lily.”

At that moment he spotted the phone between them, with his free hand he picked it up and handed it to Julia. He looked her in the eye and said, “Facetime her.”

“What?”

“Facetime her; if she can’t be here I want her to see it.”

Julia watched the knife, twitching in his hand. “No.”

“I’m not kidding, bitch, I want her to see.”

Julia held the phone in her hand, she knew she would never dial that number, she would never allow her daughter to see what Dylan was doing. Suddenly the anger she felt towards this man, whose actions would most certainly leave emotional scars on Lily, were too much. Looking right at him she whispered, “To hell with you.” Julia took her phone and smashed it against the porcelain bowl of the toilet, it shattered into several pieces.

Dylan shouted at her, “You fucking bitch!” he stuck the blade of the knife into her thigh.

She screamed and clutched her leg. Julia felt a sort of frenzied energy engulf her. Her hands grasped the knife. Ignoring the excruciating pain and the grotesque sound it made, she pulled it out of her leg. Dylan looked at the blood spurting onto the hem of her shorts. He seemed mesmerized. The officers were yelling, asking if she was okay.

Dylan shook his head repeatedly, mumbling "No." Then, he reached for the knife, leaning over her bloodied limb. Her hands were shaking, she was filled with nerves and in her effort to stop him from taking possession of it, she jerked her hand upward. Her intent was to move it from his grasp, but at the same moment he lunged forward. Their combined actions caused the knife to plunge into his abdomen. He shuddered and gave an inhuman scream.

Julia pushed herself as close to Dylan as she could, so that the door could be opened. As the police entered behind her, she looked at the bathroom floor. A puddle of blood was growing, a mixture of hers and Dylan's.

Julia didn't remember too clearly the events that immediately followed. Ambulances arrived. She went in and out of consciousness. They must have put her out, because she awoke in a hospital bed. When her eyes opened she was in a semi lit room. She moved as if to sit up and a hand gently pushed on her shoulder, "Stay put." It was Luke.

Julia shook her head, confused. "What are you doing here?"

"This is where I should be." He leaned over and kissed her forehead, "How are you, darling?"

"How did you know?"

"I couldn't get you to answer your phone for over an hour, so I got worried and headed down. I think I aged twenty years when I pulled into your driveway and saw police cruisers. You were already here."

Julia was quiet for a moment, recalling the night. She looked up at Luke, "Dylan?"

He shook his head, "The knife severed his aorta. He didn't make it to the hospital."

Tears slid down her cheeks. "Baby, this isn't your fault. It's all on Dylan." Luke kissed the top of her head. "The doctors say you're going to be fine."

Julia nodded.

43

Julia held the phone awkwardly in her left hand. She was right handed, but her arm was still weak. Tim was bringing Lily to the phone. Julia dreaded this conversation, would have preferred it in person, but she wasn't allowed to travel, and the story was getting out. She had to tell her daughter what happened. When she heard her daughter's, "Hello," she began to cry.

Lily's own voice was cracked, she knew.

"Lily, baby. You know what happened?"

Now there were sobs on the other end. "Mom," the word was more of a wail. "I loved him, Mom."

"I know you did. Honey, I'm so, so sorry," the sobs were choking her.

"He hurt you?"

Julia felt a new onslaught of tears, concern for her was not what she had expected, "I'm okay, sweetie"

"Where are you?"

"I'm still in the hospital, I should get out tomorrow.

Her daughter was silent for a moment, "Mom, I want you to tell me everything," her voice was stronger.

Though Lily couldn't see her, Julia shook her head, "Oh honey, not yet."

"Yes, please tell me everything that happened. I don't want to hear things in the news or online. I want you to tell me. Mommy, I have to hear it." And Julia told her. By the time she got to the part where she woke up in the hospital, both women were choked with grief. Julia was glad that she had waited to be alone to make this call. Lily had finally said she loved her and they hung up. Julia barely had the energy to lay the phone on the table next to her hospital bed. Just as her eyes were closing, a text chimed in. It was from Lily. She had made some decisions.

**

By the time the other kids were through with camp, Julia was home and moving fairly well. The leg hurt when she walked, but it would heal. The doctor had sadly informed her that she would be stuck with the "L" scar unless she opted for plastic surgery; but this wasn't the time to worry about that. Tim had brought Lily home the morning after she spoke with her mother.

**

It was after midnight on Friday. Julia came slowly down the steps. Her kids were all tucked into their beds and she felt peaceful. Lily had done better than she had expected. Now Julia moved past the closed bathroom door, she could smell the bleach. Luke had come in and cleaned it before she got home, after the police had done the rest of their investigation.

It made her shudder as she passed the door. Julia saw the screen door was open. She heard the porch swing and joined Luke outside. He helped her sit down, and then pulled her close for a kiss. Julia caressed his cheek, her voice thick with emotion, "Luke, I wouldn't have survived this without you in my life. If this had all happened before you, I don't think I could have coped."

He kissed her forehead, "Yes you would've, you're strong. Look at everything you survived alone. I wasn't here that night, and you kept yourself alive." At his own words, he pulled her close. "Just thinking about it terrifies me again. To think it's took me a lifetime to get you back and I nearly lost you forever."

"You didn't, though."

They moved so that her head was resting on his shoulder, the swing moved lightly. After a moment she spoke, “The night I told Lily, she later texted that after the funeral she wanted to leave Seneca. I didn’t want to commit to anything until the entire family was home. The kids are all in agreement. They want to start school at Tri-Lakes.”

Luke stopped the swing with his feet. He turned to face her, “Are you serious?”

She took a deep breath and nodded, “Yes I am. They want to move to the lake.”

“And you?”

Julia brushed at the hair on his forehead, “Do you really have to ask? Of course, I want to. I’ve wanted to be there since that first morning you floated in on your boat.”

He kissed her. “And what about this place?”

“Let’s call a realtor. It may be a tough sell now.”

“Good point. But we’re in no hurry to sell it. We’ve already got a house.”

Julia looked at her hands, then up at him, “Luke, I think we should be married before the kids and I move in. It’s more appropriate.”

He grinned, “Okay, I’m free tomorrow.”

She smiled, “You mean that don’t you? “

"How long have I wanted you to be my wife? I think I started proposing when I was seventeen."

Julia touched his cheek, "You're a very patient man, but the wait is over." Luke reached for her face and pulled it to him for a kiss.

44

The movers climbed into their truck and pulled away. Julia leaned on Luke's arm, "I still don't know what we're going to do with my stuff when it gets to the lake." They had carefully chosen things from her place that would blend with his and make the kids comfortable in their new home.

She looked at the realtor's sign sitting in her front yard. This was bittersweet. She was really leaving this home that held so many memories, good and bad. The girls hugged their mom, both a bit teary.

Seth looked around, "Can we go now?"

Luke came up to them, "I think we're ready." He glanced at the driveway filled with his vehicle and the other three. "It would be a lot more romantic to travel with my new wife and my family in the same car."

Julia laughed, "Sorry, all four cars are going. Seth are you coming with me?"

Seth looked from her to Luke, “No Mom, I’ll go with him, okay?”

She saw the pleased look on her husband’s face, “That’s a great idea.”

Epilogue

Luke looked at his watch, "Okay, eleven hours and thirty minutes. We should arrive in Munich at approximately..." he glanced at his wife. She was engrossed in a text conversation on her cellphone, "Hello, darling. Are you with me? Soon enough, you'll have to shut that down."

With a smile, Julia focused on him, "Sorry, I was just checking with Lily. She and Mackenzie arrived from Michigan State an hour ago. Wish I'd been there for her return from her first year of college." Her husband reached over and squeezed her hand. "I know, she'll be home every day now for three months. I'm so happy about that."

Though he was going to take that opportunity to express his own happiness, he knew his wife. She would want to update him on the other two children. As he had expected, Julia continued, "Seth and Cody have a game. Kelsey is working. I'm so glad that both of my daughters will be working at the country club over the summer. It's nice to think of them riding together when they get the chance." She took a satisfied breath, as if this final rundown of the kids helped her put the thoughts of them aside. She powered down her phone.

Mr. and Mrs. Lucas Thomas were aboard a plane that would take them to Munich, Germany. In two days, they would climb onto a train and travel to Neuschwanstein Castle. They were taking a late honeymoon, one that they had dreamed of as teenagers. Her love of history and his of architecture had always been met by the photographs of this famous German castle. Now here they were, married at last and headed to visit it.

Julia pulled a light cardigan out of the bag at her feet. Her arms were chilled. Luke rubbed her exposed skin with his fingertip, stopping to trace the artwork on her arm. Just last month, a talented tattoo artist had turned the hideous red scar left from that horrible night, into something beautiful. She had insisted that it remain an "L" but now it was entwined with flowers and vines. Lily had chosen to go with her mother. Though she had cried when the tattoo was complete, her whispered word, "Gorgeous" was all Julia needed to know she'd done the right thing. Luke reached for the sweater and helped her cover up her arms. The sound of the engines started, and he spoke, "Are you glad we're taking this trip?"

Julia turned, her eyes meeting those of the man she had loved for most of her life. He was here in this moment, living breathing proof that the good in the world would always prevail. "I wouldn't want to be anywhere else."

Also by Linda Van Meter

Worth Losing- For ten years, the focus on Delaney's life has been her wine bar. Peace of Wine is a place of harmony for Delaney and her two partner, Cheryl and Hunter, and the friends spend almost every hour of the day running it. It's their dream, but it's time for a break. Careful scheduling has been done so that Delaney can join Cheryl and her family for their vacation on the Atlantic shore. Delaney will meet Cheryl's recently divorced brother there, hoping it will be a match. Peace of Wine is fulfilling, but Delaney craves someone to share her life with.

Temperatures rise at the beach, but not with the man that Delaney's supposed to be spending time with. As this forbidden attraction increases, she must consider the risks. Once back at Peace of Wine, this new secret threatens to expose even darker ones. Past mistakes could destroy the life that she has created. Can Delaney choose what is valuable and what is *Worth Losing*?

Available on Amazon and Kindle

93471803R00235

Made in the USA
Lexington, KY
14 July 2018